THE GHOST OF SPRING

MEL STONE

The Ghost of Spring

Cover by **MiblArt**.

To Dell and our December to May romance. I love you, old man.

Chapter One

Subdolous ‑ *Cunning; subtle; sly*

REGINALD LUKE POLK, Duke of Fenwick, sat in his study in front of a warm fireplace with a brandy and a book. Since his seventieth birthday, it had become a habit to doze off in his chair for the night instead of properly seeking out his bed. One involved moving from his warm and cozy position, and the other didn't.

A hard pounding on the door roused him from his thoughts and before he could speak, his steward, Henry Church, burst into the room. Henry's usually calm demeanor was marred with a heavy scowl. "Excuse the interruption, Your Grace, but there is a situation at Fairley Park."

Luke waved for Henry to approach. Henry brought a wide-eyed woman clutching a handkerchief into the room with them.

"Now, tell His Grace what you told me." Henry pushed her forward.

"Beggin' Your Grace's pardon," she stammered, her gaze on the floor instead of on Luke. "But terrible things are going on with the Fletchers."

"There usually is." Luke had little love or tolerance for his neighbor. Lord Marcus Fletcher was a weak-willed man who should never have inherited the title in the first place.

He's also Mary's son. The unwanted reminder pricked Luke's conscience. Damned old age. Always stirring up memories when it wasn't wanted.

"The baron is dying. The doctor and the vicar don't think he'll live to see the dawn," her voice was meek. "His son, Mr. Fletcher, has come home, and he's brought nothing but debt and a carriage full of friends who are not exactly gentlemen. They are celebrating the baron's death as we speak."

Luke frowned. "This is all quite ghastly business, I agree, but I fail to see what it has to do with me."

"It's Miss Mary, Your Grace. Mr. Fletcher is auctioning her off to his friends...to repay his debts. I'm her lady's maid, sir, and I...please." She finally peered up at Luke, her eyes full of tears.

Miss Mary Fletcher. The name flooded Luke with memories that warmed his heart. *Why did they have to name her Mary too?* He missed his Mary. His lover and best friend had been gone for over a decade now. He would have done anything for that woman. The least he could do now was rescue her granddaughter.

He tossed the light blanket off his lap and tugged his waistcoat down. "The carriage, Henry."

"Yes, Your Grace." Henry hurried away.

Luke strode to his desk and opened the bottom drawer. He pulled out a stack of papers and shuffled through them, muttering. He was sure he had a common license somewhere, and when did he let his desk get so unorganized? Old age was making him lazy.

"There it is." He found the piece of paper he was searching for and tucked it in his pocket.

"And your name?" Luke asked the maid when they walked into the hallway.

"Agnes, Your Grace."

"Agnes, you did say the vicar was there?"

"Yes, he's up with the baron and the doctor."

"Well, let us go and make things uncomfortable for Mr. Jonathan Fletcher, shall we?" He shrugged into the coat his butler held out for him. "Please prepare rooms for Miss Fletcher and her maid, will you?"

"Of course, Your Grace." The butler strode away with quick steps.

Agnes wiped a tear from her face and her whole body deflated. "Thank you for saving my girl, Your Grace."

"*Your* girl? I was under the impression Miss Mary's mother fled to the continent with her lover."

"I was her wet nurse, then nurse, then lady's maid. I don't know how you nobles expect a human being to raise someone and not get attached." Agnes chewed her lip and lowered her face. "Forgive me, Your Grace. I shouldn't speak so boldly. But she's my girl."

"I see." Luke motioned for her to lead the way.

Henry appeared at the door with a couple of footmen, George and Peter. The two ex-pugilists had saved his life one night during a robbery. Even though their behavior was often impudent, they had hearts of gold and fists of steel that protected Luke and his family. They'd make sure everyone involved in this escapade remained safe.

"They are bringing your carriage around now," Henry said.

"Excellent. Please join us, Henry. This should prove to be amusing, if nothing else." Luke walked out the door and climbed into his carriage.

The ride over to Fairley Park was blissfully short. Agnes wrung her hands while Henry gazed out the window at the setting sun. His leg jostled up and down. Luke had never seen his steward so agitated.

"Thoughts, Henry?"

"I'm wondering how we are going to get the young lady away from her family, Your Grace. She turned nineteen last month. With her mother gone, her father dying, and her brother..." Henry's fists clenched.

"You know the young lady then?" Luke asked.

Henry was silent for a moment. "I've seen her in the village and have spoken to her a few times at church. She is a lovely young lady, despite her family."

"So was her grandmother," Luke said. They rumbled over the cobblestones to the entrance of Fairley Park.

He approached the steps and inhaled deeply, preparing for battle. He hadn't been this excited about anything in a long time. Old age had begun to put him in a state of ennui. The titillating decision on whether to sleep in a chair or a bed was not a fitting retirement for a man.

The Duke of Fenwick was going to raise a rumpus once more.

"I don't think we'll bother with knocking." He walked up to the door and entered.

Sounds of revelry filled the halls. Drunken shouts and laughter drifted from the dining room. The servants slunk through the shadows, giving each other horrified grimaces while they fetched and carried food and drink for the raucous party. Luke would bet most of them were packing their bags and waiting for the word that the baron was dead.

"Henry, do we have any empty positions to fill? Talk to the baron's butler, see if there are any of his staff willing to come to Fenwick."

Henry went off in search of the man.

"Agnes, if you would please lead me to your mistress." Luke followed the maid up the staircase to the family rooms. The hallways were dark and the furnishings sparse. The baron had made several bad investments and did not update his holdings to increase his coffers. His home reflected his poor choices.

Luke marched his way through the dimly lit halls, pulling his gloves off. There was a little light at the end of the hallway and the sound of sniffling.

Sitting in a chair outside her father's bedroom door with tears running down her face, was Miss Mary Fletcher. She furiously wiped her eyes and flinched every time a loud roar of carousing rose from downstairs. Her simple gown was patched in a few places, her curly hair in a loose braid. She was folded into a ball and her feet were tucked onto the chair beneath her like a child.

She looked so much like her grandmother, with shiny copper hair and deep blue eyes bright with tears. He hated the sight of her sorrow.

He pulled out a handkerchief. "Here now, let's dry those tears."

Mary saw him for the first time and leaped awkwardly to her feet. "Oh, Your Grace. I didn't know...you...were here." She broke down into loud sobs. "This is not a good time for a visit."

He pulled her slowly into his arms and after a moment of

hesitation, her arms wrapped around him, gripping him tightly for support. He stroked her hair and spoke calming words. "Now, that's enough tears. Agnes has apprised me of the situation and I'm here with a course of action."

"I don't know what to do," she sobbed. "My father's very ill, and Jonathan is... he's..."

"He's a villain," Luke said, anger inflected in his voice. "And your father is going to do right by you, or I'll make his last moments linger in misery." He released her from his embrace and took her hand. "Come along now."

He opened the door to the baron's bedroom and pulled Mary inside with him.

It was gloomy inside, hot from the blazing fire and ripe with the smell of medicine and sweat. The doctor was asleep in a chair, waiting patiently for the baron's death. The vicar was seated next to the baron's bedside, praying.

"I'm afraid there's no redemption for him, Vicar. I'd save your breath." Luke's voice boomed through the room. The doctor awoke and the vicar dropped his Bible.

"Your Grace! What..." The vicar came to his feet with the doctor following.

Luke strode to Marcus's bedside. The unfortunate man was wheezing for air. He was barely recognizable as the stout, balding man who'd run Fairley Park into ruin for the past two decades. Now he was a pale and thin-skinned ghoul.

"Open your eyes, man. I will speak with you." Luke's voice was soft but firm.

Marcus's eyes fluttered open and shock spread over his face. "Fenwick. What... are you..." He couldn't gasp out the last word.

"Doing what you should have done, you spineless cretin. I

am taking care of your daughter." He motioned for Mary. She came to his side with a sniffle and wiped her face.

"Mary..." Marcus gazed upon her fondly. His withered state made his smile appear ghastly.

"Yes, Mary. I'm glad you can drum up some feelings for her. Your son is currently downstairs auctioning off her virtue to the highest bidder," Luke announced.

The vicar gagged and the doctor gaped. The vicar found his voice first. "Your Grace...are you sure? We knew there was no love lost between Lord Fletcher and his son, but..." He glanced quickly at Mary and then dropped his gaze to the floor.

The dying man whimpered and a single tear filled his eye. "Mary," he whispered.

"You have no funds to send her away to safety. You have no friends or family to care for her." Luke pulled out the paper from his pocket. "You will do the honorable thing and give her to me." He passed the paper to the vicar. "I'm here to marry your daughter."

Mary gasped loudly and Agnes staggered next to her. The doctor fell into his chair and the vicar slowly took the paper from Luke. His hand trembled as he read. "It's a common license."

"Yes, good for this county, so you can fulfill it. Simply write in the correct names." Luke glanced at the door when Henry entered the room.

Luke cheerfully greeted him. "Ah, Henry! Your timing is perfect. We need another witness."

Henry's brows furrowed and he walked towards the dying man's bedside. "Witness to what, Your Grace?"

"My upcoming nuptials to Miss Mary Fletcher. Taking place as soon as the baron signs his name."

Henry's jaw tightened and his eyes flashed.

Interesting. Was his right-hand man more attached to Miss Mary Fletcher than a mere soul to save? "Henry, you seem appalled. My wife has been dead for thirty years. Am I not an eligible bachelor?"

Henry exhaled and brought attention to Mary's pale face. "I'm not sure your bride-to-be is so amiable to such a match, no matter how eligible you are."

Mary clutched her hands to her chest and gaped at Luke. "Your Grace...I couldn't...we wouldn't..."

"Oh, come now, you don't think I am unaware of the considerable years between us? I'm old, not daft." Luke took Mary's hand. "Unfortunately, I haven't a better plan at the moment, and time is running out. You are not of age yet and will be your brother's chattel unless we do this. You need the protection of my name." He took her other hand. "I will take care of you, Mary Fletcher. I make no demands, no pressures, or expectations. I only want what's best for your welfare."

She met his gaze and was silent. He would wait as long as it took for her to make her momentous decision while willing her to make the right one. Hopefully, before her father expired.

Finally, she let out a shaky breath. "I'll do it."

He squeezed her hands and faced Marcus. "There now, it's settled. Get your signature on the paper and I'll let you get on with dying peacefully."

Marcus managed a glare for the duke, but stretched forth his hand and took the license. A pen was produced and in a shaky hand, he signed his consent.

"Well done, Fletcher." Luke took the license. "I'll see her happy."

"Ssssafe," Marcus managed. His eyes closed and his breaths became labored. He writhed in pain.

"Oh, Father!" Mary began sobbing.

Luke put an arm around her shoulders. "I'll give you all the time for tears you wish, my dear. But first, we need the vicar to do his part."

With Henry and the doctor as witnesses, the vicar read the vows and pronounced them husband and wife. When it came time for the kiss, Luke pressed a chaste peck to her forehead. "There now, that wasn't so difficult."

He motioned to Agnes. "Take your mistress and go pack up her belongings. We'll be leaving as soon as we can."

"I should stay with Father." Mary took Marcus's frail hand.

"My dear, I'm touched by your love for your father, but we need to leave while your brother is distracted. I'll stay here with the good doctor and the vicar. We'll watch over him." His view met Henry's over her head with a silent command.

"Come along, Your Grace." Henry clasped Mary's elbow. "I have two footmen below to carry your things." He ushered her out of the room with Agnes.

Luke found another chair and sprawled into it.

"Hell of a night, Your Grace," the doctor said.

Luke exhaled. "I agree." He contemplated his new father-in-law dying in the bed. *Mary's son.*

With gasps and gargles, Marcus twitched on the bed. Occasionally, his arms and legs would thrash violently. It was a dreadful sight.

"How much longer does he have?" Luke asked.

"Minutes... hours... I doubt he sees the morning."

"Is he in pain?"

"Yes. But he refuses anything." The doctor glanced down

at his patient. "Frankly, right now anything I give him would relax his system to the point it would stop."

"Do it," Luke spoke in his most commanding ducal voice.

"Your Grace!"

"I'm telling you right now, young man, if you ever preside at my deathbed, I want you to hurry up the process as much as possible. Even though Marcus is a waste of flesh, he deserves some dignity in dying. There is also a young lady who will be returning to say her goodbyes to her father, and I want him sedated and peaceful when she does."

The doctor scowled but administered a dose. In moments Marcus ceased thrashing. His gargling and gasping slowed to deep, slow breaths. The doctor straightened the bed and made the dying man appear more presentable. "Perhaps you are right, Your Grace."

"A duke is never wrong." Luke snorted.

Downstairs, the party became louder. Voices rose and the sound of breaking glass followed by braying laughter penetrated through the bedroom door.

Luke shook his head and slapped his gloves against his thigh. "I can't imagine you and the vicar want to spend much more time here either. Marcus will have to have the good manners to die quickly."

"I can't believe you married her," the vicar whispered.

"Believe it. Spread all the rumors and scandal you wish, how the lecherous Duke of Fenwick has taken a child bride on her father's deathbed." He slapped his gloves again. "But kindly spread your gossip out of Mary's hearing. She's already going to hear enough gossip from the *ton*. I would hope a man of God would be more generous with his slander."

"I care for Miss Fletcher."

"You mean Her Grace, The Duchess of Fenwick," Luke corrected.

The vicar sighed. "I pray you have done the right thing."

Luke shrugged and repeated, "A duke is never wrong."

Mary returned to a resting father. Luke ushered everyone out of the room except him to give her some privacy. She caressed her father's thin face and planted a kiss on his pale skin. She whispered comforting words Luke couldn't hear. She was calm and straightened her spine when she finished her goodbyes.

"Good girl," he praised and took her hand. He tucked it into his elbow and led her from the room. "Let's take you home now. Your father is in good hands."

The revelers downstairs didn't even take note of the departure of Mary Fletcher Polk, Duchess of Fenwick.

George and Peter tensed when the duke and his new bride exited the house. Both men held small batons, waiting for action. Luke nodded at them and they relaxed.

Henry and the coachman finished strapping Mary's luggage to the carriage. "Any problems?" Henry opened the carriage where Agnes was waiting inside.

"Not one. We've carried out a successful covert operation. Well done, lads."

They were a silent group returning to Fenwick. Even though the hour was getting late, the servants met them at the door. Word spread quickly and they were all ready to fawn over their new mistress when she stepped into her new home. Supper was ordered to her room, along with warming pans and a bath. Agnes promised to have Mary fed, cleaned, and tucked in bed before she worried too much about the evening's activities.

Luke placed a hand on Henry's arm and stalled him while

Mary and Agnes climbed up the steps. Once they were out of earshot, he addressed Henry. "Tomorrow, send a summons to my solicitor. I need to make some changes to my will."

"Yes, Your Grace."

"I need a list of the unentitled estates I have. Also, hire a dressmaker tomorrow. I have a feeling she'll want to mourn properly, and her clothes are barely staying together."

"I'll see to it," Henry said.

Luke clapped Henry on the shoulder. "I need your support in this, Henry. It was the right thing to do, but there's going to be hell to pay."

"Whatever you need, Your Grace."

Chapter Two

Vernal - Belonging to the spring.

MARY AWOKE in the most comfortable bed she'd ever slept on. She inhaled deep and enjoyed the crisp scent of lilacs. Lovely and fresh. Like spring and new beginnings.

She took a moment and fully examined her new bedroom. The night before had given her glimpses of grandeur in the dim light. The ceiling was twice as high as her old room. She glanced at the giant fireplace employed to heat everything. She probably could hold afternoon tea in it without the crackling flames keeping the room warm. The paper on the walls was bright yellow and new and the windows flooded the room with light. Fresh flowers sat on a table next to her washbasin.

Not a lilac in sight.

She pulled the covers off and stepped onto the plush

carpet. Although the clock said it was almost ten, she was still exhausted.

A duchess! She was a duchess. But she only knew the basics of running a household. She'd been able to juggle the needs of Fairley Park while her father was ailing. But it was only one estate. And she'd never entertained, even a simple picnic. How would she manage to be the wife of a peer? What did it even entail?

The duke didn't need an heir. That thought was comforting. He didn't seem inclined towards any intimate marital relationship with her. The night before he treated her more like a daughter than a wife, even sealing their marriage vows with a kiss on the forehead.

Her life had changed overnight and it was more than overwhelming. What would the duke expect from her as his wife? Entertaining other peers? A caregiver as he aged? Would she be hidden away in some far-off estate?

Her ever-practical mind regrouped. One thing at a time. The duke would not want an ignorant wife, so she would strive to better herself with what little she had.

"First things first." She reached for the little dictionary she'd placed beside her bed. Her morning routine of finding a new word to learn soothed her jangled nerves for a moment. She let it fall open and found the first word on the page that didn't have a little check next to it.

"Commence," she read aloud, "To take beginning; to take a new character.' Oddly fitting, isn't it." She sometimes believed the little abridged dictionary carried more words of wisdom than the Bible. She checked a little pencil mark next to the word and closed the book.

A faint noise came from the dressing room, catching her attention. A woman's voice hummed an old lullaby that

Agnes once sang to her in the nursery. When did she come in?

Mary padded to the little room. "Good morning, Agnes. How long have you been..."

The dressing room was empty.

Mary entered it slowly and made a complete turnabout. She was certain she'd heard something. Creeping closer to the walls, she pressed her ear against it. Maybe someone in the next room was singing?

Silence.

Agnes appeared behind her, bearing a tray of coffee, tea, and chocolate. "Anything wrong?"

"No, I thought I heard you in here." Mary glanced one last time around the dressing room and left.

"New house with new noises. You'll get used to them. Come and get something warm into your belly. Cook wasn't sure what you wanted, and insisted I bring it all," Agnes said.

Mary contemplated the offerings on the tray. It was an easy choice. She hadn't had chocolate in years. Not since Mama left for the continent with her lover and Papa banned it. She took the dark drink and hummed with delight when it warmed her insides. "Chocolate is exactly what I needed today. Have you heard any word about my father?"

Agnes shook her head. "Nothing yet. Sit down and finish your chocolate. I was going to bring you a breakfast tray, but the duke insisted you eat with him when you woke. I suspect he has news."

The maid rifled through the wardrobe. She held out a muted brown wool dress with the fewest patch jobs for Mary's approval. "Did you read your word for the day?" she asked.

Agnes had started the tradition while Mary was still in the schoolroom. With her brother's volatile temper, a governess had been hard to find for Fairley Park, so Agnes made Mary read the children's dictionary aloud and practice using a new word every day.

"Today's word is: commence. I shall now commence being the new Duchess of Fenwick." The words churned her stomach anew. "Agnes. I'm terrified."

Agnes handed her a pair of stockings. "Nonsense. I'm sure you're well qualified for whatever is expected. You devoured every book at Fairley Park before Mr. Fletcher sold them all. You know French, write beautifully, and you do things with numbers on a ledger that is astounding. You're the smartest lady I know."

"I think I'm the only lady you know," Mary mumbled and tugged on her footwear.

"I am sorry about bringing your trouble to the duke. I didn't know what else to do last night but turn to Mr. Church for help. He's always been kind and caring towards those in the neighborhood, even if they don't live at Fenwick. I was desperate to help you. He's the one who asked the duke for a solution."

A rather drastic solution, but one that would hopefully keep her safe from Jonathan.

Mary took Agnes's hand and squeezed it. "You did the right thing. You are more than a servant to me, Agnes. And you always will be."

The maid's face relaxed and she quickly kissed Mary's cheek before slipping a corset over Mary's head. They did their dressing routine quickly before she trod downstairs to the breakfast room and her future.

Mary didn't find the duke at breakfast, but Henry Church was sitting at the table tucking into a meal. He rose when he saw her. "Good morning, Your Grace."

Glancing behind her for the duke, she realized he was speaking to her. Her cheeks flushed. "Good morning, Mr. Church."

He assisted her with a seat while the footmen brought her breakfast.

"His Grace will be along shortly. He likes a morning walk before breakfast." Henry waited for her to take a bite before continuing his meal.

"I was told to meet him for breakfast." She poked around at the plate. Her appetite was nonexistent as a cloud of anticipation hung over her. "Is there any word about my father? Did he linger much longer?" Her voice caught and she tried to clear her throat.

Mr. Church put down his utensils. "I think His Grace wanted to be the one to catch you up."

"Please, Mr. Church. Don't make me wait."

Mr. Church frowned and tapped his fingers on the table. His dark brown eyes contemplated her as she silently begged him for answers. "The vicar stopped here before he went home late last night. Your father died an hour after we left."

Tears splashed onto her plate. Sorrow mixed with relief in her chest until it bubbled up into her throat. She stifled a sob when a warm hand took hers and squeezed it. She looked up into Mr. Church's kind face, taking strength from his grasp. Even when he was a youth and she a child, he'd always shown her tenderness.

"All will be well, Your Grace," he whispered. "I promise."

"Henry! What are you doing with my wife's hand? Have I been cuckold already?" The duke's booming voice caused Mary to jump. Mr. Church chuckled and squeezed her hand briefly before letting it go.

"I was lending my support to the duchess, Your Grace."
Mr. Church stood and assisted the duke with his chair.

Mary didn't want to start her new marriage with trouble.
"He was simply comforting me, about my father."

The duke waved it off. "It was a poor attempt at a joke, my
dear. All will be taken care of. I've had an army of undertakers
bombard your brother this morning. Your father's remains are
being prepared for burial."

She exhaled a shaky breath, and a little sunshine broke
through darkness surrounding her. "Thank you, Your Grace."

He wrinkled his nose. "Your Grace. We'll have to change
the way you address me. I can't have my wife 'Your Gracing'
me for the rest of my life. It will put me into an early grave.
You shall call me Luke, and I shall call you 'my dear,'" he
proclaimed. "Unless I am cross, then you will be Mary."

"Very well...Luke." His given name barely tripped off her
tongue correctly.

"There we go. It sounds better already. Now eat up. You
have a busy day ahead. The dressmaker is scheduled to be
here around noon. I presume you need new mourning attire.
And I want you wearing everything new, befitting a young
duchess bride."

"Yes, thank you." Mary managed a bite of toast at his
command.

"I'm not quite sure what to do about your mother, though.
Do you want me to try and hunt her down now that your
father is gone?"

She was amazed at his thoroughness. "It won't be necessary. I'm sure she'll stay wherever she is. I haven't heard from
her in six years." Her cheeks heated. "What you must think of
my family."

"You are rather tame compared to some. I will regale you

with tales of the scandals from the *ton* someday when you are in need of distraction."

The butler entered the room and walked to Mr. Church's side. He spoke into the steward's ear and Mr. Church rose from his seat. "Excuse me, it appears Squire Morris is conducting a search for the missing Miss Mary Fletcher. I'll go enlighten him."

The duke laughed. "If he needs proof of life, send him in for some breakfast." He sent Mary a stern stare. "I see you pushing those eggs around like a cuckoo about to shove them from their nest. You'll need your strength for the upcoming week. We need to bury your father and do something about your brother. Your new position as my wife will have a number of odd relatives popping out of the woodwork wanting money or favors. I will use your father's death as an excuse to give them the boot, since my wife is deep in mourning. Unless there is someone you'd want to visit?"

She shook her head. "No, they... they're all as you described them. I'm afraid you've taken on a great burden."

"Bah! I was getting too complacent in my retirement. This will be an exciting challenge to take on. Not to mention the scandal of our age difference. I look forward to hearing all the speculations on my sexual prowess." He waggled his grey brows at her like a scoundrel.

Mary bit off a smile. It would only encourage him. "You are a bit of a rascal, Your Gra..." she cut herself off.

He laughed. "Not even one day as my wife, and you already have me sorted out. Well done, my dear," he praised with a mock toast from his teacup.

Mr. Church returned to the table, followed by a timid Squire Morris. The squire relaxed at the sight of Mary. "Miss Fletcher, I'm greatly relieved you are well."

"She's Mrs. Polk now, Duchess of Fenwick," Luke announced, motioning for the squire to take a seat at the table.

"Duchess of... oh. Oh my." The squire dropped hard into the chair. Mr. Church poured him some brandy.

"We have rendered the good squire speechless, my dear." Luke beamed while the man took a healthy gulp of liquor.

"Duchess! Are... you sure?" The squire's face was more active than a tennis match trying to meet everyone's gaze.

Mary didn't fault his surprise. She was still coming to terms with everything changing around her. "Yes, quite sure."

The efficient Mr. Church presented the squire with the marriage license before sitting down again to his meal. The man had been on the move ever since she'd entered the room.

"Would you like a new plate, Mr. Church? Your food must be cold by now," Mary asked.

Mr. Church's eyes danced with merriment and he glanced at the duke. "I haven't had a warm breakfast since I started working for His Grace, and I don't see it happening any time soon."

"I am unfairly abused. Do you hear this rubbish? You would think I chained the man to my side and whipped him hourly," Luke grumbled and the squire took another gulp of brandy.

"This is quite a revelation." The squire examined the marriage license. "Both the doctor and the vicar witnessed this?"

"And Mr. Church. I wanted everyone to sign it so there was no confusion on the authenticity of our union. Mary Fletcher Polk is my wife and will be afforded all the dignity and protections that come with it," Luke declared.

The squire set the license down. "I can't think of a better way to protect her. That brother of hers is a waste of skin."

Mary's cheeks began to flame. "I'm quite aware of my family's flaws, Mr. Morris."

"My apologies, Your Grace. I've been searching for you since sunup and your brother has been flanking my every move with those 'friends' of his. I'm tired and cross, and I am not looking forward to telling him about your new status. He is rather volatile."

Mary rubbed her wrists where her bruises were finally fading. She knew exactly how volatile her brother was.

The butler entered again and spoke into Mr. Church's ear. Once more he rose to his feet. "Find George and Peter for me and have them meet me at the front door," he directed the butler.

"It appears the new Lord Fletcher has arrived, searching for the squire and his lost sister. I'll go inform him Her Grace is indisposed and doesn't wish to be disturbed."

"Squire Morris and I will join you." Luke stood and straightened his coat.

Mary went to rise and was pressed down by her new husband. "Stay here, my dear. This is sure to be unpleasant."

Waiting until they all left the room, Mary slipped out and followed them. She was near the entryway when the raised voices became clear. Slowly, she continued forward, flinching every time her brother cursed and shouted. Fear left bumps on her arms and she hugged herself. The last time Jonathan had been so angry she'd been beaten and locked in her room.

The butler blocked the door and her view with his body. Crouching down for a better view, she saw Luke and the squire on the porch. She stayed in the shadows and peered around them to find Jonathan.

Mr. Church was toe to toe with her brother in the drive. Jonathan's face was a brilliant red while he bellowed at Mr. Church. He was flanked by two of his cronies. Her heart sank. She wondered which one 'bought' her.

"This is ridiculous!" Jonathan shouted at Mr. Church. "I want my sister now."

"Her Grace is in mourning for her father and is not receiving visitors," Mr. Church calmly replied.

"She's not a duchess, she's a disgrace. This entire farce has gone on long enough." Jonathan stabbed a finger into Mr. Church's chest. "I'll have you arrested for kidnapping!"

"As the good squire has verified, she is in excellent health, and is no longer your concern." Luke's voice carried across the drive. "You will leave now or I will have you escorted off my property."

Peter and George, the two footmen who'd helped her pack last night, appeared behind Jonathan and his friends. He didn't notice them when his voice became shrill.

"Even if my father agreed to this, he was out of his mind at the time. It won't hold up in court. I'll have it annulled!"

Mary put her hands over her ears and closed her eyes, sinking all the way to her knees. She couldn't return to her brother's clutches. He'd beat her, then toss her away to be used. He'd already told her all he thought she was good for.

A warm hand rested on her shoulder. "You shouldn't be here. Come away."

It was Agnes. Her faithful companion pulled her to her feet and tugged on her arm to lead her away.

"No, I need to face this. I need him to know he has no power over me, not anymore."

Mary took a deep breath; it was time to *commence*. She

straightened up tall and forced her gaze forward. She was a duchess now. There was no turning back.

She pushed past the butler and stood at Luke's side, linking her arm with his.

Jonathan stopped his tirade. "Finally. Come along, Mary. You have work to do." One of his friends snorted with a lecherous sneer at her.

Mary shook her head. "I'm not going anywhere. I'm staying here with my new husband." Luke put his arm around her shoulder and pulled her into his side. His warmth was comforting and she tried to keep her voice from trembling. "It was Father's last wish. He wanted me to be safe, and the duke will take care of me."

"I'll take care of you," Jonathan snarled.

"No. You will only hurt me. It's all you've ever done. Please leave." Her voice quivered on her last word when Jonathan's eyes narrowed.

"You stupid little whore!"

Mr. Church's fist flew so fast Mary wasn't sure she actually saw it. She did see it the second time when he planted it again in Jonathan's face and knocked him to the ground.

Both of his cronies hollered in alarm when Peter and George detained them. Alone on the ground, her brother moaned. He spit out blood and rose to his feet.

"Henry," Luke called out.

"Yes, Your Grace?" Mr. Church's eyes did not leave Jonathan's form.

"Hit him one more time."

Mr. Church planted a hard punch into Jonathan's gut that doubled him over.

"Thank you. I think he now understands the consequences of disparaging my wife."

Jonathan glowered but remained silent, clutching his belly.

"If you would like to pursue something as ridiculous as an annulment, I wish you the very best in trying. I doubt you'll find a barrister to take your case with the debts you owe." Luke grinned like a Cheshire cat. "Why, I believe I bought up those debts this morning. Didn't I, Mr. Church?"

"I believe so," Mr. Church answered, never taking his focus off her brother.

"A benevolent act toward my new brother-in-law, don't you think?" Luke pressed.

"Very generous, Your Grace."

"I thought so. Pity he's not as gracious as I am. Do you think he'll like Australia, my dear?" Luke asked Mary. "I'm sure it's much lovelier there than Fleet Prison."

Jonathan's face paled. "No. You can't."

Luke's expression was stone. "I can and I will if you bring up this nonsense of annulment ever again. I'd like to see you in chains being marched across a gangplank. But the decision is up to my wife." He addressed Mary again, "What would you like to be done?"

She didn't face her brother but kept her eyes on Luke. *Commence! You're a duchess now.* "My recent grief has made me think of my father. He would like for his son to have a second chance. But I want him to leave me alone. I don't want to see him again, ever." Her voice was loud and clear while her heart thundered against her ribs.

"The lady has spoken," Luke announced. "Be grateful for her generous heart. Now take yourselves off my property and don't darken my doorstep ever again." Luke guided her inside. She glanced one last time over her shoulder. Jonathan and his cronies sauntered away under the watchful eyes of George, Peter, and Mr. Church.

Chapter Three

Unlibidinous - Not lustful

HENRY ALBERT CHURCH was in love.

But being in love wasn't Henry's problem. The problem was who he was in love with.

Henry's heart belonged to Mary Fletcher Polk, the new Duchess of Fenwick. Even before that horrible night when they spirited her away, he'd been in love with her. He'd seen her at church and in the village helping small children and war widows with her own meager supplies, smiling and lifting spirits while the sadness in her eyes never faded. He'd watched her grow from a child to a gangly youth to a charming young woman. He'd seen her quiet strength while she took care of her father's illness and stood up to her bully of a brother.

How could a man not fall in love with such a soul?

He was content to love her from afar, like a knight of old pining after his lady fair. Now she lived under the same roof and he was finding it harder and harder to hide his affection. Or maybe it was his affliction?

Henry almost struck the duke when he'd announced he was going to marry her. But he was right. She needed the protection of the duke's name. Lord Fletcher wouldn't dare try to do anything against the Duke of Fenwick. Mr. Henry Church, however? He'd probably be assaulted, killed, and Mary would be in the clutches of her rotten brother.

A month had passed since her father's death and he'd been watching Mary deal with her grief while he stood by, feeling helpless.

Some days she spent the day crying in her room. Other times she would descend on the piano and play until he thought her fingers would begin to bleed. And sometimes she would start the day slamming doors with anger.

Today was an angry day.

She'd been marching outside around the manor all morning. She'd pass the window of his office with a scowl on her face and her fists clenched while she wore a new path through the lawn.

Why did no one stop her?

Because she was the duchess, that's why. No servant would approach her with words of comfort. Even her own maid was at a loss of how to help her. The duke was no help either. He patted her on the head and ran from the room at the first sight of tears.

Henry debated if he should do something; if there was even something to say that would be of comfort to her.

"It's not my place," he mumbled and returned to his ledgers.

She passed his window again, muttering angry words through the open pane. He heard a sob before she disappeared.

He gripped the armrests of his chair to keep from chasing her.

"You're setting yourself up for more heartache." The numbers on his ledger were his priority now. Not Mary.

One glance at her tear-streaked face on her next pass found him out of his chair and making his way outside.

"You're a fool, Henry. An idiot. This is lunacy," he berated himself aloud and quickened his steps to catch up with her.

She was still trooping ahead of him when she tripped on something and stumbled. He ran to her as she regained her balance.

"Alright there, Your Grace?" he called out. She bent down to pick up the offending object.

"Yes, I'm fine." She hissed and contemplated the small rock in her hand. "I tripped on this stupid..." In a fit of pique she threw the stone toward the trees shading the manor.

She had more strength than either of them thought when it bounced off a tree trunk and returned to smash a hole into a nearby window.

"Oh no!" She covered her mouth with her hands.

Henry blinked a few times while he found the right words. "I must say, I'm impressed. I did not expect the tree to fight back."

He was rewarded with a little laugh, and she dropped her hands. "I did not expect it, either." She gazed at the perfectly round hole in the window. "I suppose destruction is the usual outcome of anger. I thought I had it well contained. I don't want to be like him."

"Like who?" He asked.

"My brother. He did the most horrible things when he was in a foul temper." She hugged herself. "I'm so angry."

"Why are you angry?" He wished to pull her into his arms and hope she'd find comfort there. His limbs ached with wanting to hold her.

"I feel so worthless. Mama left us for another man. Papa's gone now. Jonathan wants me as a..." She stopped and shook her head. "Even the duke doesn't need me. I'm more of an indulged daughter—or granddaughter—than I am a wife! When will someone want me for me?" Tears spilled from her eyes.

Henry chomped down on his lip hard enough to draw blood. Instead of giving in to his base desires and kissing her senseless, he bent down and picked up another stone. He didn't dare speak. An errant stream of endless devotion would trickle out. He handed it to her and nodded towards the broken window.

Her eyes widened a little before she furrowed her brow and threw the stone at the window with the shout of a warrior. It smashed through with a little tinkle of glass hitting the floor inside. He handed her another, then another, and wished he could throw a few himself.

On their ninth stone, the window next to their destruction opened and the duke's head poked out. "By Zeus's beard! What goes on here?"

Mary's tear-streaked face looked at him with guilt, her shoulders deflated like she was awaiting punishment. Henry answered for them both. "We're letting out a little pent-up aggression, Your Grace."

The aged man nodded like a sage. "And you're taking it out on a window so that I'll board it up and save money on this year's glass tax. Good thinking, my dear. So frugal!" His head disappeared into the house.

Mary visibly relaxed. "He really does have a kind heart, doesn't he?"

"He's all bluster," Henry agreed. "Now go wash your face and I'll have the window taken care of."

"I should help."

He took the last stone out of her hand and tossed it away from the house. "You might cut yourself. Let me tend to it."

She nodded and walked away. Wary servants started poking their heads around corners and out of windows once she departed.

"Apologies, everyone, Her Grace is still working through her grief," he announced. Mutterings of "that poor thing" and "fewer windows for me to scrub anyway" were all he heard from them.

He returned to the study and found the duke waiting for him there.

"Henry, I think we need a change of scenery for my wife. We'll leave for London next week. I know David and Miriam are staying at the townhouse with their children, so we'll need to find someplace else to stay."

"I'll set things up," Henry promised. His feelings were mixed. As much as it pained him that Mary was leaving, it was probably the best thing for her and for him.

"I don't know how long we'll be staying, so you'd better pack for a lengthy visit," the duke directed.

Henry blinked. "Me? I should stay here and see after the estate." He gestured to the piles of bills and ledgers stacked on the desk.

"Pish-posh, those can come with us." The duke waved

them off. "I'm certainly not young enough to keep up with a blossoming lady in London! I'll need your help."

Henry's heart soared while his brain railed against the directive. He managed to force out the correct words. "I'm at your service."

The duke patted his shoulder like when Henry was six years old and working in the gardens with his father. "Good lad. It'll be an adventure for all of us." He swept out of the room and called for his valet.

Henry slumped into his chair and muttered, "More like torture."

MARY FOLLOWED her nose all morning and she still didn't find what she was searching for.

The gardens at Fenwick were in full bloom. A riot of colors and smells led her down various pathways and through a variety of different emotions when she was alone with her thoughts.

Excitement was first on her mind. She was going to London as the Duchess of Fenwick to be part of the whirlwind of parties and balls and operas with Luke and his family.

But with excitement came fear. She was a little country mouse who married an old lion. Even with their considerable age difference she constantly felt she was running to keep up with him. Embarrassing him and his family was always at the forefront of her thoughts. Throwing stones at windows because she'd tripped on a rock was not her finest moment.

And last of all, grief. She'd taken Agnes and skirted the edge of Fairley Park after Jonathan left. The shabby old manor was boarded up and the servants all dismissed. She wasn't surprised Jonathan put it up for sale when he hadn't been able to sell her. Neighborhood rumors circling about her family and marriage had been hurtful. She was grateful to Luke and Mr. Church for their unfailing support.

Now she was searching for lilacs to take to her father's grave before she left for London. Father had loved the smell of the little purple blooms in the spring.

The scent of a thousand blooms filled her nostrils and not one of them were lilacs, and she couldn't understand why. She smelled them every morning when she woke up. The fragrance lingered in the air throughout the day in various rooms of Fenwick.

Mary roamed most of the garden paths before the morning slipped away and she quit her search for the elusive blossoms. She needed to visit the cemetery before it grew any later. She'd have to settle for roses or some sweet peas.

She drew a pair of scissors out of her pocket and knelt down to cut some blooms when the soft patter of footsteps came from the pathway. The stranger drew nearer; she heard a deep voice singing a somewhat bawdy song.

Until at last he got too much,
From one that was quite seedy
He was obliged to apply
To famous Dr. Eady.

SHE CLUTCHED THE SCISSORS. No one she knew would be singing about the French Disease in proper company. Was it a trespasser? Or had Jonathan sent someone to abduct her?

Determined to stab anyone who might try, she called out. "Who's there?"

The voice and the footsteps stopped. "It's Henry Church, Your Grace."

Mary lowered the scissors along with her tense shoulders. "Mr. Church, I'm sure your mother would not approve of such a song."

He appeared on the pathway, grinning like a naughty child. The tips of his ears were pink. "You've caught me. She would most assuredly be washing my mouth with soap if she heard my tune. I'd get the switch if she knew I was singing it in front of you."

His grin was infectious. "I'll keep your secret if you will assist me."

"I'm at your service."

"I'm looking for lilacs."

Henry's brows furrowed. "Lilacs? They're no longer blooming this late in the season."

How could that be? "Are you certain? I smell them in the house every morning."

"As the son of the head gardener, I can confirm that lilac blooms are long gone."

Confusion washed over her. Was she wrong? Was there another similar flower blooming now? She'd spent all morning searching for that distinct fragrance and none of the other flowers came close.

"I'm sorry to disappoint you. I'll show you where they are if you wish." Mr. Church offered her his arm. She slid her hand over his sleeve and appreciated his warmth that seeped through into her fingers. His arm was muscular and firm, so different from Luke's thinning limbs.

He navigated the garden paths easily, taking trails she

hadn't discovered in her exploration of Fenwick. He walked at her pace. The little act for her comfort was not out of the ordinary for the servants, but from him it felt special.

"I forgot your father is the head gardener at Fenwick. I should have asked you for a tour of the gardens when I arrived," Mary said.

"I learned to walk on these paths; they've imprinted on my brain."

"How does one go from the gardener's son to the duke's steward?"

Mr. Church chuckled. "The first time I met His Grace I was helping my father weed the beds. He kept staring at me, and it made me uncomfortable. So I started tossing the weeds at his feet to get him to leave."

"I'm sure he was impressed."

"He laughed and asked Father for an interview. I was sent to the duke's study and we had a serious conversation about schooling and my ambitions. I can't say I was brighter than any other boy at Fenwick, but His Grace sent me off to school. The least I could do was repay him with my service."

"You seem fond of him."

"We have an unusual relationship. He's more of a mentor than an employer." Henry led them one more turn around a hedge and swept his arm out in a grand manner. "Here we are, Your Grace, lilacs. This piece of the garden is called Sarah's Circle."

Screens of greenery spread out in a circle around a stone bench tucked under the leaves. Not a single bloom in sight. The broad green leaves of the lilacs shimmered in a slight breeze against the sunlight. Outside noises were muffled. Mary was instantly in love with the little plot of land.

"Sarah's Circle? A relative of Luke's?" She dropped his arm

and walked to the middle of the copse and slowly spun around, tipping her face up to the sun and letting it warm her cheeks.

"I'm not sure. It was before my time. But this is where all the lilacs in the garden are."

"Now I'll know where to come in the spring." Mary walked to the bench. She sat and wiggled her way into the foliage. The view was private and cozy. A perfect little place to tuck her feet up and hide from reality.

"I believe I shall claim this spot for myself. A few cushions and a blanket and I'll be quite set."

"You'll have to share it with the bees in the spring." Mr. Church warned.

"We'll have to learn to get along." Mary inhaled. Still no scent of lilacs, but a feeling of peace swept over her.

"Henry! Have you seen my bride? It's time for lunch and I'm about to perish with hunger." Luke strode into the hedge circle with his usual flair. His gaze rested on Mary and his eyes widened. His face paled and he stumbled backward, gasping. "Zeus's beard, a ghost."

Mr. Church grabbed him before he fell. He lowered Luke slowly to a seat on the ground.

"Luke?" She rushed to his side. "What's wrong?"

"I'm fine. Help me up." The color slowly returned to his cheeks and he grabbed them by the arms.

It took her and Mr. Church a moment to put the older man up on his feet. Luke trembled and reached out to embrace her, resting his balance heavily against her. His laugh was shaky. "Forgive me, my dear. Tucked into the shadows you looked exactly like your grandmother. I was momentarily stunned with memories." He took a few deep breaths and straightened.

"Are you well now?" Mr. Church asked. He held a hand on the duke to steady him.

"I'm well, thank you both." Luke straightened and placed Mary's hand in his elbow. "I'm not too weak to escort you to lunch."

She wouldn't damage his pride any further, even if she was a bit worried. "I didn't know you knew my grandmother. I was named for her."

"I thought as much. She was the epitome of a perfect woman." Luke's bold manner returned.

"I'm afraid she would find me quite lacking."

"Nonsense, she'd be impressed with you."

The words warmed her heart. "Would you tell me about her?"

"Gladly. Come along, Henry. You both need to know all about the greatest lover the world has ever known."

Mary's cheeks flamed. "That's not quite what I imagined."

"Her cheeks used to blush like yours. One of her most charming attributes. That and her hips."

Mr. Church roared with laughter and followed them into lunch.

Chapter Four

Harbourer - One that entertains another.

"APPROPINQUATE." Mary rolled the word around in her mouth while she waited for the carriage to arrive at their destination. The word was not in her little abridged dictionary. She'd been delighted when Luke showed her his two-volume set now residing in the London townhouse library.

"That is quite a mouthful for such a young lady. What does it mean?" Luke asked from his seat. He was always attentive to her, no matter how childish her actions were.

"Appropinquate—To draw nigh unto; to approach. I am waiting for the coach to appropinquate my new stepson and his wife's house." The thought brought more butterflies fluttering in her belly. She'd seen the younger Polks once or twice attending church at Fairley Park when they were visiting the duke but never held a conversation with them. Her new stepson was the same age as her father. The thought changed the butterflies into bees.

"Appropinquate," Luke said the word with an exaggerated roll of his tongue to make Mary giggle. "I like it. I'll make a bet at White's for who uses *appropinquate* in their next speech in the House of Lords."

"I'll be anxious to know how they use it." Her nerves rattled when the carriage stopped. She fidgeted with her gloves and straightened her bonnet.

"We're here," she said. The bees in her belly mutated into hornets. "How do I look?"

"You are perfection itself," Luke assured her.

The carriage opened and Luke led her to the front door of the large family townhouse. It was still Luke's house, but he'd moved to Fenwick full time when David took up his seat in Parliament.

They were admitted, announced, and Luke presented a nervous Mary to his family.

Lord David Polk was tall and lean, like his father. His dark hair was peppered with silver, and a scowl sat on his face.

Lady Miriam Polk was the complete opposite of her husband. Her face radiated sunshine at Mary. She was pretty and perfectly plump. Her clothes were neat and flattering. Mary's apprehension increased. Maybe she should have worn a mob cap to try and appear more mature?

David crossed the room with twice the powerful presence of his father. Head high, eyes bright and searching, shoulders back, posture firm. A man ready to take charge of everything in sight, if he so desired. Had Luke been a great dynamic force in his earlier years? She tilted her chin and braced herself to meet him.

David's steps halted and he scanned her from head to toe and up again. "Caesar's ghost, the rumors are true. My father has become a lecherous old man."

Mary's skin flushed hot from her toes to the tips of her ears. "I haven't...we don't..." The words she loved to learn failed to produce themselves.

Luke laughed. "As you can see, my child bride is still an innocent."

"You are both horrible," Miriam chided and swept to Mary's side. She took both of Mary's hands. "My dear girl, welcome to the family."

"I will never refer to her as my stepmother," David groused and advanced to the side bar for some brandy.

"A grandmother too," Miriam added and led Mary to a seat. "So many accomplishments for someone of your age. How old are you again?"

"Nineteen," Mary said softly. Her voice seemed to have left her.

Miriam's face wavered between shock and merriment. "Oh my! Our eldest son Josiah is only four years younger than you are."

"Luke told me you have three children."

"Yes. Josiah, Cassandra, and little Adam. He's barely turned four, and Cassie is ten. They will be joining us for dinner."

Mary emitted her most earnest face, trying to portray all her desire for a happy relationship with them. "I hope we will all be friends."

Miriam squeezed her hand. "Of course we will be friends. Put your mind at ease. I find this all to be a delightful novelty rather than the domestic tragedy my husband would proclaim it to be."

David grunted and slugged his brandy.

"Ignore him, dear. I always do." Miriam shot her husband a scowl and scooted closer to Mary's side. "We need to plan a visit or an outing with the children. My mother died before they were born and they are most anxious to have a Nana to spoil them."

Mary gulped. She was sure her face drained of color while she contemplated skipping completely over motherhood and falling directly into grandmotherhood. Was that even the right word? She'd check the dictionary later.

"I didn't mean to frighten you." Miriam put a soft, warm arm around Mary's shoulder. "I was only trying to convince you they are excited to have you join our family. You and I will go and buy them some little baubles for you to give them, and they will be your devotees for life."

"I rather hoped you would take my new bride shopping," Luke said to Miriam. "She has never been to London before and her wardrobe is seriously lacking."

"With Lord Fletcher as her father, I'm sure most of her is seriously lacking," David muttered.

Enough of the Polk family defaming her father! She would take it from her husband and savior, Luke, but not from anyone else. She stood to her full diminutive height and glared at him across the room. "That is unfair of you to say. My father may not have been a financial genius or a wise man, but he loved me and I loved him. He did his best for me, and I will ask you kindly not to disparage him anymore in my presence."

Both Luke and David blinked at her, both chagrined.

Miriam stood with a glare. "Well said. And since the duke has given us the power of his purse, you and I will leave them to contemplate their bad manners while we deplete their fortunes on Bond Street." She looped her arm through Mary's and led her from the room.

Mary mimicked Miriam's stance, tipping her head up and

doing her best to "look down" at the two tall men when they passed. Her frame straightened with power and the heady emotion washed over her. She'd stand up for herself more often.

As they left the room she heard David mutter, "She has a spine. I like her." Mary stopped in her tracks. Had she heard that correctly?

"I apologize for David's behavior. He was testing you." Miriam sighed. "He's afraid you'll fall to pieces underneath the scrutiny of the *ton*. I told him it wasn't necessary to test your mettle but he's..."

"He's Luke's son." Mary shrugged. In a brash way he'd instilled some courage into her, but she wasn't in the mood to be grateful at the moment.

Miriam hugged Mary briefly. "Exactly. You've got them both figured out. You'll do fine as the new Duchess of Fenwick. Now, let's spend enough money to make them flinch when they get the bills."

Shopping was a whirlwind and meeting the children was a delight. Dusk came quickly and Luke took her on a tour of the house while the children were put to bed.

Mary slowly walked through the portraits lining the gallery in the Polk townhouse. Eyes of the past occupants gazed out across the room at each other in the silence.

She stopped at a more recent portrait of a lady in formal wear and a bored expression she recognized on David Polk's face during dinner.

"My wife, Annette," Luke said from behind Mary's shoulder.

Grinning, she faced him with a saucy look. "I thought I was your wife?"

He produced an exaggerated eye roll. "Yes, of course you

are. I was married twenty years with her and have only had three months with you, so you'll need to be forgiving of an old man's mind."

Mary admired the lady in the portrait a little longer. Annette was dressed in high fashion for the time with an elaborate gown, her hair piled high and powdered, her skin pale and creamy, a hint of a smile on her pink lips. She wore several pieces of jewelry from the cache of jewels Luke had offered to Mary. She thought Annette did them more justice than she ever could. "She's lovely. Were you very much in love?"

"Annette and I in love?" He frowned and tilted his head. "It was an arranged match and we both made the best of it, I suppose. There was no fighting or disagreements between us. It was all civil and proper. And boring. She and I both agreed to take secret lovers to break up the monotony."

Mary gasped and then laughed at his unrepentant smirk. "You're teasing me."

Stepping over to the next portrait, Mary tapped the frame with a familiar face staring back at her. "This must be you."

Luke's chest puffed up a little. "Quite dashing, don't you think? I hated powder and wigs, so I went *au naturale* for my portrait. My mother was vexed with me for months."

His dark hair was pulled into a queue without any false curls for his picture. His face was softer, carefree, and bold. A man ready to take on the world. An ugly three-legged hound dog lay at his feet.

"And who was your companion?" Mary asked.

"Talbot." Luke's face spread into a fond grin. "Mother was especially cross at me for adding him to the picture. She refused to pay the artist, so I doubled his salary and hung it over the front entrance for her to see every time she visited.

Told her it was the most expensive piece of art I owned and needed a place of prominence."

"You are a rascal."

"Through and through." David's voice agreed.

David and Miriam walked into the gallery with their arms around each other's waists in a casual but intimate pose. Mary's heart sounded an empty thump, wishing for the closeness a husband and wife shared.

You didn't have a choice. The alternative was much worse.

Luckily, if she moved a little closer to Luke, he'd instinctively tuck her arm into his and pat her hand. She enjoyed the affection, even if it wasn't what she'd wanted in a marriage.

"I haven't done a thing in the gallery yet," Miriam said. "I wanted to know if there were any portraits you wanted to be moved to Fenwick before I started rearranging things."

Luke pointed at his likeness. "I think Talbot and I should enjoy rusticating in the country together." He took a few more steps before his pace slowed and stopped at another portrait.

His face softened, the lines around his eyes and mouth settling into something more melancholy while he gazed at the young woman in the painting. He swallowed hard and his eyes shimmered. "I'd like to take Sarah home to Fenwick as well."

The woman in the painting seemed familiar. The eyes and shape of her nose were recognizable, but Mary couldn't place them at the moment. Her hair was a light chestnut color and up in curls. Her blue velvet gown was more modern. Her face was soft with full lips and her eyes sparkled. Was this the Sarah of Sarah's Circle?

David's voice wavered a little when he spoke. "Of course

you should take her home. She loved Fenwick better than London. Stupid of us both not to have done it sooner."

Mary wanted to speak, wanted to ask questions, but the air was too heavy to break. Miriam drew her away while both men stared at the portrait, David's hand resting on his father's shoulder.

"Sarah is David's older sister. She died in childbirth along with her son." Miriam's soft voice didn't disrupt the quiet. "David and Luke, they both adored her. Still do."

Mary identified the mixture of Annette and Luke in the lady's features. "Did you know her?"

Miriam shook her head. "I wish I had. David let me read all her old journals. I might be able to find them for you if you wish. She was a delight. Kind, compassionate, but a bit of a rascal."

"Like her father?"

"Quite a bit like her father."

THE STREETS WERE DIRTY, thick with mud and garbage. The crowd of bodies pressed close and dug into each other's pockets. Drinks and coins were passed freely. Men and women laughed to cover their misery. It stunk like sweat and piss.

There was no place in the world like London's secret boxing matches, and Henry was glad to be a part of them. Breaking away from society and joining Peter and George in their world always filled him with a sense of freedom.

"You going into the ring tonight?" Peter asked.

"A course he is," George answered before Henry opened his mouth. "I got five pounds on him. He won't let me down."

"Where did you get five pounds?" Henry demanded, scowling when George merely shrugged.

Peter scouted above the heads of the crowd. "Five pounds...as sure a thing as ever. Where's the books?"

Henry shook his head. "You should both save your money and not waste it betting on me."

After spending his week in the quiet and clean of Mayfair, Henry was itching to get into the ring and pound out all his frustrations on someone who would return the punch.

But the time wasn't right to enter the ring, not yet.

"I ain't worried. You've never let me down yet. Still my best pupil." George patted him on the shoulder.

Henry's ears still rang from the lessons George and Peter gave him when he'd been a child needing an outlet for his temper. He'd been born with a fire in his belly and a need to strike when it got too hot. The former fighters found an adept student and spent the same amount of time coaxing out his feelings as adjusting his fighting stance. They'd guided him into using his fire for something productive instead of destruction and taught him how to cool his head. Peter and George molded him into a gentleman as much as any lessons at Cambridge had.

The stakes were up and the ropes were set. Sand was spread for grip and to sop up the blood. Someone drew a shaky chalk line down the middle of the ring on the uneven cobblestones. A few torches were set up high for more light on the dark street. The crowd grew louder and pressed tighter for a clear view of the fight. Excitement crackled in the air.

"Where's Tommy? He'll get you set up. Oi! Tommy, I brought the Vicar with me tonight!" Peter shouted across the ring.

"Look'ee here! Welcome, Vicar!" Tommy shouted back.

Other spectators began to shout greetings at them and make their way towards the books.

Henry groaned. "I have not now or ever will be a vicar," he said.

"Your name is Church, ain't it? That's as good as the Archbishop around here." George laughed and pulled a flask out of his coat pocket. "Here, take a swig of this, it'll put a fire under your tail."

Henry opened the flask and took a whiff. "Zeus's beard, man!" His eyes watered.

"My mum's homemade brew right there. She's lost all her teeth and most of her eyesight, but she still makes the best batch of homemade gin."

Peter dove for the flask and took a chug before passing it to Henry. "Ah Georgie, boy. Your mum always makes the best 'Mother's Ruin' in town."

"Does she strain it through her stockings?" Henry asked and both of the older men laughed. Henry shrugged and tipped the flask to his lips. He gasped and coughed as the fiery concoction slid like hot coal down into his belly. Wiping the tears from his eyes, he returned the flask to George. "I don't ever want a taste of it again." His voice came out in a strangled whisper.

"You'll do, Henry Church." Peter clapped him on the shoulder. "Ready to get in the ring now? The purse has doubled since you joined the crowd."

Henry shook his head and tugged his cravat loose. The sign still hadn't come to him. "No, not yet. I'll watch for now."

His two teachers passed a glance between them but didn't push. He'd tried to explain it to them once, the focus he needed to get into the ring. The rush of adrenaline and knowledge his limbs were somehow faster and more sure, accompanied by a wave of calmness and the ability to almost "see" beforehand what his opponent was going to do. He'd gone into the ring once before without waiting for the ethereal sharpness to wash over him and gotten the thrashing of his life.

"Come to fight where it's fair instead of punching a man unawares, Church?" a voice sneered in his ear.

Henry glanced over and his blood boiled at the sight. He kept his composure and managed a nod at Mary's brother. "Lord Fletcher. I shouldn't be surprised you're here in the slums."

The weasel glared at him and then scanned the throng. "Where's my sister? I'd expect her to be working in a place like this." Lord Fletcher waved towards the rough-mannered women who mingled in the crowd.

Heat flushed through Henry and he strove to keep his fists down. Without the duke's protection, he couldn't punch Lord Fletcher in public. Not unless...

"Care to step into the ring and say that?" Henry kept his voice calm.

Fletcher scoffed. "You wouldn't last in an even fight. I've trained with London's best. It's only because of your cowardly actions you got the best of me last time."

"Oh ho! Hear that, me boy-o. Trained with London's best." Peter slapped both hands on Henry's shoulders with a hearty squeeze.

"London's best." George echoed and elbowed Henry.

His two mentors wouldn't be talked down now. It didn't matter if he did get splattered, he wasn't going to let this idiot keep that smirk on his face. "Sign me up, would you please Peter?"

With a gleeful shout, Peter skipped to the lists.

"I look forward to your comeuppance." With a final taunt, Fletcher left Henry to rejoin his cronies.

"Too bad we can't go below the waist anymore. Like to pull his balls off so there will be no more Lord Fletchers."

Henry laughed loudly at George's statement and his rage diminished slightly.

He kept his eyes on Fletcher from across the ring. *Never take your eye off your opponent, 'cept you got blood in 'em.* Peter's advice from years ago rang true for more than the ring.

The baron greeted his friends, partook of some drinks, flirted with a colorfully dressed doxy, and every other minute he was eyeing the growing purse at the side of the ring.

"He's under the hatches," Henry said.

"If he needs this win badly. It'll be down and dirty." George also followed the baron's every move. "He'll pull every trick he can. You feelin' it yet, my boy?"

"Not yet, I'm just angry right now. I can't believe Her Grace dealt with him for so many years. It makes me sick to think about what she..." Henry trailed off as awareness began to flow through him. His limbs tingled and the roar of the crowd was muffled. Everything was brighter, clearer; his motions sharp and distinct.

He inhaled as much of the pungent air into his lungs that they would hold. Mingled with the acrid scents of humanity was the subtle hint of spring. The scent of victory.

He ripped off his cravat and unbuttoned his waistcoat. "I'm going to destroy him."

Chapter Five

Concupiscible - Impressing desire; eager; desirous; inclining to the pursuit or attainment of any thing.

LUKE CONTEMPLATED his right-hand man at breakfast. The usually casual Mr. Henry Church was wearing gloves while eating and would not fully face Luke when speaking. His gaze was firmly focused on his plate.

It was time to reveal some truths to the lad.

"Late night?" Luke asked.

Henry's hand paused mid-bite. "I hope you didn't need my services while I was out."

"Not at all. A young man in London should be able to stretch his wings a little without a dour old duke demanding things from him at all hours." Luke snapped his napkin and laid it in his lap while Henry resumed eating.

Silence, then, "Do a bit of gaming?" Luke asked.

Henry cleared his throat but still wouldn't face Luke directly. "A bit. I made out all right."

"It's always a good evening when one comes out ahead. I had a little wager going myself last night. Time to find out if it was fruitful." Luke motioned for a footman to come closer. "Would you summon George to me?" He nodded and scurried off.

Henry was as still as a statue.

Luke bit into some toast. "Lost your appetite?"

"Maybe." Henry placed his white-gloved hands down on the table and curled them into fists.

George followed the footman in. His face lit up when he saw Luke and Henry sitting together.

"Good morning, George," Luke welcomed. "How did my investment do last night?"

"Safe bet, as always." George pulled a small purse from his pocket. He handed it to the duke. "Five pounds increased to ten. Minus my fee."

"Five pounds." Henry's head bowed so low to the table that Luke thought he was going to start banging it against the surface. "That's where you got the five pounds."

George winked at Henry and snapped the duke a proper salute. "Been a pleasure, Your Grace," he said and left the room.

Finally facing Luke, Henry pulled off his gloves and exposed his damaged knuckles. Small dark bruises rested right underneath both his eyes.

"How long have you known?" Henry asked.

"The first time you knocked one of Peter's teeth out when you were sixteen," Luke smirked. "I felt it was a healthy outlet for a young man to have, and encouraged them to continue your shadowy career. I make a nice little pile of blunt whenever you fight. Although, you haven't returned with bruises and bloody knuckles for quite a few years."

Henry rubbed his wounds before picking up his fork again. "Rough competitor. Things got a bit out of hand."

"I'm sure I wouldn't know. Ghastly business, pugilism. Downright barbaric."

"Good morning." Mary's sweet voice proceeded her entrance. "I hope all is well with...Oh, Henry, what on Earth happened?" Her eyes widened to the size of saucers and she covered her mouth at her misspeak.

A smugness warmed Luke's insides. Ah ha, Mary was comfortable shouting out Henry's given name and was concerned for his wounds. Luke's matchmaking plan was moving along perfectly.

"Forgive me, Mr. Church. I should not be so familiar with your Christian name."

"It's quite all right, Your Grace. I took a tumble last night and got a little banged up trying to break my fall." The younger man helped her to her seat.

"Sometimes we do more damage trying to keep our feet." Her face lingered on Henry's a moment before she shook her head and reached for the tea.

Luke's conniving brain saw a way to further his plot. "Of course you should call Henry by his Christian name. I've done it regularly since he was a small boy. Every time you call him Mr. Church, I turn about the room searching for his father. I say we put an old man's mind at peace and you call him Henry from now on." Luke declared.

Mary's face drained of color, and Henry's bruised eyes widened as they both gaped at Luke. He stifled a chuckle.

"I don't think I should..." Mary started.

"Nonsense. You'll do it. For me. Please?" he added.

The color returned to Mary's face and her cheeks blushed a pretty color. "If you insist. But only when we are not in public."

"Henry?"

Henry cringed at his name coming from Mary's lips. At the same time, it warmed his blood. Damn and blast! Why did the old man have to remove another degree of separation from her?

He stood up from his ledger with what he hoped was a neutral expression. "Yes, Your Grace?"

Mary's cheeks flushed. The duke was right. She was lovely when she blushed. "It feels so odd when you call me that. You've known me since I was a child."

I've loved you since you were a child, and the feeling keeps growing. "What do you need, Your Grace?" *Move it along, don't be alone with her. Keep it proper.*

"I tried to give Luke my bills, and he said I should take them to you personally. He said he's afraid he will lose them."

The old man hasn't lost a thing in his life, except his mind. "Of course, I'll be happy to take them." He held out his hand and she placed a small neat pile of slips in it.

"I'm trying to be frugal; please let me know if I overstep my budget. Every time I try to get an exact allowance from Luke he says, 'If I have to sell everything I own to get you what you want, I will.'"

Her higher-pitched voice tried to imitate the duke's. Henry let out a small chuckle. He glanced over the amounts and saw a glimpse of revenge against his employer's odd behavior. "This is hardly a drop in the bucket for him. I'd take advantage of his generosity while you can. Be outrageous. Redecorate every room in the house with something gaudy. Buy perfume and jewels and gowns." *Please, make the old man pay for being so erratic all of a sudden.*

Her ever-practical brain caught onto his last statement. "I don't want to buy gowns until I'm out of mourning. It would be such a waste to buy an entire wardrobe of black. I hate wearing black. It makes me feel smothered and swallowed up thinking of death, and then my belly starts to ache because Luke is not a young man and I wonder every day how long I'll have with him." Her eyes widened. "Oh, dear. I hope you don't think I have mortiferous thoughts towards Luke. He's been nothing but kind and..."

"Mortiferous?" Henry interrupted her. He bit his lip to keep a straight face.

"Mortiferous—Fatal, deadly, destructive." She recited the definition perfectly, her innocent face sweetly contradicting the dreadful words.

Again, Henry hid a laugh. "Your vocabulary is... prodigious." She smiled, and he hated the little twist his heart did at the sight.

"I'll have to look that one up. You're sure I'm not spending too much?"

Henry fanned the bills. "You could spend this amount every day and not make a dent into his fortune."

She visibly relaxed. "Thank you for letting me know. I feel much better. I retrenched so many times with the household budget when Father put me in charge at Fairley. I couldn't justify ending a servant's employment when all I needed was a new dress. It feels odd to me to not keep re-patching my clothes and instead give them to the servants. I'm sure they didn't think my first cast-offs were worth much."

They went into the rag bin, and the servants were all disgusted by your family for neglecting you. "I'm sure they made good use of them," was all he said.

There was a heartbeat of silence between them. It extended into two, then five, then ten. Ten glorious seconds where all he had to do was admire her face.

"Thank you again, Mr. Church. Er, Henry." Her smile wrenched his heart and left him with another fond memory to lock away tightly.

———

"YOU HAVE A CALLER, YOUR GRACE." The butler presented the card to Mary with a slight bow. She placed her embroidery to her side and took the card off the salver.

"On a Sunday? Who would call for you on a Sunday? It's not that worthless brother of yours, is it?" Luke placed down his evening paper and removed his spectacles.

Sundays were for family visits. If it was from her brother, she'd tear it up and tell the butler she would never be "at home" to him.

The name on the card made her heart fall like a stone into her belly. "It's not my brother. It's my mother." Her voice barely carried across the room.

Luke was at her side with remarkable speed for one his age. He took the card from her hand and snorted when he finished reading it. "Still thinks she's a baroness, does she?"

Excitement, wanting, forgiveness, and anger all battered against each other in her heart, and she rubbed her chest. The child desperate for her mother's attention warred with the older and apprehensive woman she was now. She shouldn't have feelings towards her mother. She *couldn't*. Her mother would use any emotions against her.

Mary's tongue was dry when she spoke. "I don't know what she wants. She left six years ago and I haven't heard from her since." She peered up at her husband. Her heart raced and her stomach plummeted into her toes. "What should I do?"

Luke handed the card back to the butler. "Let's see what she wants. Although, I can already hazard a guess."

Money. She was here for money. Money that wasn't Mary's to give. Money she wouldn't give if it were.

"I'm sorry," Mary whispered.

Luke chucked her chin lightly. "Cheer up, my dear. Pretend you're madly in love with your ancient husband. This will be a fun performance if we play it right."

"You are always so contrary to how I think a duke should act."

"Yes, well, this duke's been on the earth long enough to be as outrageous as he wants." Luke returned to his chair, holding his paper to hide his face.

He gave her no time to figure out the game he played when the butler entered with her mother.

"Mary, darling!" Naomi Fletcher, Baroness of Fairley, had not aged well in six years. She embraced Mary and kissed both her cheeks with paper-thin lips. Mary stared at the skeletal creature. Her mother was wearing a gaudy lavender gown more fit for a debutante than a mature woman. Bright red rouge stained her pale cheeks and lips.

Her mother grinned with rotten yellow teeth while she examined Mary from top to toe. "You are beautiful." Naomi's yellow smile widened to reveal black spots creeping around her gums. Her breath was terrible, and Mary subtly tipped her face away.

"I must admit, I'm at a loss for words right now." Mary was unable to keep the wonder out of her voice as she studied the woman before her.

Naomi's eyes were too bright, darting around the room in a feverish frenzy. Mary saw her mentally tallying what everything was worth.

A loud rumbled cough came from behind the newspaper in the chair, and Mary's attention darted toward the duke. Luke hadn't stood when Naomi entered. It was a cut.

Naomi frowned at the older man and placed her scowl on Mary. "Well, aren't you going to introduce me to your new husband?"

"We've met. When you first were married and came to Fairley Park. I wasn't impressed then, and I'm less impressed now." Luke's voice was bored, and he flipped a page of his paper without glancing up.

Naomi's glare tried to burn a hole through the paper.

What was he playing at?

"Please sit down. I'll ring for tea." Mary woodenly walked to the bell pull. The raging torment in her morphed into something cold and solid in her gut. Was she in shock? Going to faint? Or was she a little girl again, and cowed by her mother's presence?

"I came as soon as I learned of your father's death. You poor lamb." Naomi strut across the room to the couch. "Your brother told me your father had cancer. The dear boy is beside himself with grief and his new responsibilities."

"I'm sure he is." Mary rang for tea. Why had her angry feelings suddenly ceased? Where had her emotions run off to?

Were they hiding now? She'd rather feel turmoil than the cold, hard pit settled in her chest.

Her mother seated herself on the edge of the couch beside Mary. She touched the black silk of Mary's gown, rubbing it between her fingers. "And you're still in black? As a new bride? It's not 'the thing.' Clearly, you need my help to put things right for you."

Mary shook her head and gently tugged the fabric out of her mother's grasp. "I'm going into half-mourning tomorrow, and I wanted to honor Father. My husband has been very supportive of my wishes."

Naomi glared again at the newspaper across the room. "Yes, your husband. Quite a catch there. I can't believe our old neighbor had his eye on you."

"I didn't. But someone needed to run to the rescue when your son was selling her to the highest bidder." Luke's tone was bored and dismissive. He turned a page of his paper.

"My son would never do such a thing. He loves his sister." Naomi's voice rose a little.

The newspaper was slowly lowered, revealing Luke with his spectacles perched on his nose and wearing a fierce glare. One eyebrow hitched when he finally took in the sight of Naomi. "Zeus's beard. This is worse than I thought," he muttered.

Her mother pointed a finger at Luke. "I won't have you slander my Jonathan. He's a good boy. Why, just last evening he rescued a young family from a pack of thieves. They stole all his money and beat him soundly. He has a broken nose and two broken ribs to show for his heroism."

There was a pause and then a grin of realization washed over Luke's face. "Ha! Beat soundly, was he? Broken ribs and nose? Well done, Henry."

Henry? What did Henry have to do with...Oh! "Henry didn't fall." Mary's voice was monotone. And then something trickled up from her cold belly, past her throat and out her lips. She giggled.

Luke beamed at her. "He didn't tell me either. I knew he'd been in the ring last night, but I didn't know your brother was the other competitor."

"What are you talking about?" Naomi demanded.

Another feeling burst out of Mary's lips. Courage. "Jonathan is lying to you. He tried his hand at pugilism and got a sound drubbing for it." The cold knot started to dissolve. Henry gave Jonathan a beating. She had champions in her life now, and she would stand up to her mother.

Naomi gasped. "Your brother would never do anything so vulgar."

Mary snorted and shook her head. "You really should have written in the last six years, Mother. So much has changed."

"Your brother hasn't changed one bit." Naomi pressed her obsolete point.

"No, but I have." The desperate young child in her mixed with the sullen and shy adult and out emerged a different woman. One that wouldn't be bullied by those who were supposed to love her.

Rising to her feet, Mary pointed at the door. "I think you should leave now."

Naomi stood as well. "What are you saying? You're a young woman who has recently married a rich duke taking her first turn in London and mingling with the *ton*. You need my help now more than ever."

Mary caught her mother's gaze and didn't waver when Naomi began to glare. "I needed you four years ago when Father cut off Jonathan's allowance and my brother beat me for not giving him money from the household budget. I needed you three years ago when my father got sick and the doctor told me he was going to die. I needed you two years ago when I was adding cloth to my hems instead of buying new clothes to keep food on the table while Jonathan stole and sold everything he got his hands on while my weak father could do nothing but watch. I needed you one year ago when my bedridden and dying father required me to do everything for him to keep his dignity because I couldn't afford a nurse to care for him."

Hot tears streamed down her face, but her voice never wavered. "I realize now I never had you to begin with."

Agnes appeared in the doorway with the tea tray in hand. Her eyes widened when she witnessed the end of Mary's condemnation.

Mary pointed at her beloved friend. "Agnes was my mother. You gave me to her."

"*I* gave birth to you." Naomi protested.

"Since you ended your obligation to me early, please allow me the same generosity." Mary wiped her eyes. She faced a stunned Luke. It was rare that he was shocked into silence. "Luke, I do not want any relationship with either my mother or my brother. Would you please assist me?"

Luke cleared his throat and dug a handkerchief out of his pocket. He crossed the room to her. "Of course, my dear."

She took the cloth and wiped the tears that wouldn't stop. Mary glanced over at the woman she once admired and doted on for the last time. She locked her eyes with her mother when she spoke. "And never give either of them a single farthing."

"Never," Luke vowed.

The heavy silence in the room broke when Naomi let out an unholy screech. "I hate you! I've always hated you!"

Mary braced for a blow that never came.

Henry was there. Strong and capable as always. Mary wasn't sure when he'd entered the room, but she wasn't surprised. He was always there when she needed him.

Henry grabbed both of Naomi's wrists and then spun her around to be locked in his strong embrace.

"I'll remove this for you, Your Grace." He picked up Naomi's emaciated form without much effort. She screamed and thrashed and spit while he hauled her toward the door. Agnes opened the door for him, cast a sorrowful expression at Mary, and followed Henry from the room.

Mary's breath shook. Luke wrapped his arms around her. She promptly began to water his waistcoat with her tears.

"I owe you and your father an apology. I will never disparage your father again. Not if he had that creature for a wife," Luke said.

"I don't know what's happened to her. She's half the woman I knew."

"She's an opium eater. And from the look of her, she has been for quite some time." Luke took a step back from her and tipped her face up to his. "There's nothing you can do for her. I know your gentle heart will rattle around in a bit and appeal for mercy and compassion. But please. Please, I cannot stress this enough. There is *nothing* you can do for her."

Mary wiped her face once more. "I think I have quite a collection of your handkerchiefs stained with my tears; you must be running out."

He gently tapped her nose. "I'm hoping you'll get all your tears out now, my dear, and have nothing but happiness from now on."

Chapter Six

Concitation - The act of stirring up, or putting in motion.

WITH A FLOURISH, Henry signed his name to the last letter of correspondence sitting on his desk. He groaned and indulged in a delightful stretch, staring at the mural on the ceiling. Were there naked cherubs up there? How had he not noticed them before?

He hadn't time for anything except Mary. The duke made sure of that.

Once Her Grace was out of mourning, Henry was called in to accompany her everywhere. Everywhere! He'd taken her to Gunter's for her first bite of strawberry ice. Her eyes lit up and she radiated over the new sensation. He'd struggled not to take a bite for himself. A bite of her lips.

The next day, it was a drive in the park so she could be seen in her new wardrobe. She protested the need, but the duke insisted. He also insisted Henry be the one to take her, making a bald-faced lie his hands shook too much to drive himself. She'd sat next to Henry, close enough to brush against him while she pointed out all the beautiful colors of the flowers and fabrics and horses. He'd struggled not to laugh with her when she snickered at someone's outrageous fashion choices.

Again, last night, when Lord and Lady Polk came for supper and wanted to play whist afterward. The duke suddenly retired early and who was called to be Her Grace's partner? Him. Henry Church. Hopelessly in love and unable to utter a word.

There was a plot against him. Henry wasn't sure what the duke was planning. Was this a test of his loyalty? Perhaps he wanted Henry to quit and work somewhere else, away from Mary. Then why didn't he dismiss him? Or was the old man toying with his emotions for fun?

Too many questions and not enough answers.

But he would no longer be a part of whatever madcap scheme his employer had. His resolve to remain a loyal servant was becoming shakier with every second he spent with Mary. He'd threaten to resign and see if the old man called his bluff.

He folded from his stretch into a normal posture as Agnes appeared in front of his desk. "Forgive me, Agnes. I've been in the chair too long today."

"His Grace is asking for your help in the green parlor."

Suspicion flooded his veins. "Help with what?"

"He's teaching Her Grace to dance. Lord and Lady Polk are throwing a ball next week."

Henry's eyes narrowed. "I'll *bet* he needs help." He rose to his feet and with a march that would have impressed Wellington, strode into the green parlor.

"Ah, Henry. Thank you for coming so quickly." The duke sat in a chair with one foot resting on a padded ottoman, wearing a gaudy green woolen sock. Mary stood next to him, fussing with a blanket to lay over his lap. Two strangers, a man and a woman, stood at the piano.

"May I introduce Mr. Louis Travers, a dancing master from France. And his sister and accompanist, Miss Travers." The duke motioned to the strangers in the room.

The plump and fresh-faced Miss Travers bobbed from the piano. Henry rested his gaze on Mr. Travers and froze when the green-eyed monster poked at his brain. Mr. Travers was young. Young, lithe, and handsome. He bowed at Henry. "Your servant, monsieur," he said with a thick Parisian accent.

Henry returned his gaze back to the duke, raising a brow.

"We were teaching Mary how to dance, and doing splendidly, but my gout is flaring up something fierce."

Gout? Since when did the old man have gout?

"We were about to learn the waltz. But I can no longer keep my feet. Would you be so kind as to step in for me?" the duke asked.

Anger bubbled up into Henry's chest. "Your Grace, I'm getting tired of this farce."

The duke frowned; his eyes wide with innocence. The old man should tread the boards. "Farce? What do you mean?"

It was the worst possible moment to confront his employer. Miss Travers gazed on with interest, Mr. Travers with amusement, and Mary, innocent Mary, was the only one who appeared truly confused.

Henry grit his teeth and searched for the most diplomatic way to extract himself. "I am a little behind in my work at the moment. I've been *delighted* to escort Her Grace to various activities for the past week, but I really must return to my duties or your estates will fall to pieces." There. That sounded plausible. Downright responsible if he wanted to push it further.

The older man's face melted into one of abject apology while his eyes sparkled with mischief. "You're quite right, Henry. I have been making unusual demands of your time. You are such a wonderful asset to me; I forget my place at times."

Henry's heart twisted. The old fox was cunning. Henry glared while the duke blinked with complete purity.

"It's quite all right, Your Grace. I will lead Her Grace in the steps myself." Mr. Travers volunteered and held out a hand to Mary with a charming smile. Mary lowered her eyes and reached out to accept.

The green-eyed monster walloped Henry upside the head. Waltzing required much more touching than a quadrille or a reel. Hands were placed on shoulders, on waists. He'd be damned if the young pup touched his Mary.

"Stick to teaching, Mr. Travers. I'll dance with Her Grace." Henry's voice was more of a growl than actual speech.

Mary's lips twisted into a frown. "Mr. Church. I don't want to take up any more of your time on needless activities. I can take instruction from Mr. Travers."

Damn and blast! Now Mary was out of sorts with him.

"Don't listen to me grumble in the gizzard. I will always have time for you, Your Grace." He held out his hand for her, hoping she'd accept.

She hesitated a moment before sliding her hand into his. Her skin was warm, her touch soft but firm. It sent a bolt of excitement and heat through his limbs. He silently cursed; he'd fallen into the duke's trap once again.

"Splendid. We shall begin." Mr. Travers clapped his hands and Miss Travers began to play softly.

———

LUKE ADMIRED the way they danced together. Henry's muscular form and darker complexion contrasted nicely with Mary's smaller frame and ivory skin. He wasn't too tall; she wasn't too short. Henry put his hand on Mary's waist and she relaxed into his grasp, trusting him to guide her.

A quiet celebration was in order.

Unfortunately, the only thing within reach was cold tea. And he wasn't about to give up his 'gout' charade yet to fetch anything else.

"Your steward is dancing with your wife." David's voice came from over his shoulder.

He glanced up at his son who was standing behind his chair and motioned for him to take a seat next to him.

"Don't they fit perfectly? I'd like to call for brandy and cigars, but I'll settle for tea and biscuits." Luke caught Agnes's eye, pointed at the tea tray, and she scurried off to fetch a fresh pot. "Delightful servant. It's like she reads my mind."

David gestured toward the dancing couple. "There's a Frenchman. In your parlor. Teaching your wife to dance the waltz. With your steward. And what's this nonsense about your foot?" He tapped Luke's ugly green sock with his walking stick.

"Clearly, I've come down with a horrible case of gout. It's common for a man of my age."

David rolled his eyes. "You've never been sick a day in your life."

"I didn't realize how wonderfully useful it was until now." Luke settled into his chair. "Things are coming along nicely. Look at the way she beams at him. He's no longer a savior, he's a friend. And if the blushes in her cheeks mean anything he will easily become more. We'll finish the Season here, and go back to Fenwick before I start on my annulment."

"What!"

David's outburst was loud enough to stop the music and have everyone in the room stare at them.

Luke slapped his son against the chest, causing him to cough. "Carry on, my treasures. A fly flew up his nose."

They all stared at David who coughed again, glared at his father, before flicking his wrist they should continue.

"Annulment. Whatever for?" David hissed once the music resumed.

"Because, as you said, I haven't been sick a day in my life and I won't sit around waiting to die before those two can have their happily ever after."

"You are mad."

"That's one reason for annulment, but I rather thought you'd like me to choose fraud instead."

"Fraud?"

"Seems to be the easiest. I will claim the license was no good, or her father's deathbed signature was coerced. Enough blunt to go with my claim and I'm sure the bishop will sign off on it."

"And you haven't thought of me and my family and all the rumors we'll have to deal with?" David grumbled.

"Would you rather I go for a divorce instead?" Luke countered.

"Caesar's ghost, no. That would be much worse than an annulment."

"Now you're seeing the light." Luke reached for the hot cup of tea Agnes placed beside them. "You've got plenty of warning now. Plan ahead. Come Christmas time, I will be an old, dour, single man once more."

———

"I WANT to try once more to persuade him I should stay home tonight." Mary's gaze met Agnes's in the mirror.

Agnes shook her head and fastened up another copper curl into the updo she was creating. "If there's anything I've learned in the last six months it's that what the duke wants, the duke gets."

Mary slumped, and then straightened when Agnes poked her with a hairpin. "I don't need to go to the opera, especially now David and Miriam can't go. I can wait until Luke's foot is better. I should stay home and take care of him."

Agnes grunted. "He does like it when you fuss over him. He's still wearing the ghastly green sock you made him." She pinned the last piece in place and admired her work before patting Mary on the shoulder. "You'll do."

"Such effusive praise, Agnes. Please refrain or it will all go to my head." Mary covered Agnes's hand with hers and squeezed. "In all truth, I'm afraid."

"Afraid? Of what?" Agnes asked.

"Of Mr. Church. Henry." Mary heaved a deep breath. "I'm having some...feelings toward him. Feelings a married woman shouldn't have toward another man." Holding his hand all afternoon while she learned the waltz was magnificent. His hand on her waist while he led the steps felt amazing. He stared into her face as if she was the most important thing in the world. Was she starved for attention or was this something more?

Agnes pulled up a stool and took Mary's hands. "I see why. Mr. Church is a wonderful man. And he cares for you, he always has. But now you're seeing him through the eyes of a woman instead of a child."

Mary squeezed Agnes's hands and released her. "You always bring me back to reality. I'm married to another man, and Henry probably still sees me as a child. I shouldn't have such thoughts towards him. But I feel I've done nothing but annoy him all week. Tonight feels like icing on the cake."

Agnes handed Mary a pair of long white gloves. "I have a feeling he doesn't mind."

Mary grabbed on to a bit of hope. "Do you think so?" Doubt still clouded her mind. Henry was both working and escorting her around town for the duke. He deserved a night off. "I can try again to stay home with Luke, and take some pressure off of Henry."

"I think you should go to the opera; you've wanted to go for years." Agnes clipped rubies to Mary's ears.

Mary did want to see the opera, and the gardens, and the palace, and the parks, the theater, the food, the balls. She wanted to experience everything. But not if Henry was uncomfortable. He looked like he was about to throttle the duke during her dancing lessons. "Maybe I should find a companion to take me places. I'll talk to Luke about it."

Agnes helped her to her feet and walked around her, taking in every inch of her new gown, tucking and smoothing away any creases. Her eyes swam a little when she finished. "You're not my little girl anymore. You're a beautiful lady. Your father would be so happy."

Mary pushed down the rising pressure in her throat. "Stop, Agnes, or I'll become watery-headed and make Henry even more cross with me." She picked up her reticule and a silk shawl. With one last glance in the mirror, she stepped out.

"You are doing me a great service tonight." The duke told Henry while they waited for her in the foyer. Mary got a peek of him and liked what she saw. He was decked out in formal wear for the evening. Black coat, golden waistcoat, buff breeches, white gloves, and black Hessians. A walking stick and top hat were tucked under his arm. He was scowling at his employer.

"Bad case of gout." Luke continued, pointing at his foot still encased in the ugly wool sock she'd made him. "But I don't want to disappoint Mary. She's enjoying herself more and more every day. I like seeing her happy."

Henry's face softened. "I like her being happy too. Put your feet up and rest, I'll take care of the duchess."

Mary wouldn't keep him waiting any longer. Both men went silent when she swept into the foyer.

"Red." Henry gasped.

She brushed a hand down the red gown. Agnes said that the color brightened her copper hair and skin. Her curls were styled high and sophisticated. The Fenwick rubies hung at her ears and throat. She did a slow turn for Luke to view her new purchases. "I hope you like it. Miriam said red was my color. I like it so much better than black."

Henry gawked at her while the duke loudly kissed both her hands.

"Stunning!" Luke declared. "You'll be the most beautiful creature at the opera." He took her hand and tucked it into Henry's arm. Henry gazed down at her, blinking before shaking his head and firming up his jaw. Was he clenching his teeth? Oh, dear. It was not a good start for the evening.

"Have a good evening, both of you." The duke ushered them toward the door. He waved at them from the porch as they entered the carriage.

The carriage door shut and the duke returned to the house, where his limp mysteriously disappeared.

———

LUKE LIT every candle in the study to get all the light he needed for his aging eyes. He ate a simple dinner prepared on a tray sent to him and asked for a cup of coffee for some extra vigor.

He had no qualms about abusing Henry's time to insert him with Mary. But the least he could do was help the boy with the books.

A stack of ledgers, bills, and correspondence awaited him. A depressing sight he'd been happy to foist onto Henry for the past decade.

With a sandwich in one hand and a pen in the other, he donned his spectacles and began signing a stack of bills. His heart warmed at every one he saw for Mary. She was becoming bolder and bolder with her choices and habits. Her bills told him the parlor was getting new drapes and plush expensive carpets. Good girl.

He downed another cup of coffee before taking up the pile of letters awaiting him. He began separating them by personal, business, and solicitations when he noticed a thumping sound in his ears. Sitting back in his chair he took a couple of deep breaths and placed a hand over his chest. His heart was galloping.

Noticing a numb sensation on his tongue, he licked his lips. He set down his cup of coffee and wiggled his prickling fingers. So very odd.

He sipped his coffee again. It was strong and sweet, the way he liked it. His lips began to tingle and he tried to shrug off the sensation. Time brought a variety of strange sensations to an aging body, poor circulation being one of them. He was probably just cold.

A letter from his solicitor was the best place to start his evening of work. Poor Merrill barely kept up with all the changes to his will. And now Luke was throwing in another ball for the man to juggle. Annulment.

He picked up his pen and his fingers trembled violently when he tried to press it to the paper. The pen fell from his hands and splattered ink across the pages.

This had never happened before. Cold fingers, yes, but never this severe. He stared at his trembling hands and his heart began to pound even harder against his ribs. His breath came fast, and he couldn't get enough air into his lungs.

A heart attack? The doctor told him last week he'd live many more years. He was faking a spell of gout, for hell's sake.

He opened and closed his fists, trying to dispel the coldness seeping into his digits and stop their quaking. It was all so odd.

Perhaps he needed to warm them up. He reached for his hot cup of coffee and froze.

Coffee. Sweet and strong, the way he liked it. Sweet enough to hide anything unusual in it. Like poison.

By Zeus's beard. He'd been murdered!

And it angered him. All his plans for Mary and Henry weren't done. There were a great many things he wasn't done with.

A sharp pain pierced him from inside his chest and he grunted. Who would do such a thing?

He wouldn't stand for it. He'd never slipped away from anything and he wasn't about to do it in his final moments.

"Trying to make the old man look like he's suffered a heart attack, eh? You'll not get rid of me quietly," he muttered, rising from his chair. He swept all the papers off the desk and threw the cup against the wall to shatter. If he was going to be murdered, he was going to do it properly.

He pushed the heavy desk over; gratified he still had the strength for theatrics while his body began to shut down. The desk thumped when it hit the ground and scattered all the contents onto the floor. Ink splattered on the carpet along with the rest of his dinner.

Falling to his knees, he gasped for air from the exertion. It was still not enough. He must show them, everyone needed to know that the Duke of Fenwick had been murdered.

The paper knife lay on the floor in front of him. It wasn't sharp but with enough force...

"Explain this." His pulse pounded in his ears as he grabbed the dull implement. His hands trembled so hard he almost dropped it. With his last bit of strength, he jammed the makeshift weapon into his ribs, letting out a cry when it pierced the skin. He fell onto it, burying it deeper into his body.

The servants came into view while his rapid heartbeat spilled out his blood. The world got darker and darker when shouts and screams filled the air. The numbness began to overwhelm him and he allowed it to take him.

Chapter Seven

Enerve - To weaken; to break the force of; to crush

HENRY HADN'T ATTENDED the opera since his Cambridge days. Admittedly, he'd gone with a group of friends to view the dancers but found the ordeal somewhat boring. He glanced at Mary to see if she was having the same type of experience.

Mary was on the edge of her seat, eyes wide, lips parted in awe, clutching her reticule tightly while the Queen of the Night sang her aria about blood and death. He found the sight of his lady fair much more appealing than whatever was going on stage or in the audience. He sprawled into a comfortable position, one ankle resting on his knee, supporting his head on his hand, and observed her instead. Much better view.

He'd started to doze when she rose to her feet and

applauded, clapping with an exuberance that was muffled by her gloves while the players took their bows.

"Oh, Henry, it was delightful." She took in his casual posture. "Obviously you were not as enchanted as I was."

"I wouldn't say that." He rose to his feet. Giving his waist-coat a tug into place, he held out his arm.

She set her hand on his forearm. "Have you seen 'The Magic Flute' before?"

"Once, back in my college days. The view was somewhat cramped from the floor, and I think I was three sheets to the wind before the First Act."

Giving his arm a little slap with her fan, she laughed. "You shouldn't say such things, you'll break my hero-worship illusion of you."

Her words hit like a kick from a mule, but he managed to keep a smile on his face. It was best she thought of him as a hero. A knight in shining armor who used his fists rather than a sword. He would practice his courtly love from afar, running off to do errands to prove his bravery while knowing the lady would never be his. A Lancelot to a Guinevere, although he would never betray his King Arthur.

But he and King Arthur would have strong words before the night was over.

He forged a path through the throng of audience members for them, enjoying the way her grip tightened around his arm whenever she was jostled. They broke through the crush and into the outside world. He waited for Mary to adjust her shawl before escorting her down the street toward the carriage.

Peter and George were leaning against the vehicle, waiting for their return with smug expressions. They flashed a full purse at him. He wondered if cards, dice, or an actual fight occupied their time tonight while he played the noble.

"Does George have a mark on his eye?" Mary asked when they got closer.

Henry snorted. A fight, then. "Probably. He's getting a little old and slow."

"Oy, but my hearing's perfect. I can still whip you, me boyo." George opened the door to the carriage and Henry helped Mary up the step. She froze in the entrance. "Henry, the seat is missing." Her voice inflected almost like a question.

"What?" He lifted her down from the step and poked his head inside the carriage.

There was a gaping hole in the rear of the carriage where the seats and cushions used to rest. Now it was a bare stretch of wood and nails. The front seats were untouched.

"You dunderheads! Didn't you pay anyone to guard the carriage?" Henry shouted.

George and Peter both peered into the cab.

"Wouldja look at that!"

"Impudent stealing at its finest."

"Bet they didn't make a sound."

"Professional job right there."

Henry seethed. They both sounded much too relaxed with the current situation.

"Oh well, guess you'll have to sit cozy next to Her Grace in a dark carriage all the way home." George hopped up on top and Peter sniggered.

He'd been set up. Again. Damn and blast! Had the duke done this as well?

"Henry." Mary's soft touch rested on his arm. "We can hire a cab."

"They're all full and it might be hours before one becomes available." He'd give both men a drubbing when he got home. "I'll send you on ahead and then they will return for me."

"I don't want to leave you behind."

"I'm quite good at navigating London's streets."

"He'll be robbed for certain." George piped up from on top.

"Fancy cove like him? Naked and in the Thames by morning." Peter added.

Mary's grip tightened and she stepped closer to him. "Please Henry. Let's go home together. I couldn't bear it if anything happened to you."

He was sunk. "Very well, Your Grace." He handed Mary up into the damaged cab. He would spend the time traveling home planning the perfect punishment for his traitorous friends.

Climbing into the carriage he sat next to her, trying to keep a proper distance on the seat. It was impossible to do, and his leg rested snugly against hers. The door was shut, and they were alone. And by the size of the crowds, they'd be trapped in streets for a bit before the traffic moved.

She squirmed a little beside him as she settled into the squabs. Her legs brushed against his and brought a rush of heat to all his limbs. He leaned away from her and began bouncing his leg nervously while staring out the carriage window.

The scent of her perfume was released every time she moved. He wondered if the smell was stronger on her neck if he nuzzled her there. *Get your act together, man!*

Mary cleared her throat. "I remember when you left for Cambridge. Your parents were so happy. Said you were the first in the family to go to school."

"I was, thanks to His Grace. He sent me to the vicar's local school, then Eton, then off to Cambridge. Told me I was too bright to let my brains go to waste on gardening."

"Luke's not stupid. He knew what he was doing. He told me he has a long-term plan in mind for my future. I wish I knew what it was."

Me too. "He likes his schemes. And won't reveal them until they are fulfilled." *Did the old man* want *him to create a scandal with Mary?Ridiculous.* Henry loosened his cravat. Blasted heat was making his neck itch.

The carriage moved forward a few feet before stopping in the heavy traffic. Mary waved her fan, wafting more of her tantalizing scent towards him. "We probably will be here for hours. I hope you will be able to endure my company a bit longer."

"I enjoy your company."

"You do? I have been underfoot all week. I was certain you'd begun to tire of me."

He couldn't let that go. "I will never tire of being with you." He was glad of the darkness. If he had been visible she would have seen a moonstruck calf gazing at her.

The mood between them was comfortable now. His leg stopped bouncing and his anger subsided. They still hadn't moved more than a few feet and he saw a long night stretching in front of them.

Mary began slouching next to him. Her body would jump into wakefulness and then slowly descend into dozing.

He'd had enough of the duke's meddling. If His Grace orchestrated this charade with the seats then Henry was going to oblige. Just a little.

His mouth was dry but he managed to speak. "Rest your head on my shoulder."

Mary didn't hesitate. With a happy little sigh, she nestled into his side. Her head weighed lightly on his shoulder and her curls brushed his cheek. "Thank you."

He'd wallow in guilt later. For now, Henry would enjoy the moment.

IT TOOK a long time for the traffic to start moving. Mary didn't mind one bit. She leaned against Henry's broad shoulder and melted against him. If holding his hand and dancing was magnificent, then resting against his strong, warm frame was absolutely glorious. She'd never felt so snug, and cherished. The best experience of her life was happening and if it wasn't so disloyal to Luke, she'd order the coachman to circle for the rest of the night so she wouldn't lose the feeling of perfection.

She felt no need to break the silence in the carriage. For the moment she pretended she was the sleepy young bride of Mr. Henry Church. They'd finished at the opera and were returning to their own comfortable home. He'd steal kisses from her in the dark carriage and whisper words of love. She'd blush and return his affection, knowing she was the most loved woman in all of London.

The carriage started moving and her daydream was interrupted. She lifted her head off his shoulder and glanced out the window into the foggy London night. "Henry?"

"Yes?"

"Do you think you'll ever get married?"

Silence. "No."

The response found her both relieved and sad. "Why not?"

"I'm devoted to His Grace."

She buried her little dream as Mrs. Church deep into her heart, locking it up and throwing away the key. "He's lucky to have you."

A commotion outside alerted them long before the carriage stopped. Henry leaned out the window to investigate the noise.

"Something's amiss at the house," he said when the carriage rolled to a stop.

There was shouting, wailing. It came from everywhere, surrounding them with confusion.

"Stay here," Henry commanded.

She waited for him to exit the carriage and poked her head out the door. George and Peter stepped down from the top and stood guard on either side.

"Any idea what's going on?" Mary asked. A little shiver of fear crawled up her spine.

The two men glanced at each other and George took point. "I'll go find out."

"Help me out, Peter," Mary said and took his hand.

He helped her down, but kept a grip on her hand. "Mr. Church wants you to stay here, Your Grace."

"I will," she stared at the house. Every window was lit up and the shadows of bodies moved quickly through each room.

"Do you think we've been robbed?" The fear going up her spine radiated into her limbs.

Peter scowled. "It's possible. Awful lot of people for a burglary."

She thought so too when the neighbors began to congregate in the street. She rested her hand against Peter's arm for support as the fear settled into her belly.

A loud cry came from the open door, one of horror and despair. Henry.

Mary lifted her skirts and ran.

"Your Grace, stop." Peter's hand on her arm was firm, stopping her from continuing across the street.

"Peter, let me go. I have to find out." She struggled from his grasp when George exited the house.

His face was pale while his eyes sought out Peter and Mary. "Don't let her in," he shouted across the street and disappeared back into the house.

Mary thrashed harder. "Let me go! Peter, let me go!"

He shook his head and carefully held her in place. "I can't do it, Your Grace. I won't."

George reappeared with Agnes. Her face was pale and streaked with tears.

Mary stopped struggling when she saw her friend and Peter released her. Agnes searched through the dim light and ran towards her when their eyes met.

"Oh, my dear child! I'm so sorry." Agnes embraced Mary tightly.

"What's happened? What's wrong?" Mary demanded.

"His Grace has been murdered." Agnes wailed.

Mary's mind went blank and she froze. The information didn't make sense. Luke? Murdered? How? He was staying home to put his foot up. How could he be murdered?

Her legs wilted, and Peter stepped in, holding both her and Agnes upright until Mary found her footing.

"No. No, you're wrong." She wriggled from Agnes's arms. "He's not. He can't..."

Another unholy howl inside came from Henry. It was drowned out by the sound of hooves when a horseman made a jarring stop at her porch. Lord David Polk leaped from the saddle and stormed into the house.

There was a beat of silence. The whole world waited for what he would do. His voice began to carry from the open door, shouting, demanding, screaming, and then crying.

Mary sank to her knees, her beautiful red gown pooled into the dirty street as tears raced silently down her face. This had to be a nightmare. She was still in the carriage, dozing on Henry's shoulder and would wake up at any moment.

Tiny pebbles dug into her knees as reality sunk in. She fell forward, bracing herself up while despair washed over her. Luke couldn't leave her too.

Agnes tried again to embrace her. She didn't want any contact. It was too much. Everything was too much. She pushed Agnes away. "Please don't touch me. Don't, don't..." she gulped before her voice cracked.

Henry walked from the house. His eyes were red and he wiped his face furiously on his sleeve as he searched the crowd.

He morphed into the duke's right-hand man once again, and took charge of the scene. "George, clear off the onlookers. Peter, go for the constable." His voice was firm and sharp and the two men sprinted into action. Henry strode towards Mary with long steps. He crouched next to her and lifted her hands from the street, the heat of his grasp filling her cold fingers with warmth.

"Mary." His voice quivered again.

"Please, tell me it's not true," she begged.

He closed his eyes and let out a trembling breath. "It's true."

She began to sob, folding herself over and hugging her aching belly. Strong arms surrounded her, and this embrace she welcomed. She inhaled Henry's familiar scent and pushed herself into his warmth while she sobbed.

He stroked her hair and face gently. "Please, Your Grace. We need you to move from the street. Lord Polk and I are sending you to his home while we deal with this."

She found his handkerchief stuffed into her hands. He pulled her to her feet.

"Agnes, take care of your mistress." Henry's voice was commanding once more and Agnes's slender arm draped across her shoulders and led her to the carriage.

Chapter Eight

Internecion - Massacre; slaughter.

HENRY DIDN'T SEE Mary for days after the murder. She'd stayed with the new Duke and Duchess of Fenwick while the constable and his men picked through the house. Henry answered all their questions about their whereabouts that night, with George and Peter to testify as well. The constable promised not to question Mary after some knuckle cracking and subtle threatening motions from all three men. She'd been through enough.

He'd been too busy to go and pay his respects, trying to answer the constable's questions, help the butler and house-keeper with the servants in an uproar over their master's death, and make a seamless and painless passage of his duties to David's steward.

The new duke requested his attendance in the funeral

procession and asked him to be a pallbearer for his late employer—and friend.

Mary was sitting vigil next to Luke's body when he arrived for the procession. Her posture was low, defeated. She was dressed in black, with her face veiled. Silent tears splashed onto the handkerchief in her lap. She appeared small and alone while she passed out sprigs of rosemary wrapped in black silk ribbons from a basket at her feet to each mourner who came through the parlor.

Henry wanted to embrace her, to take her away from this sorrow and kiss her until she never thought of crying again. He'd seen enough of her tears. He tried to catch her gaze, but she never raised her eyes above anyone's waistcoat. When they closed the coffin, she burst into sobs and ran from the room.

The funeral march was a spectacle, with mourners coming out of the woodwork to gawk at the murdered duke's transport to the church. The new duke hadn't taken any chances with his father's body being attacked and hired a security detail to escort them to the cemetery. The words of the sermon blended together into a background hum. Henry waited for the proper words to be said before he would be needed to take the body to its final resting place.

Henry's head began to nod and jerk while the service droned on. "You're dead on your feet," someone murmured in his ear. Henry straightened and glanced at Lord Polk, er, the Duke of Fenwick, standing next to him.

"Forgive me, Your Grace." Henry rubbed his eyes. "Things have been a mess and I haven't rested much."

The duke's gaze rested on the clergyman who was raising his voice and arms to heaven to ask the Almighty to accept the newly deceased into his bosom while he leaned toward

Henry. "I need to impose upon your time a little more. The solicitor is going to read the will tomorrow at my home, and your presence is required for it to go on. Father wanted a show with the dispersal of his earthly possessions and, damn him, he's going to get it." The new duke growled and was silent for the rest of the sermon.

THE BLUE PARLOR of Fenwick's townhouse was brightly lit by the sunshine, and Henry was glad it was no longer draped in black. There had been too much darkness in his life recently. He gazed over at the few occupants who arrived earlier for the will reading and stopped when he saw Mary.

He hated seeing her still dressed in black. She'd forgone a veil and her face was exposed. There was a little light in her eyes, and it pleased him. She sat next to Miriam and the children, pulling little Lord Adam into her lap for a hug.

Henry took a place leaning on the wall next to them, standing with his arms crossed and facing the door to identify who else was invited to the old duke's afterlife performance.

A few of the servants shuffled in, dressed in their best clothes. They appeared a little lost, as if they should be cleaning and organizing instead of sitting on the furniture they usually tended to.

Mary stood every time someone new entered, thanking them for coming and helping them find a seat where they would be comfortable and offered refreshment. He admired her strength and poise. In a short time, Mary had become a strong and capable woman.

Henry smelled a strong whiff of lilac and wondered which lady was wearing the strong perfume when Lord Maxwell

What had Luke done? Why hadn't he told him?

A soft hand gripped his sleeve. "Oh my dear boy, please. Please don't hate me."

He peered down into the face of his mother. His mother? "I could never hate you," he said. "I need to go." He brushed her aside and paused when David Polk demanded from the vicar and the doctor from Fenwick to tell the truth.

"Henry Church is the true son of Sarah Carroll," Dr. Smith said. "I was there when Sarah died. She gave birth to a healthy young son who was given to the care of Mr. and Mrs. Church, the gardeners at Fenwick."

The vicar verified it. "I baptized baby Henry Albert Carroll and then hid the records away at the request of the duke."

The noise started up again as Henry stormed out of the parlor. He inhaled the fresh air deeply. Once. Twice. His head spun. He charged down the hallway and into the library. Once he was alone, he crashed onto his knees and let the wave of emotions sweep over him.

Shock, betrayal, anger, sorrow. All of these things at once drew out a cry of agony from his gut and he curled into a ball.

"Henry! Henry Church, where are you!" a loud voice demanded from the hallway.

He couldn't answer, he couldn't even breathe.

He saw a pair of legs and a strong hand gripped his shoulder. "Up with you, lad. You're a Polk and we're made of stronger stuff than this."

He was forced to his feet and came face to face with His Grace, David Polk, Duke of Fenwick. His uncle.

The duke searched Henry's face for a moment, his eyes wandered over every single feature. Henry waited for him to finish. Long fingers reached up to his cheeks and Henry saw tears swimming in the duke's eyes.

"You have her face. I never really looked at you before, but you have her face. The old fox kept you from me."

Henry blinked a few times. "I don't expect...I can't know what you think..." Sentences wouldn't form right and he ceased trying.

"You are my nephew. You are Sarah's son. I claim you. I'll declare it to the world," the duke vowed.

Henry was overwhelmed once more and almost toppled over. "Please, Your Grace."

He received a shake from the older man. "David. I am David. Never call me that again. We are family." David released him and led him to a chair. Henry gladly dropped into it and hung his head down toward his knees.

"I'll go dismiss everyone. Catch your breath. Oh, I'm sure the old man's having a good old laugh watching this unfold." David stormed out of the room.

DAZED.

Mary's morning word described her current mindset. *'Dazed - To hinder the act of feeling by too much light introduced.'* In this case, it was the light of knowledge, and everyone in the room was dazed by it.

Mary picked at the black lace gloves covering her fingers while the rest of the room murmured and whispered like angry bees in the background. Someone should go after Henry, to make sure he was safe, to let him know he still had friends. But her feet and limbs refused to move. *Dazed.*

"Your Grace, I'm so afraid." Isabel Church cried in the

seat next to her. Mary shook off her fog and wrapped an arm around Isabel.

"I hope Henry doesn't hate me. I didn't take care of him for money. I love him. He's such a good son."

Mary shook Isabel gently. "I don't think Henry can hate anyone."

Isabel nodded and sniffed. "He's a good boy, like his mother. How someone raised a hand to that sweet creature..." She broke down again into noisy tears. Mary embraced her until the older woman was able to regain her composure.

"Thank you, Your Grace. You've always been such a sweet girl," Isabel sniffed and stood. "I won't keep troubling you."

Mary squeezed Isabel's hand one last time. "You are never trouble, Mrs. Church. And I hope you will call me your friend Mary instead of 'Your Grace' from now on."

Isabel placed a tender kiss on Mary's cheek and left.

Wiping away an errant tear of her own, Mary rose to her feet. There wasn't any reason for her to stay any longer. There was a townhouse to pack up, her own servants and living to arrange, and a constable still investigating the murder of her husband. Agnes appeared at her side from the shadows and discretely squeezed Mary's arm a little before dropping behind her as a servant should.

"We should go to the townhouse and start packing for our new home," Mary said softly. She hadn't returned there since the night of the murder and she didn't plan on staying there long. She was more than ready to leave London and its memories of Luke behind.

"I'll send for the carriage." Agnes left with a quick pace.

Mary walked toward the parlor door when Miriam appeared in her path. "My darling girl, you take all the time you need to get things at Fenwick organized for your departure." She took Mary's hands. "And let me know what help you need."

"Aren't you worried I'll steal the silver?" Mary tried for a lighthearted tone that broke off into a sob. Miriam's arms embraced her tightly.

"He loved you," Miriam said. "Not the way a husband loves his wife, but a grandfather or a friend. You brought him great joy and delight in his old age, and I thank you for it. David does too, but he won't say it."

Mary released herself from Miriam's grip. "Thank you. I'll let you know my timeframe when I figure it out." She and Miriam exchanged sober smiles and Mary left the room.

As she was passing the library, a strong hand grabbed hers and pulled her inside, shutting the door behind her. She managed a squeak of protest when Henry's voice calmed her. "It's me, Your Grace."

The room was dim with the curtains drawn but still light enough to view the sorrow on the face of the downtrodden man before her. He slumped into a chair and towed her onto his lap.

"Please," his voice was weary, "Please let me hold you. Just for a moment."

Hold or be held? She slid her arms around him and pressed his head to rest on her shoulder. Her dear friend and savior had never looked so sad before. She wished there was more she could do. He sighed deeply while she gently stroked his soft brown hair.

"That feels lovely, thank you," he whispered.

The comfortable silence between them stretched on. Conversation was the last thing either of them needed. She drew strength from him as he surely pulled the same from her.

His arms tightened around her and he buried his face against her. She held him close and selfishly wished for the moment to never end.

Henry swallowed hard and broke the spell, lifting his head. "I'm so angry at him right now."

"You have a right to be."

"And at the same time, I miss him terribly." He buried his head into her shawl.

She stroked his neck. "I felt the same way when my father died. I was angry at how he left me so defenseless. And yet there was a large hole in my heart where he should have been."

"I wish... we had more time together. He should have told me so I could have been a better grandson to him. I wish I had known so I could have helped Lady Carroll..."

Taking his face in her hands, she forced him to face her. His brown eyes were brimming with different emotions threatening to spill forth. She couldn't stop from rubbing her thumb tenderly across his cheek.

"He adored you," she said firmly. "He told me dozens of times he couldn't be without you. I daresay he was overly selfish and made you his steward so you wouldn't part from him, to keep you for himself." She brushed his hair away from his eyes. "He helped you become a strong, smart, and honorable man. I am grateful to him; I am grateful he kept you from that monster."

Henry closed his eyes and clasped her to him. Tight, so tight her rib creaked. His shoulders shook a moment while he gasped for composure. She held on just as firm, cherishing the feelings between them, wishing to run away with him.

But too much was revealed. He was no longer merely Henry Church, son of the gardener and steward to a duke. He was so much more now, and he needed to find out where he fit in his new world. He was the grandson of her deceased husband; she was doubtful there was a place in it for her beyond friendship.

With one last sigh, Henry pushed her from his lap and rose to his feet. He adjusted his waistcoat and jacket and his face shifted into the persona of Henry Church, the Duke of Fenwick's unflappable right-hand man. "Thank you for your kind words. They mean a great deal to me." His voice was steady now. "I shouldn't detain you any longer."

She was dismissed. They'd shared a heartfelt moment and now it was over. It was time to resume their roles again as friends, and nothing more.

"Good luck to you, Mr. Chur..." What did she call him now?

"Henry," he said forcefully, "Remember? He wanted you to call me Henry."

HENRY RETURNED to the blue parlor. Everyone left except Mr. Merrill and his uncle David. The new duke walked to a cabinet and pulled out a little bottle of clear liquid.

"Vodka, from some Russian friends of mine. It gets the job done quicker." He poured a finger's worth into three glasses and passed them around.

Henry gulped his down quickly and let the fire in his belly burn. He closed his eyes and heaved a deep, heavy groan that came from his toes.

Mr. Merrill sipped his at first and then downed the rest of it. "You and I are the trustees for Lady Carroll's house and her children, Mr. Church. It makes a fair living if Lord Carroll cuts them off."

Henry guessed as much. He stared at his glass and then glanced at his uncle who poured him another.

"Keep drinking, son, there's more."

"I don't know if my brain can take any more." He took a swallow of the vodka with a humorless chuckle and relaxed into his seat. "Let's have it."

Mr. Merrill continued. "With the exception of what's in the will and the entailed estates, he left you everything."

"Everything?" The weight of it squashed Henry. There were more estates, mines, forests, and some investments in canals and a railway. He glanced up at his uncle. "I don't want..."

David snorted. "Neither do I! I haven't been an idle man waiting for my inheritance. I have plenty and to spare for what I need and want to pass on. This is Sarah's legacy, your legacy."

Henry groaned. "It's enormous. My brain is in such a dither I can't see straight."

"You'll stay here until you do," his uncle declared. "I feel I have been robbed from knowing my dear Sarah's son and I won't waste another day." His eyes shone brightly while he swallowed his drink.

After clearing his throat, Mr. Merrill pulled an envelope out of his breast pocket. "There was one last bequest in the will. I was to give you this."

Henry examined the thick red seal with his grandfather's signet. "Do you know what it is?"

Mr. Merrill shook his head. "And after today's debacle, I'm fairly certain I don't want to know."

Henry broke the seal. He pulled out the single sheet inside and unfolded it.

It was a marriage license. One obtained from the Archbishop at a considerable sum. It had already been filled out. He was the groom. And the bride was Mary Fletcher Polk.

Chapter Nine

Capricious - *Whimsical; fanciful, humoursome*

THE CONSTABLE PACED in front of Mary. His frustration and helplessness radiated into her. "There was no forced entry, no suspicious activity reported by the neighbors or staff. No questionable deliveries at a late hour. The windows were all intact and locked. Not even a scrape on a keyhole to be found anywhere. I simply have no place to start looking."

Mary shoved down her own frustration and did the only thing she was able to think of. "Please, sit down Mr. Frost, and have some tea." She motioned toward a seat at the small garden table set for her meeting with him. The townhouse was a torrent of activity and outside was the only place to find any peace to receive his update on the investigation into Luke's murder.

"I'm sorry, Your Grace." He dropped into the chair while she poured him a cup.

"I know you are doing your best, and I thank you for

doing such a thorough search. I was waiting for you to question me as well."

He scowled and picked up his cup. "Yes, well, Mr. Church warned me off from you. Said you had nothing to add he hadn't already told me."

Mary stirred in her milk. Her cheeks warmed along with her heart. Even in a crisis, Henry took care of her. "That may be true, but it wasn't his place to interfere with your investigation." She took a sip of the hot tea to settle her thoughts. "Do you have any questions for me? Anything I can do to help?"

The constable set down his cup and exhaled. "I have questions, but they are not pleasant ones."

"Murder is rarely pleasant." Poor Luke. Was he surprised and frightened? Did he fight to the end? No one would tell her any details. Her hand trembled when she pushed a plate of biscuits toward Mr. Frost.

He took one and bit into it. She waited for him to gather his thoughts.

"Did your husband have any enemies?" he asked once he'd swallowed.

"No, not that I know of."

"Do you have any enemies, Your Grace?"

"No, I -" she stopped. "My brother and my mother are not too fond of me at the moment. They were both seeking funds from my husband and he refused to give them any."

He took out a small paper and pencil. "Lord Fletcher?"

"Yes, my mother is staying with him."

"Did they ever threaten you?"

Her throat began to tighten. "Not threaten, but they both have expressed their disdain for me. My brother was...physical with me before my marriage."

He grumbled something under his breath and kept writing. "And the new Duke. How was his relationship to his father?"

"David? They were two peas in a pod, truth be told. They would argue and disagree, but they would laugh and joke with one another just as often. I believe he loved his father." The sound of David weeping over his father's body laid out in the parlor was something she would never forget. "I know he did," she added.

The constable nodded while he wrote. "The night of the murder, you were not at home. You were at the opera with Mr. Church."

"Yes. Luke was complaining about his foot hurting and didn't want to go. I'd never been to the opera, but I was more than willing to stay home. He insisted Mr. Church take me instead." She frowned. Luke had been pushing her and Henry together, finding every excuse to put them in proximity and even be seen in public. Was it on purpose? What was he thinking? He said he had a plan for her future. Was some kind of scandal part of his plan?

No. Luke was kind and caring and showed her nothing but love and affection. She wouldn't allow any other thoughts to take root.

The constable, however, wasn't so sure. "Did Mr. Church often take you places for your husband?"

"Yes," she answered, her voice small.

"How often. Once a week?"

"Almost daily." She flinched. This was sounding worse and worse.

The constable glanced up from his pad. "Are you in love with Mr. Church?"

Yes. "No. Mr. Church has been a friend since my childhood. Luke trusted him with everything, including me. His behavior is exemplary toward me and nothing but professional."

The constable tapped his pencil against his pad, focusing on her hands, then her face. "Is Mr. Church in love with you?"

I hope so. "He has never expressed anything to me beyond the bounds of propriety," she answered firmly.

He jotted down something on his pad and tucked it into his jacket. "Thank you for your time, Your Grace. May I call on you again if I have more questions?" He rose to his feet.

"Of course, thank you, Constable. I am leaving for my new home tomorrow, but you will be received if you call." Mary told him the address and bobbed politely when he bowed. He left the garden, heading toward the house.

She collapsed in her chair once he'd left. What had she done? Did they now suspect Henry? He'd been with her at the opera, not stabbing his employer with a paper knife. And he'd loved Luke as much as she did.

A female voice drifted over the bushes to knock her out of her reflections. "The constable barely left next door. Oh! I wish I could know what things he's discovering about our neighbor."

Mary sat up straight and held as still as possible. The voices carried as if they were being channeled directly to her ears.

"Gossip is unseemly. But I am glad she's in mourning now and we won't be expected to make calls or see her," an older voice spoke, and there was a clatter of dishes. Someone was taking tea outside on a beautiful summer day in their private garden next door. What a perfect place to be a busybody, even if Mary was the object of their gossip. Since she was the subject, she'd indulge in eavesdropping.

"Yes, but the Fenwick's ball has been canceled! And I had

such high hopes for it being a successful evening of meeting new people."

"New men, you mean. You should spend more time on your studies so they won't think you an absolute featherhead."

A gasp, then, "You are always so harsh with me. And yet Mother will not dismiss you, no matter how hard I cry."

"Your mother doesn't want to put up with your nonsense, and pays me to do so." The older voice was so matter-of-fact it made Mary smile.

"She pays you to instruct me. Now, tell me what we should do if I see our neighbor on the street. I'm so curious! Do you think I could wriggle any information out of her, tactfully?"

"I don't think you understand the word 'tactfully.' And any woman found at an opera with her husband's steward instead of being at home with her ailing husband is not fit company. If you see the dowager duchess, you will give her a polite nod, and move on. We don't want to foster any kind of friendship with her now."

The voices began to blend into nothingness while Mary slumped in her chair. Loneliness crept in around the edges of her heart. She'd lost her father, her kind husband, and now she was to be shunned by society as well.

And she hadn't done anything wrong!

Mary stood from her chair and marched into the house. There was one friend who would never abandon her.

Inhaling deeply the earthy scent of books, she entered the library. Her first stop was the tray of decanters on the sideboard. If she was going to be labeled improper, then she was going to do what she wanted. And right now, she wanted to discover what port tasted like and why it wasn't fit for women to drink.

She opened the bottle and poured herself a generous

amount. She sniffed the liquid for a moment and then took a sip.

Rich and thick and sweet. No wonder the men kept it for themselves. She took another liberal taste and sauntered to her timeless and true friend, the dictionary, laying on the table waiting for her to read her word of the day.

Taking another a mouthful of port, she swished it a moment before letting it slide down into her insides. Placing the glass carefully on the table, she opened the big book. The pages fell apart on their own and settled before she twirled her finger in the air and let it fall onto a word.

She read it and smiled. She read it aloud and giggled. She took another swig of what was quickly becoming her favorite drink and committed the definition to memory.

Another glass was drunk before she'd completed her task. Feeling lighthearted and free, she rang the bell pull. Agnes poked her head around the corner and Mary hiccupped before speaking.

"My dear Agnes, fetch me Peter and George? I would like to go on an outing."

———

"SHE'S OVER THERE, PLAYING PIQUET." George pointed across the smoky room.

Henry peered over the crowd. His heart sank at the sight of her. Peter showed up that evening at his uncle's house claiming to have an emergency. At first, Henry hadn't believed a word Peter told him. His sweet Mary wouldn't visit a gaming hell.

But there she was, dressed in black, copper curls in disarray and her bonnet skewed to the side, with a half-empty bottle of gin in one hand and a handful of cards in another. Mary.

Her cheeks were rosy from the heat in the room and her eyes were too bright. The first three buttons of her gown were unbuttoned and opened to reveal her ivory skin. Her opponent said something to her from across the table and she began to laugh loudly in a most unladylike manner, slapping her handful of cards on the table.

"How much has she lost?" Henry asked.

"Lost? Our Duchess? Hell, once she learns the rules of a game, she wins almost every hand. She scoffed at Hazard and Faro, said only idiots would play those." George's voice was filled with amazement.

"She's ahead?"

"She's won fifty pounds tonight. Fully foxed, she's still winning. It's like the cards and numbers speak to her." George shook his head, then smirked. "The house would like her to leave, since she's putting a dent into their winnings. Discreetly, of course. I suggested it to her, but she, er, refused, loudly. Then she lit into the proprietor about his lack of, um, manliness since he was scared of a poor little widow scraping together a living."

"She's not poor," Henry countered.

"I know that, and you know that, but the room put up an uproar against the house for being so shameful to try and kick her out. They allowed her to stay and she hasn't been without a game since."

Mary took a large chug from her glass. The three men winced when she placed it down on the table and missed. It clattered onto the floor. Mary's eyes opened wide and she gaped across the table at her opponent with shock. They both burst out into laughter while a waiter picked up her glass and returned it to her.

"How much has she had to drink?"

"More than one little body should be able to handle." George shook his head. "I've been watching over an entirely different woman tonight."

Henry exhaled. "I think I'll go try my hand at some piquet." He wove his way through the crowd of onlookers and took a place behind her chair.

"I have you now, madame." The young buck opposite Mary smirked and laid down his trick. A queen of diamonds.

Mary frowned, then scowled. Her head and body wove back and forth while she tried to keep her drunken balance. But her sharp eyes and tongue prevailed. "You can't play that queen."

Her competitor reclined in his seat. "I think you've been indulging too much, madame."

"You can't play it, because I discarded it earlier." She flipped through the discard pile and holding up the same card he'd just played. Silence fell over the table and spread through the room.

Henry swore. So did Peter and George.

"I saw you cheating earlier, but I couldn't..." Mary hiccupped, "...couldn't prove it. So I threw away a perfectly good queen to teach you a lesson." She smiled smugly before she hiccupped again.

The room erupted into chaos. Chairs and tables were overthrown. Men shouted and drew swords. Servants appeared with clubs and the smoky room devolved into a melee.

"Time to go." Henry grabbed Mary around her waist and picked her up while men swarmed in to beat her partner.

"Unhand me at once!" Her heavy reticule filled with coins slammed into the side of his face. It hit him harder than any blow from the ring ever had.

He stumbled while she wriggled and screamed. "George! George, help!"

"I'm right here, madam. It's Mr. Church who's got you," George shouted above the din.

"Mr. Shurch?" She slurred and hiccupped again. Henry righted himself and carried her through the pandemonium.

Her bright blue eyes squinted on his face. "What are you doing here?" she demanded.

"What are *you* doing here?" he countered while he carried her through the hallway and out the door, Peter and George on their heels.

"You're not a stupid man, you can clearly see I am drinking and gambling." She wriggled some more. "Please put me down, sir."

He released his hold on her and went to catch her when she stumbled a bit, her arms waving like a newborn chick trying to find its balance.

She righted herself and tipped her chin into the air. "George, I think we should find a different eshtab... estabble..." She shook her head and cleared her throat. "Est-ab-lish-ment. Establishment to spend our time tonight."

"I think we should go home, Your Grace," George said gently.

"Pssssssshhhh." Mary waved in his face and teetered down the street with the three men following. "And don't call me, 'Your Grace' anymore. I'm not 'Your Grace.' Miriam is now 'Your Grace.' I am the nineteen-year-old Dowager Duchess of Fenwick, whose husband was brutally murdered while she was at the opera with his secretly-hidden-in-plain-sight grandson.

I have been declared *opprobrious*. So there will be no more 'Your Gracing' me, is that clear?"

"Yes, Your Grace," George said.

She stopped her marching and glowered up at him. "You're kind of a cheeky man, do you know that?"

"So I've been told."

Her face softened. "I like you, George."

"I like you too, madam."

"Good! So you should have no issues in finding us a new place to be opprobrious in." She continued her pace and they all fell in line.

"I know just the place." Henry placed her hand into the crook of his elbow. She bobbled for a moment but regained her footing.

"Ooooo! Is it a fight? I do want to see you fight. I think it would be an excellent place for me to be seen at. Do they let ladies fight?"

"Rarely." He shifted their direction toward her house.

"Rarely. Probably opprobrious women, like me. I'd fit right in. You should let me fight."

He choked for a moment when his mind obligingly showed him an image of her in the ring. It was definitely time to change the subject. "Opprobrious. Is that your new word today?" he asked.

She sniffed and nodded so rapidly her bonnet threatened to fall off her head. "Opprobrious—reproachful; disgraceful; causing infamy; scurrilous. When I read it, it was a sign. A signal from the universe to throw off the bounds of propriety and be what everyone is saying I am."

"Which is why you're drunk and gambling in a dismal gaming hell?"

"Yes." She released his arm and began to stretch, throwing

her arms up high and bending her neck and back in an arc. "I feel so light." She began to spin in a circle. "So very free for the first time in my life. There's no minuscule household budget to try and scrape a living from. No sick father to take care of. No brother trying to beat me. No rich and respected husband I need to please for saving me. Just me." She laughed and twirled for a moment before her feet tangled and she fell onto her backside.

"Mary!" Henry knelt by her while Peter and George stood over them.

She was staring straight ahead, blinking repeatedly. Her breathing became long and drawn out while her torso shifted in a slow circle.

"Mr. Church, I am going to be sick."

Henry grabbed one arm and George the other. Together, they managed to get her to the side of the street before she relinquished most of the liquor she'd consumed all evening. Peter held her hair and bonnet out of the way, while Henry rubbed between her shoulders and spoke soothing words to her. He dug out a handkerchief which she gratefully accepted.

She took a deep breath. "That was unpleasant. I'm sorry you had to see it." She wiped her face and eyes, before tipping her head at an angle in thought. "Where were we going?"

"Home," all three of them answered at the same time.

Mary wrinkled her nose. "I don't think so. We were going to do something else." They all held their breath while she thought. Eventually, she shrugged. "I suppose it is getting late." She pointed at her mess in the gutter. "And apparently I'm not feeling well. Home it is."

She grinned at the audible sighs of relief from her companions. "I didn't know you gents were so tired. You should have told me earlier."

Picking herself up, Mary pointed towards her house with Henry at her side, flanked by George and Peter. They were all silent while she chattered on. "I suppose I should leave London quickly. It might be easier for David and Miriam and the children if I'm not here to stir up any more rumors about you and me. Or would it be worse if I did leave? Like I'm hiding something?"

"You have nothing to hide. And neither do I," Henry said.

"But I want them to think the worst of me. They already do, but I'm certain I can come up with something better. Opprobrious, remember? Oh, I know. I'll hide for nine months and adopt a baby and return to London. Then I'll spread the rumor I don't know if the child is yours or Luke's."

Peter let out a loud guffaw and was cuffed by George.

"You're going to be the death of me," Henry mumbled.

"What was that?"

"I said you need a good night's sleep." He spoke a bit louder.

"Wise advice, Mr. Church. I'll come up with an even better plan when I'm sober and rested."

He groaned.

They approached her house. A few lights were still on, and he imagined Agnes was sitting at the door waiting for her return. Relief swept through him at the thought of her safely tucked away.

Her steps slowed their progress until she stopped completely. She stared up at the house, the columns and cornices filled with shadows from the street lights, giving it a somewhat eerie appearance.

"It's lonely without him." They all stilled to listen to her subdued voice. "I know our marriage wasn't real. It wasn't normal, or ideal. But I did love him. He was my..." her voice caught, "my friend."

She shifted toward Henry, her eyes brimming with tears in the dim light. "May I cry all over your coat while you hold me? Only for a moment?"

"I wish you would." He opened his arms.

She fit so perfectly against him. She rested her face against his chest while her body shuddered and the occasional gasp and sob escaped her lips.

One arm snuck around her waist and the other reached up into her hair to press her firmly to him. Peter and George stepped away to give them some privacy.

His sweet Mary. Lonely and loving Mary. Words he wanted to say, promises to give her burned in his throat. But her earlier speech trapped them up tight.

A child abandoned by her mother. A young lady responsible for a household. A daughter caring for a sick father. The wife of an elderly and prominent duke. When had she ever just been Mary?

The special license in his breast pocket weighed a million pounds. How could he ask her to be his wife? Why would she want to, when at last she was free from any burdens placed on her? As his wife, there would be scandal and rumors. Hell, even he didn't know where he fit into the world anymore.

She needed a friend more than an ill-suited husband. It was what she'd always needed. Someone to love her for being simply Mary.

And he would be that friend.

"Better?" he asked when she pushed away from him.

"Yes, thank you." She made further use of his handker-chief and moved toward her house.

"Who is that?" she demanded, pointing at her steps.

A man was there, pacing before the door. Occasionally, he would stop and glance up at the upper windows, before resuming his patrol.

"Is that my brother?" Her voice rose in anger. She lifted her skirts and pounded her way toward the villain.

Henry's blood began to heat and it boiled in his ears. Perhaps Mary was going to witness him fight after all. He trotted to keep up, feeling Peter and George resume their ranks around him.

"Dear sister." Fletcher sneered when they met. "Rumor has it you had a bit of luck tonight."

Mary glared at her brother silently.

"Of course, I wasn't surprised you were in a gaming hell, or see you were with him. Your husband isn't even cold in his grave and you're already showing the world what kind of a woman you really are."

Before Henry raised his fist Mary swung her weighted reticule and smashed it into Lord Fletcher's face. She hit him squarely on the nose Henry broke a few weeks ago. Lord Fletcher cried out and staggered, grabbing his face when blood gushed forth.

Mary took off her reticule and threw it at him. He flinched when it hit his arm and clanked to the ground. He stared at the heavy purse laying between them.

"Mr. Church, would you please do me a favor?" Mary asked, her eyes never leaving her brother.

"Of course, Your Grace." This bounder would never see him treat Mary with anything less than the respect she was due.

"Would you tell my brother what is in my purse is all the money he is ever going to see from me, and if I see his face darken my door ever again it will be his last moments on this earth?" Her voice was steel.

"With pleasure," Henry pounded one fist into the palm of his hand. Fletcher yelped and scurried away from them.

"If you gentlemen will excuse me, I'm going to find my bed." Mary stormed her steps. The door opened when she reached it and Agnes ushered her in. The bolts snapped into place when it closed.

Lord Fletcher snatched up the reticule from the ground. He backed away from the three men a safe distance before he turned and ran.

Chapter Ten

Revivisency - Revival of life

MR. CHURCH,

 I must thank you for your assistance with my condition last night, and your timely arrival in my dubious place of business. I won't be frequenting any more such localities in the future, although I have found I have a new appetite for port and won't be giving it up for propriety.

 As I went to leave for my new home today, I saw Peter and George packed and ready to accompany me. The thought of taking your two friends during this time of turmoil in your life broke my heart a little, and I have released them from my service. I do hope you will retain them in yours, they are good men with good hearts and hard workers.

 Sincerely,
 Mary Polk

. . .

YOUR GRACE,

Think nothing of my services to your welfare. I offer my help at any time you need me and ask you to call upon me whenever you will.

In good conscience, I cannot accept the service of two trusted men who would leave your side to assist me. I will sleep better at night knowing they are within your household to provide security and comfort to your well-being.

I am returning them to you with a lovely bottle of port from Madeira which I think you will enjoy.

Sincerely Yours,

Henry Church

DEAR MR. CHURCH,

Thank you for your gift. I'm sure it will be something I will enjoy in my new home.

I'm returning Peter and George to you, along with the many handkerchiefs of yours I have used. Your kindness to me knows no bounds, and I am grateful for every moment I have had in your company. I still cannot, as you say, "in good conscience" take away your two closest friends when you are in a disarray and searching for new servants to fill so many new positions. Their information and insight will be invaluable to you.

I do see the wisdom in seeking out help for my security and peace of mind. I will be making inquiries as soon as I am settled to find someone suitable for the position.

Yours Affectionately,

Mary Polk

. . .

Dear Mary,

I didn't realize how many handkerchiefs I was missing. To know each one has dried your tears brings me sorrow. To also know I won't be close at hand to provide any more handkerchiefs brings me even more grief. I beg you to think of my peace of mind and I am returning Peter and George into your retainment with half of my handkerchiefs to keep on hand if you need them.

I have also sent a gift for you to the Sycamore estate. It should be there when you arrive. I hope it will bring you many hours of enjoyment. It is something I'm sure my grandfather would want you to have.

Affectionately Yours,
Henry Church

Dear Henry,

You simply must stop sending me gifts! I am too weak of a woman to return them as I should. Although, since I am opprobrious, I suppose it doesn't matter what propriety dictates. I shall keep your handkerchiefs; they will help me to smile instead of cry every time I am in need of them.

Peter and George are staying with you.

Affectionately,
Mary Polk

HENRY GLANCED up from the latest letter and saw Peter at the sidebar, pouring himself a drink.

"Help yourself." Henry chuckled when Peter plunked down into a chair, propped his feet up on the desk, and took a sip. "Where's George?"

Peter glared at Henry. "George is going with Her Grace, and I am staying here with you, me boyo. The two of you had us running around like a couple of jingle brains for most of the morning and we're putting a stop to it."

Henry folded up the letter and tucked it into his breast pocket with the others. "I don't think I've ever seen you without George."

Peter wrinkled his nose. "I don't know a time when I haven't had him at my elbow either. We grew up in Jacob's Island together. Rough place. Even you wouldn't last five minutes. He had me and I had him and we always pulled each other out of the gutter. Or into it if needed." He took another sip of brandy and sank into his memories for a moment before brushing them off. "But we got enough brains to know it won't be too long until Her Grace is Mrs. Church and we'll be together in no time."

Henry was about to make a rebuttal when the butler entered.

"You have a visitor," he announced.

"A visitor would be most welcome right now." Henry pinched his nose and rubbed his eyes. The butler held no card. "Who is it?"

"Mr. Benton Carroll," the butler informed him.

Henry rose to his feet. Benton Carroll, his new half-brother? Henry inquired about his siblings and tried to visit them after the emotional day with the reading of the will. His letters were returned and any visits were dismissed curtly by the Carroll's butler.

"Yes, show him in." Henry smoothed his sleeves and waist-coat into place.

"I showed him to the blue parlor," the butler said.

When they arrived at the blue parlor it was empty.

"I left him here." The butler scowled.

"Have Peter help us search. Ask if anyone saw him leave." Henry strode through the hallways and poked his head into the various rooms. The sight of the ballroom door cracked open caught his attention. He approached the massive room and peeked inside.

Benton's youthful wiry frame was stooped over, his hands behind his back. He stomped agitated passes in front of the door, muttering to himself. The length of his stride was much too big for the blue parlor. No wonder the boy had wandered off somewhere larger. There were dark shadows under his eyes and his clothing was rumpled.

Henry didn't know how to approach him. He was a good ten years older than the unhappy youth before him and he wondered if it was too big a gap to bridge.

But he would try.

He opened his mouth to speak and shut it. How did he even address him? Mr. Carroll? Benton? Ben?

Henry finally spoke. "You look hot and tired. Won't you join me for some refreshment?"

Benton Carroll stopped his pacing and stared at him. His eyes narrowed. "No. I want nothing from you."

If that were true, he wouldn't be marching uninvited in the ballroom. Henry took a cautious step toward his brother. "Is something wrong? Your mother and sisters, are they well?"

Benton clenched his fists. "They are fine."

"I am happy to hear it." Henry took another step toward Benton. "And you? Are you well?"

Benton was silent for a moment. Tears swelled in his eyes before he screamed and attacked. "I hate you!" the young man swung wildly at Henry.

Henry dodged the first blow and blocked the second and third.

Behind them, the butler called out for help. Henry grabbed Benton's wrist before he swung again.

Benton growled and struggled while Henry tried to bring him under control. The wiry young man got another wild hit in, smacking Henry hard across the nose and making his eyes sting.

Henry grabbed Benton's loose arm and shook him once. "Stop! You can hate me all you want, but the hitting has to stop!"

"What would you know about hitting?" Benton demanded, squirming to release himself. "What would you know about getting beat? Nothing! You know nothing!"

Henry let him go, and his younger brother stumbled away. Benton glared at Henry and continued ranting.

"You know nothing of hiding from our father when he comes home at night and listening to your mother cry after he hurts her. You know nothing about creating hiding places for your sisters to escape to when he comes home in a rage and take hit after hit, so they won't!" he screamed. The empty ballroom echoed and punctuated every word over and over, breaking Henry's heart into pieces.

Peter appeared in the doorway alongside the butler, but Henry held out a hand to stop them from interfering.

"Thank you, Peter, my brother and I are having a heated discussion."

Peter raised a brow but tapped the butler on the shoulder and they withdrew from the room.

Benton continued to fume. His breathing was rapid and he occasionally snarled. He scowled at Henry with open hostility.

Henry knew about having rage pent up in your belly until you exploded. He'd seen it plenty of times in the ring. It was liberating to pound your frustrations out on someone that hit back equally as hard with a cleansing give and take.

But there were also desperate men with nothing left to lose, ready to destroy anything for a better life. Benton was the latter.

Henry pulled off his coat, never dropping his eyes from his brother. He tossed it on the floor and unbuttoned his waist-coat. He rolled up his sleeves and then opened his arms in a welcoming manner.

"You have every right to be angry," Henry said. "I grew up with a father who embraced instead of punished, even to a child that wasn't his own. I know you think I deserve an ounce of the horror you've been living with." He took a slow step toward Benton, then another, until he was face to face with him. "If you think beating me will help you feel better, then do it. I'll stand here and take every punch you want to throw at me." He lowered his voice. "But I think you know better than anyone here, there's been far too much hitting in your life already."

"You don't know anything," Benton yelled at Henry and shoved, knocking him back a step.

Henry kept his arms open and his face soft. "You're wrong. I know my younger brother is angry and hurt. He's tired of holding up an enormous weight that shouldn't be his to bear. I'm his older brother, and I'm going to help him in any way I can. If I have to stand here while he lets all his anger out on my body, I'll do it. He's not alone anymore."

The thick silence between them was broken when Benton lunged for Henry and gripped his shirt. He didn't touch him but screamed hateful words in Henry's face while tears streamed down both their cheeks.

Henry held still and silent as Benton swore at him and called him a list of names. Finally, his brother dissolved onto the floor in a broken mess of sobs. Henry sat next to his grieving sibling and carefully reached out a hand toward Benton's shoulder. He rested it there lightly. When his touch wasn't rejected, he patted his brother softly. Once accepted, he reached out and pulled Benton into his arms, and held him.

Benton struggled for a brief moment, and then collapsed into Henry's embrace and cried.

"He won't let us leave," Benton wailed. "He doesn't love us, doesn't want us, but he won't let us go."

Henry managed to keep his rage in check. It became harder and harder with every one of Benton's sobs, until he was shaking along with his brother. He heard a soft feminine whimper and shifted to face the doorway.

Miriam stood there, tears running down her face. David held his arms around her waist, his body quivering with fury. Peter stood slightly behind him. His old friend was pounding his fist in his hand.

Henry's gut churned while his mind searched for an answer. Even the Duke of Fenwick couldn't legally separate the family of a peer. The courts and church would take too long.

This needed a non-legal approach.

"Peter, are you still in contact with anyone from Jacob's Island?"

HENRY WAS both pleased and frightened by the ability to organize a raid on a household so quickly.

He sent Benton home, with the instructions to have his sisters and mother pack a few belongings in secret. Peter left to find some help and Henry was somewhat surprised to find his Uncle David demanding to be included in the less than legal affair.

When night fell Henry found himself belowstairs in the kitchen, dressed head to toe in black, smearing soot on his uncle's face. David's eyes were filled with excitement while he did a turn for Miriam in his decidedly different apparel.

"What do you think, m'dear? Do I look like a dashing rogue?"

Miriam kneaded the handkerchief in her hand. "You look dangerous. I don't like the thought of scaring Lady Carroll and the children, even with the expected outcome. They've been put through enough."

"Benton is warning his mother. He won't tell the girls, but I'll make sure he's there when we take them." Henry rocked from his heels to his toes. He was anxious and excited like he was about to enter the ring and take on an opponent. Now if only...

Peter entered the kitchen and the scent of lilacs swept in with him. Henry inhaled deeply and relaxed. They would be successful.

The streetlights outside the Carroll house were conspicuously dark. Henry pointed to them and glanced at Peter.

Peter shrugged. "The lamp-lighter took a sop to skip this one tonight."

Henry was about to ask how much it cost when a group of men materialized from the shadows.

They were burly men, missing eyes, teeth, hair, one was

missing most of his nose. They swept around Peter with a stealthy grace. He grinned big enough to show off his own missing tooth. "There's my cronies! Best men for this job."

"I think I've become chicken-hearted," David muttered next to Henry's ear. "This has all become a little too real. Are you sure we should trust them?"

Peter spoke up. "I brought fathers and husbands only." *Fathers and husbands!* "Your family's all a rug with them." Peter's vocabulary went deeper and deeper into cant.

"Let's do this." Henry laid out a simple plan for the group. Get in, grab the children and Lady Carroll, and get out. No one gets hurt, or so he hoped.

Benton left the doors to the library unlocked. Henry silently swung the big glass-paned doors open. Benton was there waiting for him.

"Any trouble?" Henry asked his brother.

"No. Mother is waiting in her room. I told the girls we would go on an adventure tonight if they went right to sleep. That's all they know." Benton's eyes widened when the rest of the group came in.

The other men fanned through the room, silently pocketing small statues and knick-knacks. Their big forms didn't make a sound while they quietly picked the room clean of valuables.

"We're being robbed?" Benton asked.

Henry shrugged. "It's easier to explain. We can hide behind a robbery gone wrong easier than an outright kidnapping."

The silent group followed Benton upstairs to the bedrooms, taking things along the way. Benton slipped into one room and returned with a laundry sack. Smart lad.

"The girls first. Mother is locked into her rooms at night."

Benton opened the door to the nursery. It squeaked a little, and all the men disappeared into the shadows.

"Oh, they are good," David admired.

Henry followed his brother into the room. Tucked in bed together were his two sisters, curled up together and holding hands in their sleep. An empty bed sat across the room.

"Father thinks they are too old to sleep together. One always sneaks in with the other and then scampers back in the morning before they are discovered," Benton said. The thieves silently swept in behind them.

"Is there a nurse to worry about?" David glanced at the adjoining room where the servant would sleep.

Benton shook his head. "Mother dismissed her this afternoon to get rid of her. Had a big fight with Father about it after dinner. At least there was only shouting this time." He leaned over the bed and touched the shoulder of one of the girls. "Lou-Lou, Sally, wake up."

Bleary-eyed and still holding on to one another the girls sat up and took in the sight of their room being noiselessly taken apart by raiders. Their eyes widened and they whimpered, pushing themselves into Benton's arms.

"It's time to go. Remember? I promised you an adventure. These men are going to take us there. Did you pack your things and hide them?"

One of the girls pointed towards the toy chest. Henry opened it up and pulled out two laundry bags.

"Did you pack what I told you to?" Benton asked.

The other girl nodded. "Clothes, shoes, and our favorite doll. Only one each." This brought a sniff from her sister.

"I have five favorite dolls, Benton. Why can't I take all of them?" Her voice raised a little. The motion in the room stopped and melted into the shadows.

Henry knelt by the bed and took her hand. It was small and trembling, but she held still. He wished he could see her features better in the moonlight. "Are you Sally or Lou-Lou?" he asked.

"Sally."

"Sally, I'm your brother Henry. Benton and I are going to take you away to a new home, but you need to be quiet right now. If you are quiet, I'll buy you a hundred new dolls."

"Me too?" Lou-Lou asked.

"You too. Let's see who is the quietest." Henry squeezed the little hand.

They slipped off the bed with wordless enthusiasm. Both sisters took a hold of one of Benton's arms and Henry shouldered their luggage.

Now came the hard part of rescuing Lady Carroll.

Peter knelt outside her bedroom door, working with some tools on the lock. "It's a tough one," he said, scratching his face. "Brand new style. He doesn't want her going anywhere."

The thieves made their way through the rest of the house while Henry, the children, and Uncle David waited for Peter to open the lock.

One by one the burglars returned to the group. Their stealthy forms started shifting anxiously the longer he took.

"Too long, Pete, we've got to go," one of them spoke.

"Go," a soft voice came from the other side of the door. "Take the children and go."

"Mama, we won't..." Benton's voice choked.

"I'll be fine. Now go."

David pushed them all aside. "The hell we will." Before anyone stopped him, he raised his foot and slammed it into the lock. The door shook but held. The sound echoed through the house.

"Pell-mell, boys," Peter said in a loud voice and there were some sniggers.

The largest of them finished kicking the door down with practiced efficiency. Wood splintered and the door swung open. Lady Carroll cried out when they swarmed into the room.

"Benton, take the girls to the library, we'll meet you there," Henry ordered and followed the fray.

The once silent men transformed into a screaming, shouting, band of fury and they began tearing things to shreds and pocketing what they wanted.

"What is going on?" Lord Carroll's voice boomed from the other room.

Peter wrapped an arm around Lady Carroll's waist and said politely, "Best if you start screaming, milady."

She obliged. Henry wasn't sure if she was acting or out of true fear.

"Struggle a bit when he comes through," Peter directed.

The door between the bedrooms was thrown open and Lord Carroll appeared in his nightclothes. "What is the meaning of..."

David planted a fist into Lord Carroll's face. And another, then another. When the man fell on the ground David began kicking him in the ribs, cursing and swearing at him with creative language that even stopped the looters.

"Tie him up, take what you want, and get out," Peter yelled, then, "Beggin' your pardon, milady." He picked up Lady Carroll and threw her over his shoulder. She screamed again and Lord Carroll called out her name. He got another kick in the gut for his efforts.

Henry spied a familiar laundry bag and scanned its contents quickly. Satisfied it was the lady's packed belongings, he shouldered it with the rest of them. He grabbed David's elbow and tried to pull him away. "We need to go, now."

"I'm not finished." David grunted and kicked Lord Carroll again. "Go on, I'll catch up."

Henry followed Peter through the house. A few bewildered servants began to appear in the corridors, screaming and running whenever they were approached.

Benton was waiting for them at the library doors while the household began to wake with shouts and screams.

"Go, go, go!" Henry lifted Sally up into his arms. Benton hoisted up Lou-Lou and followed them out.

Peter stopped long enough to set Lady Carroll on her feet. He took her by the hand and led them to a waiting carriage in a nearby alley. Plain, black, and stolen for the evening's exploits.

"Inside, milady." Peter helped Lady Carroll up.

"I've got them, go sit with the driver and take them to Miriam," Henry said, handing Sally then Lou-Lou into their mother's arms. He pushed Benton in. "I need to get David."

Sharp whistles and shouts began to fill the streets. Dread filled Henry's heart, but there was no time to worry about his uncle's fate when Peter shoved him into the carriage and slammed the door shut.

"Take 'em home. I'll find His Grace." Peter ran off into the shadows. Henry reached for the handle and was thrown into the squabs when the carriage lurched into motion.

His heart raced, and he was about to leap from the carriage when he took in the faces of his sisters, brother, and their mother.

Fear radiated from them. Benton had tears streaming down his face. Lady Carroll held tightly to her daughters and kissed them, trying to calm them while her own sobs broke through her rational speech.

David would have to find his own way home. His little family needed him more.

"Are we running away?" Lou-Lou asked. "Or are we kidnapped?"

"We're running away." Benton wiped his eyes. "We're never going back there."

Sally's face peered at Henry from under her mother's arm. "Are you really our brother?"

Henry took the cap from his head and used it to wipe off some of the soot. "I really am your brother. I'm Henry." He held out his hand for her and she shook it. He held it out to Lou-Lou and she shook it but didn't release him.

"I was the quietest," she informed him.

He chuckled and kissed her little fingers. "You both were marvelous adventure partners."

"You said you'd buy me a hundred dolls," she reminded him.

"You would make a marvelous extortionist. Can I start with buying you one?"

"Three."

Lady Carroll managed a laugh through her tears. "Lou-Lou, you are impossible."

The little girl gazed up at her mother. "Mama, you called me Lou-Lou, and not Louise. Papa will get angry."

Lady Carroll pulled her daughters in tight and focused on her son, a bit of hope shining in her eyes. "Papa will not tell me what to do anymore. Ever again."

Chapter Eleven

Abditive - That which has the power or quality of hiding.

MARY FELL in love at first sight.

The Sycamore estate was surrounded by trees and sheep and farmland. It was tidy and well-plotted with plenty of drainage and roads for everyone to keep their feet dry. The house was large, but not enormous and the grounds were well kept.

It was everything she'd ever wanted.

"You were listening to me," she whispered to her dead husband while George helped her step out of her carriage. The staff was lined up waiting for her arrival.

The butler approached her first. "Welcome to Sycamore, Your Grace. I'm Halston, and this is Mrs. Higgins."

Mary greeted the housekeeper and followed them to the

door. She was sure to make eye contact with each servant in line, down to the little scullery maid at the end.

The sight of the little maid halted Mary to a stop. The little girl frowned at her and Mary shivered. The child's eyes were black. Shiny black orbs, with no color or white. A sliver of ice wrapped around Mary's heart.

"Is something wrong?" Mrs. Higgins asked. The house-keeper glared at the child. The girl shifted nervously, her black eyes blinking and her lips began to tremble.

Everyone in line stared at Mary, glancing occasionally at the maid. It wasn't the way Mary wanted to start her interactions with the servants. She needed to be on good terms with them and terrorizing a scullery maid was not the way to start a relationship. Since no one said anything about the child's eyes, maybe the odd orbs were normal.

Mary tried to blink the sight away. It had been a long journey and she was tired. A mere shake of the head and a refresh of her vision would set things right.

The child's visage didn't change. Black, hard, and unearthly eyes stared at her. The ice began to spread to Mary's spine, but she shook it off. A few servants began to whisper and Mrs. Higgins clasped her hands while waiting for Mary's response.

They expected her to dismiss this child for some invisible reason. To react now would be a mistake. "No. I was admiring this charming girl. I do love children." Mary forced herself to relax and spoke to the child. "I hope you have time to play on the estate between your work. What is your name?"

"Lottie," the girl whispered. Her unnerving gaze made Mary suppress a shudder. She vowed she would be calm and composed, even if it killed her.

"It is a pleasure to meet you, Lottie," she said and

continued into the house. The servants dispersed behind her, a few murmuring comforting words to the girl.

"What was that all about?" George asked, standing behind Mary with her valise.

"George, what color were that maid's eyes?" Mary asked instead.

George shrugged. "Brown? Green? I didn't really look that close. What's going on?"

That's what Mary was afraid of. No one saw anything wrong but her. "Nothing, I think I'm tired."

There was no time to think about the child. She pushed the oddity aside and took in her new home.

Her new, clean, but timeworn home. The servants tensed when she took in the threadbare carpets and rugs. The wallpaper curled at the seams. The upholstery was shiny in places of long use and in need of re-covering. The curtains were frayed at their edges. Contradicting the worn appearance was the smell of beeswax and tea leaves for cleaning. Fresh flowers brightened up the faded colors.

"His Grace never updated the house." Mrs. Higgins stood tall and ready as if to defend her old house and army of staff. She led Mary with a head held high through a tour of the clean but shabby residence.

"Did you forget about this place when my grandmother died?" Mary whispered to her dead husband. "Or did you want me to restore it the way I want it?" She had a feeling the answer was both.

The housekeeper ended the tour in the parlor where tea was set out for her.

"Please join me for a bit, Mrs. Higgins." The housekeeper hesitated a brief moment before taking a seat while Mary poured.

"The house is lovely, and I'm impressed by your ability to keep it in such neat condition despite its age." Mary sipped her tea before continuing. "I'm sure there are a few things that need updating and repairing. Would you provide me with a list of what needs to be done first?"

Mrs. Higgins' shoulders relaxed. "Of course, Your Grace."

"Is there anything I should be immediately made aware of?" Mary asked.

Mrs. Higgins set down her cup and brushed down her skirt. "Did you find something lacking in Lottie that I should address?"

Lottie with the soulless eyes. "No. Nothing lacking. She reminded me of someone and it took me a moment to remember. Please be assured her place is safe."

The rest of the day was spent unpacking with Agnes, going over the ledgers in her study, listening to requests from Halston and Mrs. Higgins to smoothly run the household, and making plans with her new steward to visit the tenants.

Dinner was delicious, with a variety of food she was sure the cook prepared to impress her. And lonely.

No one joined her at the table. A single maid stood against the wall, waiting to bring and take her plates away. Mary was the mistress, they were the servants, and everyone stayed in their places. Even Agnes couldn't break through that class distinction.

Mary poked a little at her dessert. This was to be her life now, at least for the next six months of mourning. Black clothes, no company, no calling on neighbors, no invites. Nothing. She was already tired of it.

She pushed her plate away and stood. "I'm very tired. Please tell the cook it was marvelous."

Agnes waited for her in her room. "What do you think of

THE GHOST OF SPRING

our new home?" she asked Agnes.

The maid began unbuttoning her gown. "Something's not right here," Agnes said.

Lottie's cold black eyes immediately came to mind. Had Agnes seen it too? "What do you mean?"

Agnes tugged off Mary's gown and huffed. "I don't know what I mean. It feels a bit off in this house."

"Did you...see something?" Mary continued to hope Agnes would verify the strange manifestation today.

"I didn't see anything." Agnes denied but shuddered. She brushed through Mary's hair with strokes that pulled harder than usual. "The air in this house doesn't... never mind." Agnes began to plait Mary's hair.

Mary glanced around her spacious but worn-out room. "It's been neglected, but I think we can bring it to rights."

"I'm not sure anything can bring it to rights," Agnes mumbled and placed a cap onto Mary's head.

Mary clasped Agnes's wrist and held her friend's hand against her cheek. "We have to. This is our home now. Luke wanted me here. Whatever this house has for us, we'll tackle it together. You and me."

Agnes brushed a light kiss on Mary's cheek. "I think you've always been the braver of the two of us. Don't listen to the rantings of an old woman. Get some rest."

Mary bid Agnes good night and climbed into her new bed with freshly laundered linens, wiggling down into the mattress. It was unfamiliar but comfortable.

She leaned over and puffed out her candle. The flame died with a little wisp of smoke visible in the moonlight. She pulled the blankets up around her ears and sighed into her new pillow. She would be content with her new home. Everything would feel better after a good night's rest.

Something flickered on the edge of her vision.

The candle was burning again, the little light dancing merrily on the wick.

She sat up and leaned closer to the flame, blowing with force this time. It died out, a little stream of smoke wisping around with her breath.

Laying back down, she was about to close her eyes again when the candle flared back to life.

"For goodness sake!" She licked her finger before she pinched the wick hard and rubbed off the little bit of soot left. She dropped down onto her pillow and took a deep breath to relax.

The wick of the candle began to glow, hotter and hotter until it ignited again into a full blaze. A chill swept over her while the little light cast big shadows in the room.

Mary slowly sat up. "This is an anomaly. Nothing to worry about. You're probably dreaming." She was too afraid to pinch herself and find out.

Next to the candle was a shiny silver snuffer. She took it by the handle and rested it over the flame, extinguishing the light once more. The room was plunged into darkness. She lifted the snuffer up and waited, daring the wick to light once more. She counted an entire minute of time before returning to her welcoming sheets and pillows, keeping one eye out for the return of the flame.

It stayed dark.

———

MARY APPRECIATED a dreamless night of sleep. She feared seeing black-eyed children and endless burning candles in her dreams. Instead, she woke refreshed and indulged in a stretch before Agnes walked into the bedroom with the morning's hot water.

Her usually tidy friend had hair sticking out in odd places from her cap. She wore a wrinkled dress and dark circles under her eyes.

"Agnes, are you feeling well?" Mary rose out of bed and put on her slippers.

"First night in a new house, I never rest well." Agnes shrugged and handed Mary her robe from the end of the bed. Mary slipped it on and walked to the washbasin while Agnes went into the dressing room. Their routine was calming and set Mary into a better outlook on the future. The old house needed some care and everything would be fine.

Mary poured the hot water and dipped her rag for washing when Agnes started screaming. Mary jumped and dropped her rag into the basin, running to the dressing room. "Agnes, what is it?"

Agnes clutched the doorframe, then whimpered and veered her head away. Mary pushed past her into the room. Her black mourning clothes were strewn about the floor, shredded into pieces. A few of the larger tatters were meticulously arranged to spell out the word MURDER.

All the blood drained to her toes. Mary retreated from it, reaching behind her for Agnes, searching for the comfort of her companion since childhood. When her fingers brushed Agnes, the maid jumped away from her touch.

"Did you do this?" Agnes began to cry, and Mary's heart shriveled. "Did you think to tease me because I was unsettled last night?"

Mary gasped. "What? No, I would never do something like this." She gestured at the mess, her fingers shaking. "This is horrible. You know me better than anyone else. How could you think I would do such a thing?"

Agnes moaned and fell to her knees, crawling to the scraps and gathering them up. "It's this house. I'm telling you again, something is not right here."

Mary knelt beside her to help. The candle from the night before, the black-eyed scullery maid, and now this display of destruction. Was the house...haunted?

She refused to believe Luke would send her anywhere unsafe. He and her own grandmother spent a joyful time here. It wasn't a house of dark memories or sadness. It was neglected but not haunted. Right?

Or did she bring the haunting with her? Was it Luke himself?

She handed Agnes the shredded cloth with trembling hands. She tightened her fists and took a deep breath. She'd figure this mystery out. There was no other choice.

"Take those to the rag bin." She already imagined the rumors flying from the servants. "If anyone asks you, I destroyed my mourning clothes in a fit of rage and grief. Have one of my other dresses dyed black."

"We should leave this place." Agnes sniffed and wiped her eyes.

Mary shook her head and hugged her friend, deeply inhaling the familiar scent of tea and herbs. "I know something's amiss. But at the moment we have nowhere else to go. I can't return to London and put further stress on the Duke and Mr. Church. I need to disappear for a bit while the rumors die down. And this is my home. Our home. I'll fix this. I promise." Somehow.

Agnes helped her dress in gray for the day. The food at breakfast was plentiful and delicious, but to Mary it was tasteless. Too much battered her mind for her to enjoy anything. The day before was too busy to make a thorough exploration of her house and there was one room in particular that had been touched on only briefly.

Sunshine and the smell of books greeted her in the library. She stood in the doorway and let the sight of it envelop her. This was the first room she'd put to rights. It was the brightest room in the house and held a big desk for holding all her tasks. The servants already moved all her letters and folders in from the study. And when she was done working there were only a few steps to a warm fireplace, a couch, and a book to wrap up the day.

Perfect.

A large package wrapped up in brown paper with a letter attached waited for her on the desk.

DEAR MARY,

After consulting with my uncle, he and I both agreed this would get the most use in your new home. I'm sure my grandfather would want you to have it.

YOUR FRIEND,
Henry Church

SHORT AND TO THE POINT, but his words were still sweet and soothing to her. It was good to hold in her hand something he'd touched. She refolded the letter and tucked it into her pocket before returning to the package.

She peeled off the paper and squealed with delight when

the cover of Dr. Samuel Davidson's dictionary was revealed. Both volumes were tied together. She cut the twine and flipped open the first tome to a random entry.

The first word she spotted was 'ghost' and she promptly shut the book.

"No. If you're going to be unpleasant, I simply won't read you. I'm sure your companion has something better to tell me." She reached for the second album and flipped it open.

"*Ratiocinate - to reason; to argue.* See, very good advice here. I shall reason and argue everything about ghosts before I let it consume my every thought," she told the book, her heart feeling lighter. A gift from Henry made everything better.

She sat in the worn-out chair and scooted herself up to examine the mound of correspondence and budgets set before her. Sitting up straight and tall, Mary filled her lungs with all the air and confidence she could muster. Mrs. Higgins' list of repairs and refurbishments needed was the first piece she approved. Next, the menus and expenses for the household budget. Finally, she read over what the steward said needed to be done for the tenants and estate upkeep.

The room was quiet except for the faint scratching of her pen and the shuffling of her paper. The air was peaceful and warm with the scent of baking from the kitchen and summer flowers in the air. Perhaps someone loyal to Luke was playing a mean trick on her by tearing up her clothes. She wouldn't believe the house had any malicious intent to...

She flinched when a loud thud echoed through the room.

A book fell off a shelf.

Mary laughed at herself and rose to retrieve it when the book's cover slowly began to lift. She held her breath while it gradually opened wide. The first page rose from its spine. Bit by bit, invisible hands began to tear the leaf away from the book.

Fear clutched her lungs when the leaf split off and sailed into the air. It fluttered down softly as the next page in the book rose to take its place. It was torn away faster, like a child who discovered their own strength and wanted to test it.

"Stop." Mary's voice was less than a whisper. Her frame began to shake.

Another book banged onto the floor. The cover whipped open this time and the pages started to fly.

"Stop it." Her voice gained strength. She forced herself to move to the destruction.

Another thump, then another. More books falling, more pages swirling.

"Don't do this!" She plucked up one book and cradled it to her, moving on to the next to save it. An unseen grasp struggled against her when she snatched it from the floor and held it close.

There came a massive clunk from the desk. She whirled to the sound and dropped everything in her arms when the cover of her dictionary began to open.

"No!" She raced to the desk and threw herself onto the two heavy books, clutching them to her chest. Icy invisible fingers poked and prodded her, pinching and pushing her to let go.

She curled herself tighter around her treasured books, closed her eyes, and grit her teeth. "This is a gift from my Henry and you will not touch it!"

Instantly, the invisible menace fell away. The thudding rain of books ceased and a few pages left in the air fluttered down to the carpet. Mary opened her eyes, taking a jittery breath while peace resumed in the library. She pushed herself up from the desk and slowly released the dictionaries onto the surface.

Silence.

The floor was a carpet of pages and abused texts. The carnage hurt her heart as did the thought of how she was going to repair them.

She licked her lips and spoke into the empty space. "Luke? Please. If it is you, please stop. I'll find out who killed you. I won't stop looking. I promise."

Everything was still.

Fear bombarded her and her hands shook. Her new home was haunted. Children didn't have unnatural black eyes, candles didn't light themselves, clothing didn't tear on their own, and books didn't fly off the shelves and rend apart without help.

She swallowed and collapsed into a chair. Perhaps Agnes was right. They shouldn't stay at the Sycamore estate.

But where would they go? She had no family to turn to. David and Miriam needed distance from her while the rumors died down. She had enough funds from Luke's stipend to find somewhere else to live, but it would take time.

Luke. If she found out who murdered him would his ghost leave her alone? Was that the best option?

The best option was not to sit in a chair and stew about it. She picked her way through the mess and locked the library door to hide it from the servants. Having their new mistress rip up her clothes was one thing, but tearing up expensive and rare books was another.

At her desk, she wrote a letter to the constable in London, marked it urgent, and then set about on her hands and knees to replace the precious pages into their bindings until they would be repaired.

Chapter Twelve

Troth - *Truth; faith; fidelity.*

HENRY SAT at the breakfast table with Lady Carroll and his Aunt Miriam. Both women were in a state of distress. Any loud noise would cause Lady Carroll to jump. After watching her almost fall to pieces when the servants rattled the dishes, he dismissed the help and served her food himself. Miriam hadn't touched her plate or tea. All she did was pick apart the seams of her handkerchief and peer out the window.

Peter and Uncle David hadn't returned from the evening's raid.

"Please Aunt, eat something." Henry pushed a plate of toast and jelly toward her.

Miriam sighed. "Thank you, dear boy, but I don't have an appetite this morning."

Lady Carroll chewed on her lip. "Your Grace, I feel so

guilty. If anything happened to your husband because of my family..."

Miriam leaned over and patted Lady Carroll's hand. "Oh, hush. David's been itching for a fight ever since he found out about Sarah. No one could have stopped him from helping you. He was working through the courts and the church until Benton came to us and we saw the dire situation . I think he was happier to go straight into action and get his hands dirty."

"His help is most appreciated." Lady Carroll sported an old bruise under her eye, wincing a little when she dabbed a tear away. "I'm a blubbering mess and no help to comfort you. I keep wavering between absolute relief we've escaped and then terror he'll drag us back."

"He won't have a chance. My Uncle David will still press your case through the courts and in the meantime, I'll have you all installed safely at Hawthorne with plenty of security," Henry promised.

"Security. Like the men who rescued us?" Lady Carroll asked.

Henry frowned. Had they frightened her? "No, not the same men. I was going to ask some pugilist friends of mine."

Color flushed Lady Carroll's face and her hand slapped the table. "I want them. The ones who rescued us." Her voice was strong for the first time that morning.

Henry blinked several times while his brain tried to catch up. "They are men from Jacob's Island. I don't think you want them around your family."

"I want them. I want smart and cunning men who sneak into the house of a peer, steal everything, break down doors, and beat my husband without a qualm."

"I think Uncle David did most of the beating." Henry pointed out, but he conceded her point. Peter said the group of larcenists all had families. They'd probably be happy to move out of Jacob's Island and take care of their children away from the slums. Most of them, anyway.

"I'll talk to Peter and see if any of them want a job when he comes back," Henry said.

"He'd better not show his face without my husband," Miriam groused and bit her lip when it started to tremble.

Henry took the abused handkerchief from her hands and handed her a fresh one. "I'm sure he's fine. Peter's a good man and won't let anything happen to them. If we don't hear from them by noon then I'll-"

The breakfast room doors flew open with a crash and the missing duke stood in the doorway.

"Miriam! My rib, my white ewe, my sweet nug. I have returned to you." The duke's voice boomed throughout the house. Peter stood behind the duke with an amused smirk on his face.

Henry rose to his feet while Miriam rushed from the table. His uncle was dirty and disheveled but appeared healthy. He threw his arms around his wife with abandon and kissed her, transferring soot onto her face.

"My treasure. What did I tell you, Peter? The most beautiful girl in all the world." David's eyes glowed with adoration as he held Miriam to him.

"Yes, you've told me all night, Your Grace."

"You're drunk." Miriam swung wide-eyed to Henry. "He smells like sawdust."

"Madam, I am not drunk. There is no way a woman can drink more than a duke, and since Peter's charming mother was still standing when we left, I cannot possibly be drunk." Luke wobbled on his feet and Miriam steadied him.

"You spent the night at your mother's house?" Henry asked Peter.

"We hiked off when the coves started crying beef on us. I grabbed the duke and we hid at her house for the night." Peter said in his perfect cant.

"And she gave you gin," Henry concluded.

"I didn't touch a drop, but His Grace..." They glanced over to see the duke gave Miriam another sloppy kiss. "He tried to keep up with Mother."

"You need a bath," Miriam gently pushed her husband away from her, "and then a bed."

"Capital idea, my dear, and I insist you join me in both." David winked at his wife and then saw Lady Carroll at the table. "Dear lady, I am ecstatic to see you here." He bowed, took Lady Carroll's hand, and kissed it loudly.

"He's not usually so enthusiastic." Miriam pulled David away.

"Don't tug at me, my perfect pet. I need to regale Lady Carroll with the tale of giving her husband a good thrashing." The duke pulled out a chair and sprawled into it inelegantly.

"I would love to hear the tale, Your Grace," Lady Carroll smiled at Miriam over his head. Henry saw a silent conversation transpire between the two women. Amazing creatures. "But I must be getting ready for our journey. Mr. Church is taking us directly to Hawthorne."

"Excellent! I hope you keep him there for a long time. It's right next door to the Sycamore estate. There's a young lady there perfect for Henry, and you must promise me to facilitate their joining." David turned to Henry. "Still have that special license, lad? I don't want you to return until you've used it."

The room went silent. All eyes bore into Henry and he flushed.

"The Sycamore estate is next door to Hawthorne?" Henry asked softly. His thoughts went to Mary.

"Of course it is, how else would Father make sure you didn't let her get away? He knew you would be spending time with your new family and wanted to make sure she was close by."

The cunning, crafty, sly old fox was still manipulating, even beyond the grave.

MARY LET the letter from the constable fall from her fingers onto the desk while the words jumbled in her brain.

...no apparent suspects... interviewed all the servants again and verified their whereabouts... clear evidence it was not your brother or your mother... considering the case closed unless new information comes forth.

"I don't know what to do next." She rested her head on the desk.

The quill in the inkwell on the desk began to quiver, then rattle. An icy thrill ran through her as she closed her fist over the feather and kept it from moving. A week had passed but the daily ghostly antics still terrified her. "I'm not giving up. I simply don't know what to do right now." She released the quill and sat up straight.

She needed to organize her thoughts, maybe write down what she knew about the night of the murder. If it wasn't her brother or mother, nor any of the duke's family, and the doors were locked with no forced entry, then either someone had a key, or it was one of the servants already in the house.

"But he interviewed all the servants. All of their where-abouts were accounted for." Mary closed her eyes to recall that night. She remembered feeling so elegant and graceful in her new red gown and stylish updo. She remembered admiring the Fenwick rubies at her ears and throat. She remembered how handsome Henry had looked, and the way he had clenched his teeth when he saw her. She remembered laughing when she'd caught him dozing at the end of the performance. The feel of his arm under her hand while he navigated their way through the crush of bodies to the outdoors where George and ...

George had had a black eye. And a heavy purse.

She opened her eyes and a sick feeling washed over her. Peter and George had been at a fight when the carriage seats were stolen. Or were they? How would she find out for sure? Would the pugilists all vouch for one of their own? They had no love for the law or the peerage.

Peter and George? Why would they kill Luke? Did someone pay them to do it? Someone like her brother?

Was it even possible? She liked both Peter and George. Henry trusted them. And George was now in her household acting as her security.

She groaned and pushed away from her desk to her feet. "I have to take emotion out of all this. I need to practice *ratioci-nation!*" She rolled the 'r' on her tongue when she spoke her new word aloud and paced in front of the desk.

"Your Grace?" Halston's voice stopped her steps. He approached her with a silver salver with a single card on top. "You have a caller."

Mary took the card and furrowed her brow. She didn't expect any visitors for at least five more months while she was in mourning. "Lady Penelope Carroll?" Henry's stepmother?

"She and her children have taken up residence next door at the Hawthorne estate," Halston informed her.

"Next door? Oh, how lovely. Please show her to the parlor and bring some tea. I'll be right there." Mary set about tidying her hair and changing her clothes, wishing to be seen publicly in something other than black.

A visitor. Someone to talk with, to listen to, with whom to hopefully build a new friendship. Pooh on propriety.

She straightened her mobcap before entering the parlor and her lips swept upward of their own accord. Taking a deep breath, she told herself to relax or her exuberance would scare Lady Carroll away for good.

Mary entered the room, taking a moment to find Lady Carroll sitting on the sofa and next to her sat...

"Henry!" His name burst from her lips before she stopped it. Nor could she stop her smile from growing bigger, or her heart from thumping faster.

He rose to his feet and took her hand to give it a kiss that threatened to make her knees sway. "Your Grace. I'm so very glad to see you. May I introduce to you, Lady Penelope Carroll."

Mary dipped properly and Lady Carroll did the same. Mary motioned them to the seats and took one for herself facing them on the sofa.

"I was informed you are my new neighbor." Mary began to pour the tea her efficient servants brought.

"We moved in a few days ago and are finally settled enough for visits." Lady Carroll accepted her cup.

"I am glad you are here. I hope your move was uneventful." It was the most polite way Mary could ask. Even now, she saw a fading bruise below Lady Carroll's eye.

Henry barked a laugh. "Oh, it was eventful." He started a

tale of a midnight robbery and kidnapping. Mary's tea was cold by the time he finished, sitting forgotten in her lap while she listened with amazement.

"—then Uncle David spent the night with Peter and his mother. He came home drunk as a wheelbarrow and fell onto my aunt like a love-struck fool." Henry laughed along with Lady Carroll.

"Now that would have been a sight." Mary giggled and placed her cup on the tray. She didn't expect anything less than a heroic rescue from Henry. He was quite good at them. Another reason her heart melted in his presence.

"The only thing better is if George was there. I'm sure Peter's telling him all about it now. He'll be sore to have missed it." Henry's eyes danced.

Mary's heart sank a little when Henry spoke of his old friends. How could she investigate them now? Would Henry even be open to helping her?

"I need to have a conversation with you about Peter and George, at a later date," Mary's mirth drifted away.

Henry was immediately attentive. "Is something wrong?"

"No. Nothing's wrong. Just a rather unpleasant conversation concerning your grandfather. Something I'm sure Lady Carroll would not like to be a part of."

Lady Carroll placed her cup down. "Which reminds me, I wanted to invite you to dinner tonight at Hawthorne, if it's not too late notice?"

Mary brightened. A visit and an invitation. This day was getting better and better. "As a mourning widow, I should say no, but Henry knows I am opprobrious."

Henry laughed, "You are, indeed."

"I would like to join you for dinner," Mary finished.

"Excellent. You can meet my brother and sisters. They are delightful. I've become smitten with them," Henry confessed.

"I look forward to it," Mary said.

Dinner time found her dressed in her best black dress with a bottle of wine for a gift at the Hawthorne estate. The butler took her wine and led her to a sitting room. The state of the furnishings reminded her of the neglected state of her own house. Clean, but old and threadbare. She hoped Lady Carroll would have fun redecorating; maybe she had some ideas to pass along.

She sat on a sofa and tucked her skirts about her when the curtains across the room began to sway violently.

Mary froze with fear. Had her ghost followed her?

"Stop moving. Do you want us to get caught?" A loud whisper came from behind the curtains. Mary almost collapsed with relief.

"I want to see her," another voice complained. Children's voices began to argue with each other.

"Stop! She's pretty. I told you she'd be pretty. Henry couldn't fall in love with someone ugly."

The other voice scoffed. "Papa is pretty on the outside too. Mama said his insides are ugly. What if her insides are ugly?"

Mary's heart twinged a little while she crossed the room and knelt in front of the jostling curtains. Thoughts churned in her mind. Henry in love? With her? Her heart soared until she realized the familiar pain the two little eavesdroppers were going through. Their heartache took precedence over her infatuation with Henry.

"My brother is ugly on the inside too," she told the curtains. The movement stopped and the curtains swished slowly until they were still. Two pairs of shiny little shoes poked out from the bottom.

"He used to make me cry," Mary continued, "I think it made him happy to see me cry."

"Papa made Mama cry," the bolder voice spoke, "and then we ran away with Henry."

"We like Henry," the softer voice said.

"We *love* Henry. And we're supposed to make you fall in love with him. Benton told us to."

"But not if you're ugly on the inside," the soft voice finished.

"Henry helped me run away from my brother too. I think he likes to save people." Mary's thoughts sank into the familiar territory of uncertainty concerning Henry. She'd once been a child like these two, in need of rescue. Henry didn't see her much more than a person to save.

She was tired of being saved.

"Henry's a knight."

"We dubbed him ourselves."

"And he wouldn't save ugly people."

Mary sank from her knees into a sitting position. "Are you two twins?"

"I'm ten months older!" the bolder voice declared.

"And bossier," the soft voice muttered.

Mary hugged herself with delight at the sisters. "I'm Mary."

"I'm Louise, and this is Sally," the bold voice said.

The curtain began to jump once more. "Lou-Lou! I wanted to tell her."

"I'm older, I have to make the introductions," Louise proclaimed.

"I see you're both well on your way to becoming fine

young ladies. Except ladies don't hide behind curtains when making introductions," Mary said.

The curtains shifted aside and two little bodies appeared. Both wore white lacy pantalettes under their mini-tailored gowns. One wore blue, the other yellow. Louise was a few inches taller than Sally. She carried a head of bouncy yellow curls while Sally wore her straight brown locks in a pair of braids coming loose. Both girls were smiling and staring at Mary with shy smiles.

At least she thought they were. Their eyes were black. Round sightless voids sitting in angelic faces. Exactly like the scullery maid.

Mary struggled to keep a look of horror off her face. She gasped but forced a smile to stay on her lips and not frighten the girls while her heart began to pound frantically in fear. The ghost was here.

Which meant her house wasn't haunted.

She was.

Chapter Thirteen

✥

Shriver - A confessor

"No. I don't believe it." Henry paced in front of Mary sitting on the couch in the parlor after dinner. He ran his fingers through his hair and laughed. "It's ridiculous. How could you think such a thing? George and Peter murderers? Paid assassins? Do you think I would..."

His voice trailed off when he glanced at Mary. Her head was bowed, her shoulders slumped, her hands gripping each other tightly in her lap. Her whole body was turning into itself. She raised her head to meet his gaze and he saw the trust and affection for him fading from her eyes, slipping behind a wall he wasn't sure he would ever be able to break down once it was raised.

If his grandfather had been alive, he'd be ordering George and Peter to give Henry a flogging. He'd been dismissing her, reducing her thoughts to nonsense. And she was ready to cut him off.

He'd made a huge mistake.

"Zeus's beard, I'm sorry." He rushed to her side and knelt at her feet. He took her hands and kissed them both quickly. "Please forgive me for callously dismissing your concerns, my dear friend."

He held perfectly still and mentally flogged himself for causing her pain. "Mary, I am sorry. And I will remain here on my knees forever until you forgive me."

"I forgive you." Emotion slowly trickled into her blue eyes and he could breathe again.

"I know it's incredible to accuse George and Peter," she admitted and slid her hands out of his grasp. "It would be like you accusing Agnes."

The thought of the kind and diminutive maid plunging a paper knife into the duke's chest was a far-fetched idea. As ridiculous as his lifelong mentors and friends doing the same.

"Peter risked his life to save my family. And I trust George with a precious person in my life. She lives right next door." Mary gasped and hid her face from him.

"I can feel my cheeks blushing. You should not say such things to people with light red hair, we simply cannot hide it."

"I like your blushes." The flush spread down to her neck and she lowered her eyes. Nine more months until her mourning would be over. Nine more months before he could pursue her in earnest. Nine. More. Months.

He rose to his feet. "But we must speak of unpleasant things instead. We should first eliminate George and Peter as suspects. I will make inquiries about their whereabouts without them knowing. It shouldn't be too hard to prove their innocence and ease your mind at the same time. In the meantime, will you continue to trust George with your safety?"

"I will. Thank you." The light returned to her eyes, now gazing at him in adoration. He was hard-pressed to refrain from pulling her into his arms and see how many ways he could make her blush. *Nine more months.*

"Heeeeeennnnnnnnnnrryyyyyy!" was all the warning he received before two little bodies crashed into him. He barely caught himself when they wrapped their limbs around each of his legs.

"Confound it! How did a man get two such termagants for sisters?" He gazed down at their joyful faces.

"Termagants? Is it a bad word?" Sally turned her face to her sister. "Lou-Lou, was that a bad word? I have learned so many new bad words from Henry."

Now Henry's cheeks heated.

"It means you are lovely," Mary spoke from the couch.

"Lovely indeed." He grunted when he tried to walk with the added weight on each appendage, hearing the girls giggle again. "What is the word for heavy?"

"Abundant. You are abundantly blessed to have such enchanting sisters," Mary said.

"I should never have given you a dictionary. Soon you'll have me believing these little mots are ladies."

"They are royalty. I was told they dubbed you a knight, Sir Henry. A fitting title." Her mirth radiated in her eyes.

"Mother says you have spent enough time alone together," Lou-Lou informed them.

"And Benton said Her Grace's carriage was waiting," Sally piped up.

"It appears our chaperones mean to divide us." Henry picked up each girl by an arm. They whooped with delight and wrapped themselves around Henry's torso and neck. "Say goodnight, you abundant little princesses."

The girls bobbed Mary a proper farewell before Henry released them both and they dashed away.

He held his arm out for Mary and she took it without hesitation.

"You seem to be enjoying your new family," Mary said.

"Those two will be the death of me. I thought fighting in a ring was tiring." Henry stretched his neck.

"Thank you, for checking on your friends. I like them, and I want to remove them from suspicion as soon as possible," she said. They neared the door where the butler stood with her wrap.

"It might be a fool's errand, but I will find out. I also got a letter from the constable in London with his findings. He's not solved anything." He helped Mary with her wrap, his heart plummeting a little at what he was about to tell her. "Mary, we might never find out what happened to Luke."

Mary pulled her wrap tight and shook her head. "I have to find out. I need to know the truth."

"We may never know the truth. And while it pains me greatly to have his murder go unsolved, I can't help but think he would want you to move on and be happy with your life."

"I can't accept that."

"Why not?"

She glared at him, bit her lip, and stomped to her carriage. Henry was taken aback by her sudden anger. Everything that could be done to solve Luke's murder had been done. Did she not want to move on? Was she harboring some undying loyalty toward Luke?

He followed her, pressing his hand against the carriage door before she opened it.

"I need to go, Henry."

"Mary, please be reasonable. I'll do what you ask, but you need to consider that you will not find the answers you seek."

She straightened her posture and jut out her chin. "You don't understand. I can't stop. I will never stop until I know what happened."

When did she become so stubborn? And why did that make her even more attractive? Nothing was going to be solved tonight. He'd give her time to reflect and try this conversation again later.

Henry opened the carriage door. A pair of red eyes illuminated from the darkness of the carriage. He paused, and put his arm in front of Mary to stop her from entering. Had a cat found its way into the carriage?

A low rumbling sound rose to a growl. The eyes lunged toward the carriage door. He held his arm up to defend against the creature. A gust of wind hit him and the beast disappeared. The frigid air smashed into his chest hard enough to knock him back a few steps.

"What the blazes!" He rubbed his chest where it hit him, feeling tiny shards of frost on his waistcoat.

"Are you all right?" Mary's soft hand grabbed his arm. Her face was white and she trembled.

"I'm fine. What the devil was that?"

Mary gulped and closed her eyes. Weariness swept over her features and her voice shook when she spoke. "*That* is why I must find out what happened to Luke." She brushed past him and without hesitation stepped into the dark carriage, closing the door smartly behind her.

MARY READ the caller's card again, confusion and a bit of fear rose in her chest and she swallowed it down.

Lord Maxwell Carroll was at her door, waiting for a response.

She glanced at the butler. His professional calm and emotionless expression didn't help her make a decision.

"Please show him to the parlor, and ask George and Agnes to meet me there." Mary slipped a black shawl over her gray dress and decided it was proper enough to greet her visitor.

Both George and Agnes were waiting outside the parlor door when she arrived. Her trusted maid and her currently questionable bodyguard. She'd kept her word to Henry and trusted he was right about George, at least for the moment. There wasn't a room on earth she wanted to be alone in with Lord Carroll. She apprised them of their visitor and presented her instructions.

"George, please watch him for any erratic behavior. Agnes," she took her maid's hand and pressed it. "I need your presence for support." With a deep breath, she put on her best solemn face and entered the parlor with the two servants at her heels.

Lord Carroll was on his feet when she entered, standing next to the fireplace and examining the various Staffordshire figurines lined up on the mantle.

She couldn't help but compare him to Henry. Like Henry, Lord Carroll was muscular and broad, with muscles straining through his coat. Lord Carroll's coloring was lighter, his eyes a different shade, his face lacking Henry's fine definition. Above all, she thought of Henry as a shield, a protector, and shuddered at the thought of those muscles being used to terrorize anyone.

"Your Grace." Lord Carroll formed a proper bow and she

returned a nod. She didn't motion to the couch for him to sit or ring for tea.

"I am curious as to why you are here, Lord Carroll. It is the only reason I agreed to speak with you. Once my curiosity is appeased, I will ask you to leave."

He lowered his eyes and brought up an object held in his hands. "I came to bring Lou-Lou her doll."

The well-loved object was all cloth with a worn dress and button eyes, one blue and one green and a sewn-on smile. It had been repaired several times with different colored threads. The hair was uneven with mismatched colored yarn scattered about the head. A few stains dotted the doll's hands and face and feet. It apparently had seen many adventures with Lou-Lou.

"Ugly thing, isn't it." Lord Carroll chuckled, turning the doll over in his hands. "I've thrown it away several times, even ripped it up once. I bought her new dolls to replace it. She'd always find it, rescue it, and fix it. I tried once to burn it and she threw a vase of flowers on the fire before plucking it out. Her poor little hands were burned, but I realized then she loved it more than she loved me. I was dumbfounded when I saw it left behind in her bed." He held the doll out to Mary. "I want my family."

His words were pretty, his voice smooth, exactly like Jonathan's when he justified slapping her.

She snatched the doll from Lord Carroll's fingers. "They don't want to see you."

He wouldn't meet her gaze but nodded. "I've been trying all week for a visit. I came as soon as I recovered from my injuries. They won't accept my letters or let me onto the estate. I need to apologize."

"They don't want apologies; they want to be left alone."

Mary clutched the doll to her chest. "I think they have made it very clear."

He ran his fingers through his hair and touched the yellowing bruise on his forehead. "Extremely clear. To go through such lengths to be rid of me. Staging a kidnapping and having me beaten. I'm the laughingstock of ..."

"Stop thinking of yourself," Mary snapped. "If I hear one more word about poor Lord Carroll, I'm going to be sick. I have the doll, and I can report your family is in excellent health and the bruise you left upon Lady Carroll's eye is almost completely healed. You may leave now."

Lord Carroll clenched his fists and she fought the urge to cower when George cleared his throat loudly behind them. She wasn't alone, and the knowledge filled her with bravery. She wouldn't surrender to this bully. Even if her spine pricked with fear and her knees wobbled beneath her skirts, he would never know.

"Mr. Henry Church and Miss Carroll." The butler's voice announced the newcomers before they entered the room.

Henry entered with Lou-Lou, holding her hand tightly in his. The little girl's eyes darted around the room. She clutched at Henry when she saw her father.

"We were about to leave our cards when we found out you had a visitor." Henry didn't acknowledge his sire but quirked a brow at Mary. "Forgive our intrusion, Your Grace, but Lou-Lou wanted to see her father."

Lou-Lou stared across the room at Lord Carroll. She was the perfect miniature of her mother, all blonde curls and creamy skin, except for those inky black eyes to remind Mary she was still being haunted.

"Lou-Lou, you wanted to see me?" Lord Carroll said softly.

She shook her head and buried her face in Henry's leg. "You don't call me Lou-Lou. You call me Louise."

"I'm sorry, you're right." Lord Carroll swallowed hard. "Do you have a kiss for your Papa?"

"Not right now." Lou-Lou gazed up at Henry, her lip wobbling. "I'm scared now. Can we go home?"

Henry pulled her little body in tightly to his side. "Of course, darling. Please excuse us, Your Grace."

Lord Carroll's face fell and he took a step toward them. "Louise? I thought you wanted to see me?"

"I did at first. I wanted to know if you were hurt, but now I'm scared because you called me Lou-Lou. You said to never call me Lou-Lou and you broke the rule. I know what happens when someone breaks the rules, and now I'm scared," Lou-Lou's eyes watered.

Mary bit her lip in horror when the little tear trickling down the girl's face was as red as blood. Was she the only one who saw it? Now was *not* the time for a haunting.

"Don't be scared," Lord Carroll tried to soothe. "Here, I brought you your doll." He motioned to Mary who held the doll out for Lou-Lou.

The little girl scrunched her face. "I left the doll for you, Papa."

Lord Carroll took a step. "What? Why would I need a doll?"

"She's my best, toughest, strongest doll of all. She's the one who keeps away monsters and makes me laugh when I'm sad because she looks so silly. I didn't want you to be sad and alone when we left. So I left her. For you."

The silence in the room was oppressive. Agnes sniffed behind her.

Henry detached Lou-Lou from his leg and took the doll

from Mary. In two strides, he crossed the room and slapped the doll against Lord Carroll's chest.

They stood eye to eye, eerily similar but so different. Henry's face was filled with disgust. Lord Carroll's showed uncertainty. He slowly took the doll from Henry.

"You don't deserve this doll. You don't deserve Lou-Lou. And you certainly didn't deserve my mother. I don't want to even *glimpse* your face ever again." Henry's low hiss was heard by all.

Lord Carroll's face snapped into a mask of control. He walked toward Mary and bowed, "Thank you for your time today, Your Grace. All my questions have been answered sufficiently."

He walked past the group and directly out the door, followed by the butler and George who shut the door behind them.

A loud crash made everyone in the room jump. Lou-Lou cried out and raced to Henry who picked her up and cuddled her. One of the little china dogs on the mantle fell off and shattered on the hearth. Her ghost again?

"Oh dear." Agnes walked to the mess. She bent down and picked up the pieces. "I'll find a broom."

"How on earth did that happen?" Mary asked. Was her ghost going to begin throwing things without any discrimination of who saw its tantrum? She went to move the rest of the pieces safely from the edge.

Up on the mantle was a small note tucked between a shepherdess and a cat. Mary took it and unfolded it. The contents were brief and to the point.

I know who killed your husband.
Lord C-

Chapter Fourteen

❦

Boutisale - A sale at a cheap rate; as booty or plunder is commonly sold.

THE NEXT WEEK, Henry accompanied Mary, his siblings, Lady Carroll, and Agnes to the village fair. He rode alongside their carriage, with Peter on a horse next to him.

Lady Carroll refused to attend without Peter at her side and the old pugilist was at a loss to why. "I brought a den of thieves into her house and kidnapped her from her husband. Don't know how that makes a lady trust me," he mumbled.

"It's your ugly mug. She knows it will scare anyone away," Henry said.

Peter leaned across his mount and shoved Henry hard enough to almost unseat him. Henry laughed and caught his balance before he hit the ground.

Peter scratched his crooked nose and his grin displayed his

missing tooth . "I know you're jealous of my looks. Don't worry. Someday you'll get a bunch of fives to the mouth to rattle your teeth loose and then you'll be as handsome as me."

Henry sobered a moment. "I know you've been teaching Benton to fight."

Peter sighed. "The lad is nettled about his papa. He's got a belly full of anger and is scared to death he's going to be a chip of the old block and start beating his family. Found Benton pounding the wall of the stables one morning and took care of his knuckles, like I did his brother."

Henry glanced down at his own thick, scarred knuckles currently hidden behind gloves. The thought of his brother developing the same calluses and the pain that went with it sat like a stone in his belly. "I don't want Benton in the ring."

"Ha! The old duke said the same thing about you. See how well that worked out? He'll choose his own path, like you did."

Henry didn't respond. His guts churned with the thought of his younger brother stepping into the ring, but he also recalled the fire in his own belly when he was a juvenile, needing a release before exploding onto something innocent. "Just keep an eye on him until he goes to school."

"Righto, and I'll give him some pointers on how to bob and weave and poke a sound nobbler for when he gets there," Peter said.

Henry groaned as control of the situation slipped away. "Not the face. Headmasters don't like it when you show up to class with a black eye. Have him learn to aim for the ribs instead." He ignored Peter's burst of laughter.

Lou-Lou and Sally kept poking their heads out of the carriage, keeping the occupants inside informed of their journey. When the tents and colorful flags came into view, they both squealed and the carriage rocked with excitement.

When the carriage stopped, Benton burst out of the door and glowered at Henry. "I am not riding home with them."

Henry dismounted and smirked at his brother, "You'll miss them when you go to school."

"Doubt it," Benton muttered but lifted both of his excited sisters out of the carriage.

Their chatter filled the air while Lady Carroll and Mary exited. Agnes emerged with a couple of bonnets for the girls, displaced during the drive.

"I'm off." Benton jingled the pocket full of coins that Henry gave him earlier.

"Come find us later, the ladies have a picnic prepared for dinner." The younger man waved and strode away towards the acrobats.

"Hold still, the sooner you get dressed the sooner we can go see everything." Lady Carroll held down Lou-Lou to tie her ribbons while Sally held perfectly still for Mary.

Once their bonnets were on, they grabbed their mother's hands and started pulling her in opposite directions.

"The animals!" Sally shouted.

"No, the dancers!" Lou-Lou said.

"Quiet." Henry's voice shushed them both. "I think that Mary should choose what we see first since it is her first time at the fair."

Their faces transfixed on Mary and she flushed, just like he'd hoped. "If you would be so kind to escort me, I will accept."

"Do you wish to be seen so close in public with me?" Henry asked. He hadn't heard too many rumors follow them from London, but he was sure there were a few curious onlookers.

Mary shrugged, "I'm opprobrious, remember? They're

going to think whatever they want no matter what I do. I'm also hoping if I spend enough coins here today, they will speak of me favorably."

"Money does make accusations disappear." Even the Bow Street boys turned their heads for the right price. He held out his arm for her. Mary took it and he secretly puffed out his chest with pride. Peter joined them after taking care of the horses and followed the little entourage with Agnes at the rear.

The fair was loud, crowded, and smelled amazing. The girls oohed and awed at the acrobats, and stuffed their faces with treats while Lady Carroll answered their questions at the many different sights they'd never seen.

Mary asked Henry questions about the different livestock, farming tools, while buying many things for her new estate. He enjoyed watching her give every table and tent some coin even if it was for something impractical. Whenever she saw one of her servants enjoying their day off, she paused and greeted them.

"You make it difficult for people to not fall in love with you, Mary Fletcher Polk."

Her eyes sparkled with mischief. "I will acknowledge I have a great many faults, Mr. Church. I didn't know being amiable was one of them."

"It would help if you weren't so perfect, Your Grace." He enjoyed the flush spreading across her cheeks.

"What have I told you about making such statements to people with red hair?"

"What's wrong with red hair?" Lou-Lou piped up from behind.

"Nothing, people with red hair are absolutely perfect," Henry answered.

"You must stop. I feel the color rushing into my toes. And it's time for supper, which I'm inclined to ban you from if you continue to tease me." Mary shifted their direction toward the carriage.

Agnes and Peter quickly set up a picnic for the group in the shade of the carriage. Benton joined them, folding down next to his mother to show off his purchases.

Henry tried to open the hamper for the chicken but Sally blocked him..

"No food for you unless Mary says so." His sister's grin was contagious.

"But I'm starving," Henry whined.

Sally giggled but crossed her arms firmly. "You need to learn not to tease people."

"Very well." He knelt before Mary and pleaded. "Mary, my queen, my goddess. Please let this poor starving man back into your good graces and allow him some sustenance."

Her cheeks flamed brighter. "Lou-Lou, please pass the rolls, I want to throw them at your brother," Mary said.

Lou-Lou hesitated with the basket. "At Henry or Benton?"

"Henry."

"Then can I throw one at Benton?"

All eyes, especially Benton's, gravitated to Lou-Lou. "What did I do to you?" he asked.

Lou-Lou shrugged. "It sounds like fun."

"Then we both shall throw them at Henry," Mary took a roll and lobbed it at him.

Henry spent the picnic dodging food flying occasionally in his direction. Even Lady Carroll tossed a crumb his way with a giggle. Sally possessed an especially good aim and he was wiping a blob of jam off his cheek when Peter stood up and waved. "Oi, you bunch of slags! We're over here."

George walked up with a familiar group of men, holding ropes and stakes and an assortment of tools.

"Ho there, Vicar. Where do we set up?" Tommy hefted a large mallet for the stakes.

"Just outside the village in the field. I'll show you." Henry rose to his feet and brushed the crumbs from his clothes.

"Vicar? Did he call you Vicar?" Mary asked.

It was Henry's turn to flush. "It's nothing." He glared at the broad smirks his family and Mary were giving him.

"Nothing? Our Vicar here is the best heavyweight man in the country. Shame he won't fight in any championships. He'd go down in history," Tommy supplied.

"I'm not a vicar." Henry replaced his hat knocked off by a flying chicken bone.

"Name like Church, you have to be a vicar." Tommy shrugged like the whole thing made perfect sense.

Henry bowed his head. "I beg your pardon ladies, but I need to take my leave from you. Benton, will you see everyone get home safely?"

Benton snorted. "Not a chance. I'm coming with you to the fight." The young man straightened his coat.

"You most certainly are not."

"You organized a fight?" Mary asked.

He'd been trying so hard to keep it from her. Drunk Mary had shown great interest in seeing a fight, and he was certain Sober Mary would be too. "Yes. I put up a big enough purse to attract most of my friends here." To question them about George and Peter, as she'd asked. Then maybe she'd answer his questions about that creature in the carriage she was so firmly mum about.

"That's wonderful. We'll stay and support you."

Mary's smile was so wide he hated to disappoint her. "No, you will not. You're going home," Henry pointed at Benton, "and you are taking them." He glanced over at Lady Carroll for support.

She was too calm for his liking. "Benton and I have already discussed his extra activities. I think it is a good idea for him to know exactly what he's getting into."

"I'll see the ladies get home and come back for the milling," Peter said.

Henry searched Benton's face for any signs of reluctance. Watching a prizefight wasn't for the weak, and he was afraid it would bring up bad memories for the boy. But all he saw was a young man's face radiating with anticipation and excitement.

"I've lost control," Henry muttered and clapped his hand on Benton's shoulder.

"You never held it in the first place." Benton gave his mother a peck on the cheek and stuck himself to Henry's side as they left with the pugilists.

———

MARY SILENTLY DEBATED with herself while Agnes and Peter began cleaning up the picnic.

"Peter?"

"Yer Grace?"

"We're not going home."

"We're not?" Lou-Lou asked. Her sightless eyes focused on Mary. Every child appeared the same way to her. The black, dead eyes on children had her skin crawling even as she forced an effort to not let it affect her.

"We're staying to watch Henry fight," Mary announced.

The little girls cheered and Lady Carroll laughed. "I suspected you wanted to stay."

Mary shrugged. She'd told Henry she'd wanted to attend his fights, and she wasn't sure she'd get the chance to ever again.

Agnes clutched a blanket against her chest. "Are you sure? It's not a place for ladies to be seen."

"Opprobrious," Mary answered.

Agnes huffed. "I wish you hadn't learned that word."

"We'll park the carriage on the edge of the crowd and watch from there," Mary said. "I think the crowd will be more interested in the fight than who's watching it."

They bundled into the carriage and told the driver to move them to the field where the fight was taking place. A large group was already gathering around the stakes and rope erected for the ring. A long line and a square were chalked inside it. They were far enough away they couldn't see faces, but Henry and Benton's finer clothing stuck out among the masses.

She saw Henry's arm around Benton's shoulder, their heads together while he pointed at things. She imagined in a few years Benton would be shoulder to shoulder with his brother's stature.

"Mama, I can't see," Sally complained.

"Here, you little mot, up you go." Peter took the girl by the arms and passed her up to the driver who set her on top of the carriage.

"Me too!" Lou-Lou threw herself into Peter's arms and giggled when he tossed her up.

Lady Carroll was less certain. "Peter, I'm not sure it is entirely safe for them."

"Sure it is, especially when their mum joins them to keep them in line." Peter held out a hand to Lady Carroll.

"I'm quite certain sitting on top of a carriage is not something a lady should be doing."

"Yeah, but you're not a lady right now. You're a dimber mort who's watching a milling-set-to. You'll want the best seat for it." He winked at her.

Lady Carroll blinked, and then laughed. "I have no idea what you said, but I'll assume it was flattery." She shook her head and placed her hand in Peter's. "Very well, help me up." Peter and the driver assisted her carefully to a seat by her daughters. The driver was then released to join the mob of bloodthirsty merrymakers surrounding the ring.

A resigned sound came from Agnes while she opened the carriage door. She pulled out all the cushions and pillows not attached to the squabs.

"Thank you, Agnes, you're brilliant." Mary tossed the padding up to Lady Carroll. She was about to accept Peter's help to climb up when a man approached them.

"Yer Grace?" He held his hat in his hands and shifted nervously.

"Oi, Tommy? Something wrong?" Peter asked.

"No, the Vicar asked me to come and speak with the Duchess. Bein' mum about why."

Mary took a moment to try and interpret what the man said. "Mr. Church sent you over? And he didn't tell you why?"

"Said you had some questions for me about a fight in London," Tommy said.

Questions? Oh. A burst of warmth rushed through Mary at Henry's thoughtfulness. He was going to let her question Tommy without any bias.

"Would you speak with me in private?" Mary asked.

"Yeah, er, oh! Here." The man jutted out his elbow and

Mary placed her hand in it. They walked out of the earshot of the carriage and stopped.

"I imagine Mr. Church is not happy we're still here," Mary said.

"Too right! He saw your carriage and let out a string of words I never heard before. Then he pulled me aside and told me to seek you out."

"It's about the death of my husband." Mary searched for the right words to not give her own bias. "There was a fight that night. George and Peter were there instead of watching our carriage. Please tell me if you remember that fight?"

Tommy frowned for a moment and scratched his chin. "Last time I saw Pete and Georgie-boy was them milling in town. George usually doesn't fight, just plays the books. But when he heard old James the Giant boasting with a cod of blunt that no one could get a chopper on him, George took him up on it. He beat James about five years ago, and wanted to shut his boasting gob. George took a big ogler in the gaslights before he peppered old James with a fury and won. Peter was his knee man that night."

Mary hesitated and guessed. "George took a hit to the face? To his eyes?"

"He was plenty sore about it too. Knew the Vicar wouldn't be happy about his sporting a black eye."

A rush of relief swept over Mary. She remembered George's bruised face when they met him at the carriage after the opera. Their whereabouts were confirmed. "Thank you, Mr... Tommy."

"Sutton, Yer Grace. Tommy Sutton."

"Thank you, Mr. Sutton." She opened her reticule to fish out a coin.

"No need. The Vicar promised to get in the ring if I came to talk to you. I should make a plump purse when he wins."

Mary pulled out a coin anyway and handed it to him. "Would you place a bet then, for me? On the Vicar winning?"

Tommy Sutton took the coin and saluted. "You're a rum mort, Yer Grace."

"I hope that is a good thing to be."

He extended his elbow again for her with a crooked smile. "It is."

"All right there, Your Grace?" Peter asked when they returned.

"Yes, everything is fine. Thank you again, Mr. Sutton."

The pugilist left them and Peter helped Mary take a place on top of the carriage next to Lady Carroll. The carriage swayed while Peter climbed aboard and the girls yelped and clung to their mother. Like a naughty boy, he rocked the carriage back and forth to make them scream in delight.

"Sit down Peter, you're making me sick," Mary laughed. He sat down next to Lady Carroll.

"You scared us!" Peter yelped when Sally and Lou-Lou tackled him and laughed when they overpowered him. "Promise to never do that again."

"Something amiss?" Lady Carroll asked Mary. "I kept an eye on you."

"He had some information for me, about the night my husband died." Mary sighed. Her suspicions of Peter and George were cleared but now she was back to having no suspects. And the only clue given to her was a vague note from Lady Carroll's abusive husband who happened to also be Henry's sire. Her mind muddled in different directions and a headache began to form.

"Look, they're starting." Lou-Lou leaped to her feet and

the carriage swayed again. They all shouted for her to sit and Peter pulled her into his lap.

"Lightweights first. Like you, little mot. Mostly locals trying their hand at some fisticuffs for a purse," Peter said.

"I still can't see," Sally whined.

"Oh, I forgot about these." Mary dug into her reticule and pulled out the pair of brand-new opera glasses Luke gave to her on that fateful night. "Here, try this."

Sally lifted the glasses to her black eyes. Her little face didn't fit, so she held it to one eye and shut the other. "These are amazing. I see everything." She nestled down between Mary and Lady Carroll.

Mary sat up straight when the fights began. She admittedly flinched a few times when punches were thrown, and the men staggered about. Peter began shouting advice and praise. Lou-Lou joined in with exuberance. Their voices melted into the roar of the crowd around the ring.

Punches weren't the only thing allowed by the rules. Anything above the waist was allowed. A few grabbed torsos and some wrestling occurred. One man was picked up and thrown to the ground.

Lou-Lou let out a groan. "It looks like it hurt."

"He'll be sore in the morning," Peter said. "But he's getting up. If he's smart, he'll give the man a sneezer to make his eyes water and follow up with a pepper to the ribs."

"Give him a pepper to the ribs!" Lou-Lou shouted.

Lady Carroll giggled every time Lou-Lou mimicked Peter, then spoke a halfhearted reminder for her daughter to act more like a lady.

Sally squirmed between Mary and Lady Carroll. "Benton is taking off his shirt."

"He better not be!" Lady Carroll grabbed the opera glasses

and let out an unladylike curse. "He promised me he'd only watch."

Mary sat up straight when young Benton entered the ring. He bobbed on his feet, almost hopping. Was he nervous or excited? Henry stepped under the rope and put an arm around his brother's shoulder. Benton's movements slowed when Henry spoke into his ear. Another young man about the same size entered the ring. Henry walked to the young man and spoke into his ear as well. The young man nodded and shook hands with Benton.

Henry clapped his hands and shouted at the crowd. They dulled their noise enough to listen. "I've got two young bucks getting their feet wet. No punches, grabs only, no purse available. This might be a bit boring to you blood-thirsty lot, so go and get a drink." The crowd dispersed a little while George and Tommy both entered the ring with the young fighters.

Lady Carroll relaxed slightly and handed the glasses to Sally. "Don't think for a moment I won't have words with him tonight."

The two young men clashed together with enthusiasm, chest to chest before arms and legs began wrapping around each other. They tugged and pulled; their youthful grunts reached all the way to the carriage. Henry stopped them, offered some directions, and then motioned for them to begin again.

"Meh, the Vicar's not going to let them get too feisty. I'm off for some refreshment," Peter set Lou-Lou to the side. "Any requests from you ladies?"

"Pastries and small beer!" Lou-Lou piped up.

"Candied nuts and cider!" Sally added.

Mary was about to dig into her reticule again but Lady

Carroll handed Peter some money. "Some wine for Her Grace and I."

The carriage wobbled when he disembarked and Agnes appeared below them, stretching.

"You lot make it hard for a body to nap in the carriage." Agnes turned toward the crowd. Her spine stiffened suddenly and she backed up to the carriage slowly.

"What do you see?" Mary asked, and began scanning the crowd. Was Lord Carroll waiting for Peter to leave their side to make a move?

Agnes squinted and then shook her head. "It's nothing. Someone I thought I knew, and have no wish to renew the acquaintance." Agnes leaned against the carriage and peered up at her. "I don't suppose I could entreat you to go home?"

Mary snorted. "No, we're here to watch Henry fight."

"Very well." Agnes wilted a little.

"Are you feeling ill? I'm sure I could find someone to take you home." Mary began to search the crowd for the driver.

"No need. I'm stiff from sitting in the carriage. I'll take a little walk and stretch my legs." Agnes headed toward the tables set up for food and drink.

"Now Henry's taking off his shirt," Sally announced.

"What?" Mary plucked the glasses from Sally's hands. She fumbled a bit before getting both lenses to focus on the ring.

Henry was talking to someone while unbuttoning his shirt, down the front and then his cuffs.

"Oh my," Mary whispered.

"Let me see," Sally said.

A wise chuckle came from Lady Carroll. "It's Mary's turn to look."

Mary did more than look. She ogled. Her cheeks warmed while Henry peeled off the rest of his shirt and revealed his broad chest and detailed muscles like the other fighters had. He bent over and removed his boots, giving Mary an eyeful of a well-formed backside.

"Merciful heavens." Mary quickly lowered the opera glasses and handed them to Sally. She fanned her cheeks a little with her hands. "It's become unseasonably warm all of a sudden."

Sally quirked an eyebrow at her and resumed squinting through the glasses.

Lady Carroll handed her a fan. "Ah, to be young again," was all she said.

Mary rapidly fanned her face and she scanned up and down at Henry while he further disrobed himself. Even from afar the sight of him made her body heat. "It's...not...oh fustian. Maybe Agnes was right and we should leave."

"Never. I'm enjoying it too much." Lady Carroll laughed.

Peter returned with an armful of tidbits and drinks, and Agnes followed with her own bottle of spirits. The maid disappeared into the carriage while Peter passed up the treats. The girls squealed and giggled again when he climbed up onto the carriage.

"Ah. I see the Vicar's getting ready to show us how it's done." He took a swig from his own bottle.

"Here." Lady Carroll passed Mary a small bottle of wine.

Mary took a few swallows and exhaled. "Thank you. I'm feeling much better."

"There's only one cure for what ails you. And wine is not it," Lady Carroll said softly.

Mary didn't respond but settled against the cushions and waited for the fight to resume. The crowd returned, louder and bigger. Henry bounced on his feet, while George and Benton set up in his corner.

"What's Benton doing now?" Lou-Lou asked.

"Benton is Henry's bottle man; he'll give Henry a drink if he needs it. And George is going to be Henry's knee man. Henry will sit on his knee between rounds and rest for a few seconds," Peter said. "Although Henry hardly uses a knee man."

"Why?"

"You brother's more slippery than an eel. He'll bob and weave like he knows what's coming and then give his opponent a teaser. He likes to play with them a bit and wear them down. Then he'll give 'em a poke to the brisket and a couple of rib ticklers. He never goes for the noggin until he's sure he's got a settler."

"Are you sure we are from the same country, Peter? I understand every word you said but I've never heard them used in a sentence together," Lady Carroll said.

Peter's uneven smile flashed. "Henry's fast. He'll dance around and make them tired. Then he goes for the chest and ribs. He stays away from the head until he's ready to knock them out."

The crowd roared when the two men walked to the newly chalked lines. The man was slightly taller and stockier than Henry. He glared at Henry. Henry offered a handshake that was rejected.

A bell rang and the match began. It started as Peter said it would, with Henry's opponent trying to get a jab at Henry and Henry supplying light taps to his opponent's back and arms to provoke the man further.

Mary sat up and leaned forward, anticipation and a little anxiety making her want to fidget. The crowd pressed tightly against the ring and Sally stood up to get a better view.

Mary strained her neck above the mob when Henry

received a punch to his shoulder he didn't quite dodge and stumbled a bit. He ducked the next blow and managed a light strike to his opponent's belly.

"Stop playing and pitch a chopper!" Peter shouted.

"Pitch a chopper, Henry!" Lou-Lou echoed.

Out of the corner of her eye, Mary saw a lone figure approach the crowd. She was about to brush it off when a chill ran down her spine, the tell-tale sign her ghost was about. Something was amiss.

Mary focused on the figure. A woman dressed all in white. Her clothing was loose and gauzy and her skin was as pale as her garment. Her hair was loose, dark, and long, running in matted clumps down between her shoulders. She didn't walk but floated.

Mary's mouth went dry when the creature approached the crowd. The ghost didn't stop or move around the mass of bodies but went into them, through them. Every person she touched shivered a little, but brushed it off and focused on the fight.

"May I see the glasses please?" Mary asked. Sally handed them over and Mary lifted them with trembling fingers. The woman in white didn't step over the ropes but drifted through them. She walked up to Henry, who was fending off his attacker, and paused.

Then she twisted toward Mary, as if she knew Mary was observing her from afar. The woman's face sharpened with the glasses for Mary to make out details. Her eyes were two black holes, her mouth a pit of darkness sliding up into the shape of a sinister smile directed straight to Mary's vision.

Mary quickly lowered the glasses and held a hand over her thumping heart. Was that her ghost? A woman? But what about Luke? Wasn't he the one haunting her?

"It's the white lady," Sally said quietly. The little girl was peering through the glasses again. Her eyes were the same color as the ghost's. Why did she focus on only the children?

"White lady? You've seen her before?" Mary asked. Her breath came in shaky spurts while Sally was completely calm.

"Yes. She comes to the house sometimes at night when Lou-Lou's asleep and I have a nightmare. She sings to me. She smells like flowers."

Mary shivered when the woman approached Henry's side. Her arms opened wide into an embrace and she wrapped herself around Henry's body, then she disappeared inside him.

Henry put on a sudden burst of speed. He drove his shoulder into his opponent's chest and knocked him backward. Henry landed a punch to the chest, then a series of rapid blows onto the man's ribs.

"Took him long enough to wake up," Peter muttered. The rest of the fight went the way he said it would. Henry danced and moved with amazing speed to avoid any more jabs. He landed precise strikes onto the man's chest, shoulders, and ribs. Once the man was dazed and tired, Henry landed a single heavy blow to the head and toppled his opponent to the ground where he remained motionless.

The counting started, the crowd joining in until Henry was declared the winner. Benton jumped from the corner and hugged Henry. Henry accepted the embrace and waved at the cheering crowd.

The noise faded away for Mary when the white lady oozed out of Henry's body. He leaned a little heavier on Benton while the ghost faded into the air.

It appeared Mary wasn't the only one who was haunted.

Chapter Fifteen

Whin - A weed; furze

MARY HAD plenty of time to contemplate what she should do on her trip back to London. The note from Lord Carroll burned in her pocket. She hadn't told Henry about it. He'd made it perfectly clear he never wanted to see his sire again, and she would honor his wishes.

Taking it to the constable was also not an option. Lord Carroll would dismiss it, or claim it was false, or pay them to look the other way while making Mary look like a fool.

But she needed answers. Answers to questions that increased every day. Mostly about her ghost.

The carriage stopped at David and Miriam's townhouse and George helped her and Agnes from the cab. Miriam herself met them at the door, embracing and kissing both of Mary's cheeks and ushering her inside.

"The children and I were so happy to get your letter. We've missed you."

"I've missed all of you." Mary allowed herself to rest her head on Miriam's shoulder and took a little strength from the great lady's presence.

"Cassandra and Adam are eager to welcome you to the point the governess has given up on their studies until you arrived. We should go to the nursery and relieve them," Miriam said.

"Of course. I've brought them some baubles from the village fair to give them later," Mary said.

Miriam snorted. "We heard all about the fair and Henry fighting again. I almost tied up David and Josiah to keep them from going and making spectacles of themselves. They even tried to convince me to let them go in disguise."

She opened the door to the nursery and announced, "Cassie, Adam. We have a visitor."

"Mary's here!" Her favorite four-year-old boy hurled his little body at Mary's knees and buried his face in her skirts. His face peered up into hers, his once beautiful brown eyes replaced with shiny black orbs. Her heart sank with the further knowledge she couldn't outrun her ghost. But she kept a smile plastered on her face, and ran her fingers through Adam's dark curls that were so much like his uncle Henry's.

"Want to see my new drawings? I drew one of you," Adam tugged on her hand.

"Let me greet Cassie first." Mary turned to the ten-year-old young lady with long arms and legs. Cassie formed a proper curtsey before her delighted face tipped up to Mary, her eyes also black as night.

"I've been practicing. What do you think?"

"Perfect. Please don't tell me you're ready to put your hair up. I don't think I could manage you growing up any faster," Mary said.

She was engulfed into family life once more, listening to the children chatter and show off their treasures. She listened to Miriam complain about David's antics and her troubles with Josiah not taking his studies seriously. Mary told them about her new life at the Sycamore estate and her friendship with Lady Carroll and her children.

It was easy to return to their embrace, the love and esteem they showed her. She teared up several times with joy and laughed more than she had in months. But every time she saw the children's faces, their eyes would remind her this wasn't a friendly visit, and a dismal chill would race through her bones.

When the house went to sleep, Mary crept to the gallery. A single candle lit her way and her slippered feet were silent. She opened the door to the long and tall room and shivered. Her little light cast odd shadows from the ornate patterns on the portrait frames. There was movement flickering out of the corner of her eye, and when she swung to face it, everything was still. Her hand started to tremble.

She stopped at Luke's portrait. She lifted the taper up higher to illuminate young Luke Polk. Henry's features were easy to find in Luke's visage. The dark hair, the eyes, the cheekbones, even the posture. The only thing Henry inherited from his sire was his brawny build.

"I think Henry's nose is different because he's broken it a few times," she whispered to Luke. "I wish you had told me he was yours. I wish I had instilled more confidence in my character to have known your secrets." She reached up and touched the bottom of the frame gently, needing to take a piece of his boldness for herself. "I miss you. But you're not the one haunting me."

Luke and Talbot the dog remained silent. She lowered her light and walked down the gallery. She stopped at the portrait she'd come to examine and lifted her candle up to brighten the face.

The woman in the portrait rested easily in her blue gown atop a couch. Her eyes sparkled. Eyes she had passed on to her son.

"Sarah." Mary spoke the name and quivered when it echoed through the gallery. "It's you. You're here." The spectral woman in white shifted into Henry and helped him win the fight. "You never left Henry, did you?"

The face in the portrait began to morph. The smile turned down into a frown, and the eyes narrowed to a glare.

Mary withdrew a step. Her little flame began to dance precariously before dying with a puff of smoke.

Darkness descended over her.

"Murderer..."

The word hissed through the air over and over, above her, behind her, again and again. Mary dropped the candle and hugged herself, lowering herself to her knees.

"I didn't kill him," she pleaded.

A sharp little breeze whipped her hair, pulling her braid apart. A soft voice spoke directly into her ear. "Murderer."

Mary clapped her hands over her ears. The icy wind plucked at her sleeves and skirts, teasing and tormenting. "Sarah! Stop this right now. If you want my help you have to stop." She didn't know if reasoning with a ghost was possible, but it was the only thing she could think of.

To her surprise, the wind died down. Her little candle on the floor sputtered to life and Mary picked it up before it did any damage.

She held the light up once more to Sarah's portrait. The serene lips and sparkling eyes returned.

"I'll help you find who did it. Is that what you want?"

The silence threatened to swallow her while she strained to hear something. Finally, a faint "murderer," whispered across the gallery.

Maybe it was all the ghost could say? It was all she'd been able to spell in the tattered clothing left in Mary's dressing room. She needed some kind of rule book about ghosts and their interactions with the living.

"I received a note. From Lord Carroll." Sarah's portrait lifted and banged against the wall sharply. "Yes, I know you don't like him." The portrait thumped against the wall twice. "He says he knows who killed your father. Should I question him?"

The portrait held still.

Mary waited a moment before asking. "Is that a no?"

The picture of Sarah's face began to swing back and forth, skewing itself on the wall until it hung crooked.

"This is so hard." She clenched her eyes shut and bunched her fists while she searched for an answer on how to communicate. She opened them when one came to her. "Bounce the portrait once for no, twice for yes."

The portrait straightened and tapped against the wall twice. Now they were getting somewhere.

Excitement flooded her veins and she asked in a rush. "Do you know who killed Luke?"

One tap. No. The ghost was as clueless as she was.

Deflated, Mary thought of another question. "Why are you haunting me?"

The portrait began to skew again and bang against the

wall repeatedly. She hadn't asked a yes or no question, and Sarah was probably annoyed with her. "I'm sorry, you're right."

The painting stilled.

Mary let out a soft huff. "I suppose you didn't want to haunt and torment your brother. Or Henry, since he's your son. Was I the next choice?"

Two taps.

"I don't feel honored in the slightest." Her rational brain kicked in once more. It didn't matter why the ghost had picked her. The only option was to move forward.

"I'm going to question Lord Carroll tomorrow. I would like you to come with me." The portrait thudded hard and loud against the wall twice.

"Let's see what he has to say." A cold breeze caressed her neck softly and everything went silent.

MARY SAT with Agnes in the carriage outside Lord Carroll's house, waiting for a response. George was sent to announce them with her card and the note Lord Carroll left on her mantel. It would be a clear enough indication of what she wanted to speak about.

"This is a terrible idea," Agnes told Mary for the third time.

George scowled at her when he returned from the doorstep. He was as unhappy with the situation as Agnes.

"He'll see you." George held out his hand and helped her and Agnes from the carriage.

Mary exhaled. *Chin up, eyes forward, don't let him see your fear.*

"Sarah?" she whispered before entering the house. An

invisible hand brushed her neck, leaving behind fingerprints of ice. The spectre was with them.

They were escorted inside to a large parlor with a cheery fire. It was the only truly cheerful thing in the room. Mary marveled at the fine furnishings and artwork. Not a speck of dust in sight, nor an article out of place. Everything complemented something else next to it. The room appeared like a museum instead of a home.

"Your Grace, what a pleasant surprise." Lord Carroll entered the room and bowed over her hand. "I am delighted by your visit."

"I wish I could say the same." Mary matched his bright tone.

He snorted and smirked. Was this a game to him?

Lord Carroll glanced at Agnes. "I'm sure your servant would find something pleasant to eat in the kitchen so we can discuss our business in private."

"Agnes and George will both be outside the door listening for any unpleasantness."

His voice was cool. "I'm not a monster."

"I know of a mother and three children who say otherwise." *Not to mention a dead wife.*

He glared at her and marched across the room. He opened the door where George was waiting inches away from the threshold with a broad grin for Lord Carroll.

"All right in here, Your Grace?" George asked. His eyes never left Lord Carroll's face.

"Yes George, Agnes is coming to join you in the hallway. Lord Carroll and I have things to discuss in private, but will be keeping the door open a crack in case things get boisterous and you need to intervene," Mary said.

"Right then." George took the opportunity to crack his knuckles and neck.

Agnes brushed against the lord roughly when she exited, giving him a dark glower before she left.

Lord Carroll left the door open a crack and then moved to the other side of the room, giving Mary a clear escape if she wanted. He held his hands up with innocence before he took a seat. "I assure you, I have no ill will towards you."

Mary perched herself at the edge of a chair across from him. "Let's get to our business. You left me a note."

"I did."

"A note saying you know who killed my husband."

"I do." He crossed his legs and folded his hands. The smug expression returned to his face.

"I find it somewhat disconcerting that you kept this to yourself and didn't take this information to the constable."

"Ah, but society runs on secrets. Information is always more valuable than coins. You never know when you'll need something from someone else."

Little pinpricks of suspicion tiptoed on her scalp. "What could you possibly need from me?"

His eyes narrowed and he sat forward, leaning toward her. His voice was low, quiet, and almost a growl. "I need you to stop the Duke of Fenwick from pressing this ridiculous divorce through the court."

Mary's heart skipped a beat and she forced her face to stay aloof. "I doubt I could change his mind, even if I wanted to."

"This whole ordeal is shameful and embarrassing to us all. I want my family back." Lord Carroll's voice was menacing now.

Mary leaned closer, keeping her gaze locked with his.

"They don't want to come back. They are better off without you."

He met her glare with one of his own. "I didn't do anything wrong."

The scoff came out of her mouth before she could stop it. "You have a brilliant son who pretended to be an idiot so you wouldn't send him to school in order to stay home and protect his sisters and mother from your fists. You have two beautiful and terrified daughters who flinch at the word 'papa.' You have a battered wife who won't go anywhere without a bodyguard to protect her from *you*."

"A man is allowed to guide his family. To correct his wife." Lord Carroll's voice began to swell.

Mary's voice rose to meet it. "Correction? Children living in dread of their father are simply being guided? Is beating your wife a sign of refinement?"

Lord Carroll leapt to his feet and so did Mary. She was about to call for George when the door slammed shut and the lock clicked. George and Agnes pounded on the wood and rattled the handle.

The temperature of the room dropped. The cheery fire blew out with a harsh whoosh. Mary saw her breath rise in white puffs.

Sarah.

She glanced at Lord Carroll who was staring at the door with a puzzled look. The scent of flowers began to seep into Mary's nose. Lilacs. But it wasn't the fresh scent of spring. It was overpowering and acrid as if someone spilled an entire bottle of lilac perfume in the room.

"Sarah's here." Mary folded in her seat and hugged herself. Goosebumps rose on her arms and legs and she rubbed them.

A few months with the angry spirit hadn't settled her fears at all.

Lord Carroll glanced at her and then marched toward the door. "What are you talking about?" He grabbed the handle for the door and tugged. It didn't budge.

"Sarah. Your first wife. The one you killed." Mary pulled her feet up onto the chair with the rest of her and curled into a ball. She knew Sarah's power. Every time it manifested, Mary was afraid of getting caught in the crossfire. Her heart pounded faster; fear seeped into her pores with the cold oppressive air. A slight breeze caressed her cheek and Mary shuddered. What would she do this time?

"I didn't kill Sarah," He snarled.

Mary huffed. "Of course not. You merely 'corrected' her to death." She curled herself as small as possible into the cushions. It grew so cold she could see her breath. This was going to be unpleasant.

Lord Carroll abandoned the door and returned to loom over her. "What are you doing?"

"I've experienced Sarah's visitations several times already. I think she has something special planned for you."

A vase holding a bright spray of flowers on a side table behind Mary's chair began to rattle and shake on its bottom foundation. Mary didn't hold back a whimper.

Lord Carroll stared at it a moment, watching it move. "What trickery is this? You won't scare me with parlor tricks."

"No. I won't." Mary agreed, screaming when the vase flew above her head and slammed into Lord Carroll's face. The heavy crystal fell to the ground and spilled out its contents. Lord Carroll staggered, clasping his nose while the banging and shouting outside the room grew louder.

Blood streamed from Lord Carroll's nose. He stared at the red stain in his hand and gawked at Mary. "What the devil?"

A portrait flew from the wall and smashed itself over Lord Carroll's head with such force his head tore through the canvas. He cried out and struggled to remove it when porcelain figurines started battering him from all directions.

"What madness is this?" he roared.

A rattling came from the fireplace. The poker jerked to life from the hearth and began waving wildly into the air.

Lord Carroll screamed when it smashed into his ribs. "Stop this! Stop it at once."

The furniture around her began to crack. Legs and arms separated from seats and cushions. Tables wrenched themselves apart. The upholstery fell harmlessly to the floor when splinters of wood sped through the air towards Lord Carroll. He fell onto his knees and curled his arms around his neck and face before they smashed into his body, sticking out from him like a porcupine. Little dots of red blood began seeping through his coat.

"No more! I beg of you," he cried.

Mary swallowed hard and managed to unfurl her tense limbs. She rose from her chair. It was in pristine condition, unlike the violence exacted on every other piece of furniture in the room. She shivered in the cold air but drew up all her courage. Sarah had kept her safe from the tirade so far.

Mary walked to Lord Carroll. Anger and pity warmed her blood. She enjoyed looming over him. A feeling of power joined with her anger. Was Sarah influencing her? "How many times did Sarah beg you before you stopped hurting her?"

"What?" His wild eyes filled with panic and he cowered on the floor.

"She's very angry," Mary said.

The fire poker struck him again across his shoulders and he cried out.

"I don't think she'll accept an apology."

Another vase of flowers crashed above his head, shattering on the wall and raining shards upon him. A large piece flew towards Mary's face. It halted in mid-air and then fell harmlessly to the ground.

"You should probably try, though."

"Sarah! Sarah, please stop," he begged.

The discarded upholstery began to move, ripping pieces into long strips. With lightning speed they wove into a rope which rushed through the air. A makeshift noose hung above Lord Carroll's head.

"I think she wants you to hang." Mary's toneless voice surprised even her.

"What do you want? Tell me what she wants." Lord Carroll began to whimper.

Mary crouched beside him. "Who killed my husband?"

There was a moment of silence.

"Speak, before Sarah uses the noose on you herself."

Lord Carroll began to blubber. "It was your brother. Lord Fletcher."

Mary's heart shriveled into a stone before it began pounding, filling her ears with her pulse. "Jonathan?"

"He was bragging at the club, on how he was going to inherit the old duke's money. He had to get the old man gone first. Then he would swoop in like the benevolent brother and take care of you. He was sure the courts would give him custody of your well-being. Even though you're a widow, you're still underage."

Mary staggered from him. Memories of her brother's

beatings stole her breath away while dread tore at her chest. "Then why hasn't he?" Her voice shook.

"David Polk, damn his eyes. He has his claws in everything. He trounced your brother's request and nearly beat him publicly for suggesting it." Even with his face covered in blood and his eyes swelling, Lord Carroll was a beast who thrived on fear. He started to rise to his feet and was swatted again at his knees with the ghostly poker. He cried out while it rained more blows on his ribs.

Mary's limbs trembled and she rose to her feet. She took a deep breath and released it slowly. "Thank you, that's enough Sarah. He's told us what we came here for."

The poker slashed a final vicious swipe against Lord Carroll's buttocks before clattering to the floor.

Still shaking, Mary picked her way through the destroyed remains of broken furniture and shattered artwork to the door. A chorus of voices shouted from the other side, pounding and scratching, demanding for the door to be opened. An audible click preceded the lock giving way and bodies tumbled into the room.

"Where is he?" George demanded. Agnes threw her arms around Mary and sobbed.

"He's over there. I had everything well in hand." Mary returned Agnes's embrace, strength returning into her limbs with the affection.

The butler and housekeeper fell into the room with George and Agnes. They gaped at the destruction and stepped into the chaos. The housekeeper moved in a slow circle to take in the devastation while the butler's shoes crunched on broken bits of finery the room once contained.

"How did...?" The butler was cut off by the sound of Lord Carroll's moans and he raced to his employer's side.

"Let's go." Mary straightened her stance. She grabbed Agnes's hand and led her little band out of the house before the commotion started. Shrieks and shouts from the maids and housekeeper filled the air when Mary burst outside.

George practically tossed them into the carriage and was up top before more excitement delayed their departure.

The carriage jolted into motion and Mary slumped in her seat. A tear trickled from her eye when the gravity of everything pressed on her soul. Lord Carroll's cruelty. Her murderous brother. And Sarah's draining presence.

"It was the ghost, wasn't it?" Agnes reached over and held Mary's hand. "Please, my little duck. Was it the ghost who did all that?"

Mary's mouth went dry. "How did you know about the ghost?

Agnes's grasp squeezed tighter. "I've seen her. I saw her the first day we went to the Sycamore estate. Is she haunting you?"

More tears stung behind Mary's eyes. She couldn't speak but managed to nod before she burst into tears, throwing herself into the arms of her beloved friend. Finally, someone else knew of the terror surrounding her.

Agnes held her tightly, stroking and soothing her. The maid's voice trembled while Mary sobbed. "Oh my dearest girl, I'm so sorry."

Chapter Sixteen

꧁꧂

Fred - The same with peace; upon which our forefathers called their
sanctuaries fredstole, i. e. the seats of peace. So Frederic is powerful, or
wealthy in peace; Winfred, victorious peace; Reinfred, sincere peace.

THE CRISP FEEL of fall and all the scents with it blew in the
breeze around Henry. He stood on a balcony facing the fields
and tenant homes preparing for winter. Smoke and earth filled
his nostrils and he loved the memories they brought. Fall was
busy and bustling, but it meant winter was coming. Winter
meant long nights at home with one's family. Games and hot
cider alongside pies filled with the fruits of the harvest. Cold
sleigh rides to collect crisp greenery for the holidays where
there would be music and dancing and gifts. And mistletoe for
kissing.

Kissing. There was one person he'd like to meet under the
mistletoe. He faced the Sycamore estate. It was also humming

with the activities of fall, getting ready for the changing seasons. Waiting for the return of its mistress.

"You miss Mary." A small voice spoke from beside him.

He glanced down at Sally and pulled her into a one-armed hug against his leg. "You're such a perceptive little mot."

"I miss her too. And the white lady," Sally said.

"The white lady?"

"The lady who sings to me when I have bad dreams. I think she went to London with Mary."

Henry crouched down to meet Sally at her level and rubbed her shoulders. "Are you still having bad dreams, princess?"

She shrugged. "Not so many here at Hawthorne. No one yells at each other here."

"I'm glad you have more peace here. Tell me about your imaginary friend. Does she have a name?"

Sally regarded at him like he was stupid. "She's not imaginary, she's a ghost."

"Ah, I beg your pardon. We have a ghost, do we?" Henry jostled her shoulders a little to make her giggle. "I think all the best old houses have ghosts. I think I remember a white lady when I was a child at Fenwick."

Sally rolled her eyes. "You should know best. She's your ghost. I see her hugging you all the time."

Henry slowed his caresses on her arms as a sick uncertainty trickled through his chest. "Hugs me, does she?" He bit his lip and took Sally's hands. "Does this ghost have a smell?"

Sally's eyes brightened. "Yes! She smells like springtime. Like lilacs."

Lilacs.

Henry strove to keep his face neutral while memories swarmed in. Every fight he'd ever won was preceded by the strong smell of lilacs. As a child he was drawn to the plant, spending time among the bees in Sarah's Circle to stay near the comforting scent. As much as the smell of smoke and earth meant fall and harvest, the smell of lilacs meant safety and love.

Was something deeper going on here?

"Heeeeennnnnnrrryyyyyy!" Lou-Lou's voice pealed through the air behind them, preceding her bursting onto the balcony.

Sally huffed. "I don't think Lou-Lou will ever learn to be a lady."

"It's a good thing she's a princess then." Henry quickly kissed Sally on the forehead and stood up.

Lou-Lou threw herself around Henry's knees. "Mama's crying. She got a letter and started crying, and no one can calm her down." Lou-Lou's eyes swam with unshed tears and her lower lip trembled.

Sally's little face paled. "Was it another letter from Papa?"

"No, she returns those unopened. It was from the duke." Lou-Lou released Henry and bounced up and down. "Maybe he wants this house back? And we'll have to go to Papa." A single tear escaped down her cheek.

"I can't believe you have so little faith in Henry," Sally scolded. "He'd never let us go back."

Henry handed Lou-Lou a handkerchief. "Sally's right. And before you water my handkerchief too much, let's go and help your mother."

The little girls followed him into the study where Lady Carroll did her correspondence. The lady was on a chaise, crying heartily. She clutched a bundle of papers to her heart. Benton held her other hand, patting it and speaking kind words to her. Peter was standing behind her, his hands on Lady Carroll's shoulders and massaging her.

Henry stopped at the sight and gave Peter a pointed glare at his behavior. Peter made a rude gesture and continued to comfort Lady Carroll.

"What is wrong?" Henry demanded, holding out his hand for the papers she clasped.

Lady Carroll hiccupped and shook her head while tears rolled down her face. She gasped, sobbed, and handed him the stack of papers. She then leaned into Peter's embrace and cried harder.

Henry scanned the top letter written by his uncle, muttering it aloud. "-Lady Carroll, I am pleased to present to you the enclosed documentation of your *accepted* divorce from Lord Maxwell Carroll." Henry lowered the letter and slowly addressed Lady Carroll. "You're upset?"

Lady Carroll's disjointed words came out with her sobs. "I'm ... happy!" She burst into tears again and hugged Peter, who was appearing more and more comfortable with the lady being in his embrace.

Henry chuckled. "Madame, you have the whole household in an uproar over some unknown impending doom."

"I'm ... sorry." Her children swarmed her and hugged her. She hugged and kissed them all while she regained control of her emotions.

"Peter, I think we should celebrate. Would you see if there is champagne and cider about?" Henry still wasn't thrilled about Peter's familiarity with Lady Carroll, but wouldn't push the issue in front of the children.

Peter beamed a cheeky grin and sauntered off toward the kitchen.

Lady Carroll pat her cheeks and apologized again. "I am

sorry for my outburst. I never thought they would grant me a separation. It took me by surprise."

Henry leaned over and kissed her on the cheek. "A wonderful surprise. It will take an act of Parliament to let him marry again. And I don't see Uncle David letting it happen. Lord Carroll will never have another wife." The thought filled him with relief.

"Oh, Henry, I almost forgot. Your uncle sent you a letter too." Lady Carroll finished composing herself and smiled at Peter when he reappeared with the drinks. Here was another new development Henry was not sure he liked.

He cast those thoughts aside for another time and cracked the seal on his letter.

What he read plummeted his guts like a stone to the bottom of the Irish Sea.

"I've got to go to London immediately. Mary's been arrested."

———

HENRY LEAPED from the carriage before it stopped at his uncle's townhouse. He took the stairs in long strides, skipping every other step. He didn't knock, but threw the door open and bellowed.

"David! Miriam!"

The parlor door creaked open and a beautiful, healthy, wide-eyed Mary stepped out. "Henry? What's wrong?"

Relief and passion drove him to her side, forcing his arms around her, pulling her tightly to him, and clamping his lips upon hers.

Perfection.

She let out a muffled noise of surprise and drew away from

him. "Henry!" No, he wouldn't let her get away. He pulled her into his chest, tucked her firmly under his chin, and inhaled her signature feminine scent. "Please. Let me hold you a moment. I've spent hours in a carriage imagining you in prison."

Her arms slid around him slowly, unsure, then she added pressure, until he felt her fingertips digging into him through his coat.

"I'm all right." Her words were a bit muffled until she turned her face and pressed her cheek against his chest. "David wouldn't let them take me anywhere. But I am not allowed to leave the house."

Good, it should keep her out of trouble. Henry hugged her tighter and breathed out a sweet sigh of relief.

"Ahem. Henry, what intentions do you have toward my step-mother?" David's voice brought him back to the reality where she was a mourning widow, and he was in limbo waiting for her release.

He dropped his arms and she disengaged from him.

"Apologies. Upon seeing that Her Grace was *not* in prison, I was so overcome with relief I lost my head." Henry directed his words to Mary.

Her bright eyes dimmed a little. "I am glad you hold me in such high regard. I am sorry to have caused you any discomfort."

David slapped a hand on his shoulder. "We're not completely done with this debacle of Mary's impending trial. Come into the study and I'll tell you more about it."

Henry divested himself of his outerwear and followed David to the study, shutting the door behind them.

David stopped at the sideboard and began pouring drinks. "How is Lady Carroll?

"Ecstatic." Henry took the brandy and slugged down the contents in two gulps. "She's amazed you were able to get her a divorce."

"It took me calling in every favor I had, a couple of bribes, and a few threats to get it through." David sipped his own drink while Henry refilled his. "Which means I can't use the same resources to get Mary out of the loaf she's in."

"What happened?" Henry settled into his chair with his brandy at the ready.

David threw his head back and laughed. "From the report, she almost killed Lord Carroll."

What? His little Mary?

"And not by shooting him or poison. Apparently, she beat him close to death."

Henry's mind whirled and he gaped like a fish several times. Mary wasn't as petite as some, but there was no way she was capable of taking on Lord Carroll physically. "How?"

"She won't say. Not a peep. Not to me, the constables, or anyone. She sits with a pleasantly inane smile on her face in absolute silence until we throw up our hands and dismiss her." David snickered and tipped up his drink.

"How did you keep her from prison?"

"Privilege of the peer. It should be enough to keep her safe since she didn't actually kill him and it is her first offense. Lord Carroll is also extremely unpopular right now after all of what has been made public in the divorce. I'm hoping the most he'll be able to do is successfully sue her civilly for all the damage she caused to his house."

"Damage?" His Mary was becoming more of an enigma by the moment.

"I have a list." With a flourish, David produced a paper from his desk and handed it to Henry.

Henry scanned the list and stopped. "Furniture? A couch, a settee, two chairs, and three tables? How is this even possible?"

David shrugged, his face beaming with amusement. "I don't know."

Henry slapped the list on the desk. "You're not taking this seriously."

His uncle should have been an actor. The shock on his face was nearly convincing. "My dear boy, I have been doing all I can to keep your Mary safe. But in private, I'm laughing like a Cheshire cat."

There was one question Henry still didn't know the answer to. "What was she doing at his home in the first place?" The thought of her alone with Lord Carroll had his insides seizing up.

David set his drink down. "Again, she won't speak of it. I questioned both her servants who accompanied her and all they knew was she was looking for some information. Exactly what she wanted is still unknown."

Henry slumped and drank the rest of his brandy. "How long do you think this will take before she's released from your custody?"

David sobered up and sighed. "There's other things coming into play, which makes this thornier. After she assaulted Lord Carroll, her brother began raising a turmoil to have her declared mad so he can swoop in to take custody of her and her property."

Henry's spirits sank and he ran his hands through his hair. "Devil take him. I should have pummeled his brains out in the ring."

"And I should have killed Lord Carroll when we kidnapped your siblings." David frowned into his drink. "Isn't it amazing how many people need killing?"

"At the moment I can't kill Lord Fletcher, and you can't kill Lord Carroll. So what are we to do?"

David placed both hands on the desk and leaned toward Henry, his voice low and urgent. "You need to take Mary and leave. Take her abroad and marry her. Don't come back for a few years without a pack of brats in tow."

Henry snorted, then stopped. "You're serious?"

"Think about it, my boy. You're the hidden son of a man who murdered his wife. Your grandfather is a duke but you were raised by his gardener. Now you're wealthy but untitled and everyone is betting on whether or not you try to take the title from Benton. You have scandal written all over you."

Henry slumped further and further in his chair. "Thank you for the scathing recommendation, Uncle."

"As for Mary," David continued, "even when her mourning is over technically you are now her grandson. The church won't let you marry in England, or they'll declare it void. She's got a beastly brother trying to declare her mad, charges of assault against her by a peer, an opium eater for a mother, and no other family who gives a damn but us." David's eager expression and somber voice was lacking his uncle's usual merriment and dry wit. He was serious about this plan.

"Take her and go. We'll figure out the details later," David finished.

A sliver of hope began to burrow its way into Henry's heart. "Don't push me to do this unless you mean it. I want her more than anything in the world."

David threw his desk drawer open and pulled out a purse. "I've become a bigger meddler than my old man," he muttered. He dropped the heavy bag down in front of Henry.

The coins inside rattled. "Fifty guineas to get you started. Let me know where you two land."

Henry reached out for the bag, hesitated a moment when he thought of leaving his siblings behind, and then grabbed the purse.

David clapped him on the shoulder. "Good lad."

———

MARY PACED OUTSIDE the study door. She touched her lips. They were still tingling. Or was she imagining it?

He'd kissed her!

And she'd been too surprised to kiss him back. Or should she have kissed him back?

She moaned and leaned against the door. When David appeared and saw them embracing, Henry acted once again like a worried protector rather than a concerned lover.

Would she ever be more than little Mary to him?

The study door began to open and she stepped away from it. She faced the men coming out. "Henry, may I speak with you?"

"Now you wish to speak? Will you tell him exactly how you beat Lord Carroll within an inch of his life?" David asked.

Mary lowered her eyes and took a deep breath. "No."

"Or regale him of the tale of how you destroyed an entire room of artwork and furniture single-handedly without even a splinter?"

She shook her head, keeping her eyes on the ground. It was enough that her brother was trying to declare her insane. She didn't need to add a haunting to that particular fire.

David clapped Henry on the shoulder. "I wish you luck,

lad." He motioned to the open door. "Study's open. I'll give you ten minutes before I send Adam in to chaperone."

Mary entered the study and took a seat before the desk. Henry shut the door behind them and, to her delight, took a seat next to her rather than the one behind the desk.

He reached out and took both her hands, smiling at her. Her cheeks warmed and she enjoyed the inner glow his touch ignited her. Maybe she wasn't 'little Mary' in private?

"What is it you wish to tell me?" he asked, his thumbs traced wonderful soft circles on the back of her hands.

Taking a deep breath, she dove in. "Lord Carroll left me a note saying he knew who killed Luke."

At his speechless blinking she pressed onward. "So I came to London to demand an explanation."

Henry frowned, his grasp becoming tighter. "Why didn't you tell me?"

"You said you never wanted to see him again. I was trying to protect you."

Henry huffed. "Protect me?"

Mary frowned at him. "Don't underestimate my esteem for you. I would do anything to keep you from pain."

His eyes widened and he released her hands, leaning away in his chair. "I—"

She cut him off. "I went to his home to find out what information he had. Our discussion became quite enthusiastic."

"Enthusiastic!"

"Hush, we only have ten minutes, please keep silent until I've finished. Lord Carroll revealed that Jonathan had been bragging publicly about getting his hands on Luke's money once Luke was out of the way. He's too much of a coward to do it himself, and I'm certain he hired someone else. But now

I'm confined to the house, and I need your help to investigate."

Henry stared at her a moment, then heaved a great sigh, running his hands over his face. "David has a different plan. He wants me to take you abroad."

Mary scooted to the edge of her seat. "How does that have anything to do with what I've told you? And I cannot go abroad alone with you."

"We would get married first."

Mary's heart leaped with joy before crashing down to ugly reality. He would be marrying her because David told him to, out of obligation. Like his grandfather Luke, sacrificing to keep her safe. She would not submit to another marriage of safety.

"I refuse," she said.

His brow furrowed, he paled and seemed to shrink in his seat. "What?"

"I won't run away now when I have a good lead on what happened to Luke. My brother being a murderer is a more pressing issue than a charge of assault."

"Assault against a peer," he reminded her.

She waved it away. "I outrank him, I have the privilege of the peerage, and I'd be tried in a court of women against a man who has a record of violence toward women. I'm not worried."

"You also have a brother trying to declare you mad," Henry pointed out.

"Which is why I need to prove he's a murderer," Mary countered.

Henry leaped to his feet with a strangled cry and strode across the room. His fists clenched as he began to pace.

And that's when she smelled it. The soft, subtle scent of lilac. Sarah.

The other reason Mary couldn't abandon her quest for justice. She doubted the ghost would let her run away in peace.

Taking a deep breath, she tried again to sway him. "Please help me."

Henry stopped his pacing and deflated. He closed his eyes and muttered something to himself about 'not being able to deny her anything.'

Mary waited a few heartbeats of silence before he opened his eyes and spoke. "I will help you."

Filled with relief and hope she stood up. "Thank you."

"But if things start to go badly, I'll kidnap you and drag you away from London," he warned with a finger to her face.

"I am well aware of your exploits of kidnapping." The thought of Henry kidnapping her was a somewhat pleasant one. Was she a deviant?

Henry smiled and all felt right between them again. "I'll make some inquiries into your brother's dealings."

"I'll contact the constable and see if he has anything to add from the investigation about Jonathan," she said. "Adam is going to burst in on us at any moment, so we should disperse."

She leaned close to him, stood up on her toes, and kissed his cheek. "I am glad you are here." She turned to leave when he called her name.

"How did you get the information out of Lord Carroll?"

There was one secret she wouldn't divulge, not with her brother trying to declare her mad. She wouldn't even utter it aloud for fear of being overheard and ending up in Bedlam. "You wouldn't believe me if I told you."

Chapter Seventeen

Propugn - Defend; vindicate.

A SERVING girl tripped and ran into Henry. He raised his drunken head from the pub's dirty table and she grinned at him before rushing off.

Damnation. Had she picked his pocket?

Coming to the cheaper side of town and asking questions about Luke's murder seemed like a good idea, but no one would talk to him. Even buying them drinks didn't loosen any tongues. Those that agreed to speak didn't know anything. So he started drinking in earnest to dull his sorrow over Mary's rejection.

He peered down at the empty glass that used to be full of gin and frowned. How many was this?

"Here me boyo, I got you another one." George slid a full glass to him.

"Am I beery yet?" Henry asked, lifting it to his lips.

"You're well past beery and on to sucking the monkey," George informed him.

Henry swayed a little in his seat and he emptied another glass into his stomach, slamming down his vessel and scowled at the table. "She said no."

"Wassat?" George asked.

"I asked Mary to marry me and she said no." Henry pouted.

"Did you now? Did you take her in your arms and finally declare your love?" George asked.

The drinks in Henry's belly swirled and he tried to sit up straighter. "No, not exactly. I told her I was to take her abroad and marry her."

"Ah yes, what every lass wants to hear," George smirked. "No kind words or passion. No kisses or embraces. Just told the lady you were both to be shut up in the parson's pound and that was the way of it."

Henry groaned and dropped his head to the table with a thump. He hadn't said a word of his affection to Mary. He'd more or less ordered her to marry him without a hint of his ardor. He hadn't even taken an opportunity to sneak a kiss. "Blimey, I've mucked it up, haven't I?"

"You're a fat-head." George slapped him hard on the back.

Henry moaned again when he sat up and the world tipped on its side. His belly lurched violently. "I think we'd better head to the house." He dug around in his pockets, frowning when he didn't find any coins.

"I've got your blunt." George pulled some coins from his pocket and tossed them on the table. "When you started guzzling Mother's Milk, I didn't want anyone to shake it from you. You brought us to a low part of town and I'm itching to know why."

"I need to find out if Mary's brother hired anyone to kill the duke."

"Did you find the answer in a bottle of gin?"

"Shut your bone box." Henry managed to find his feet and growled when the world swayed and George straightened him.

"You're a regular knight on a noble errand," George mocked. Henry wanted to roll his eyes but was afraid he'd lose his stomach if he did.

"If you wanted to find someone to hush a body, we're in the wrong place." George put an arm around Henry's waist and placed Henry's arm over his shoulder.

"How do you know?" George and Peter held various connections in most criminal enterprises, but murder for hire was one he thought they would shy away from.

"Most murders here are petty or 'accidents.' You want to kill a Nob; you go a professional."

The cold air outside slapped a little bit of soberness into Henry. He slid his arm off George and managed to keep his own feet straight while they walked away from the dark alley-ways near the docks and returned to the well-kept streets closer to his uncle's house.

George stopped them outside a familiar well-lit town-house. "Here we are."

Henry frowned. "This is a gaming hell."

"Right."

"This is the same gaming hell Mary was at."

"Made fifty pounds while she was chirping merry with gin. So proud. She's a smart little hen."

"You brought Mary to a gaming hell where you can hire an

assassin?" Henry was immediately fully sober and ready to plant George a facer.

George scoffed. "I'd never do such a thing. But here's where we start asking questions." He opened the door with a grand gesture for Henry to enter.

"Mary's right. You are cheeky."

They circled their way through the hallways to the center of the house. The sound of cheers and shouts and groans grew louder when they entered the gaming room. A cloud of cigar smoke and the scent of sweaty bodies made Henry wrinkle his nose.

Men swarmed around the Hazard table, a drink in every hand. A few more tables of Faro were set up prominently and the less chancy games of piquet, whist, and loo were scattered in the corners.

The room was draped in rich colors and dark wood. It was well lit and plenty of servants scurrying around to each table. Tight-lipped Crowpees were making slow rounds about the room to watch for signs of cheating.

"I'll sherry off and see what I can find around the servants' group." George handed Henry his money. He slipped away into the hallway while Henry straightened his cravat and hoped he appeared more sober than he smelled.

A handsome, well-dressed man with a charming smile approached Henry. "What's your fancy tonight?" he asked Henry.

"I'm looking for some friends. Then I might try my hand at some Faro." Henry replied.

"Excellent, the house is losing badly tonight at the Hazard table. A lucky night for you to be here."

Henry scoffed silently. The house was never losing. "Lucky night? I hope so," Henry said. *In more ways than one.*

His head started to pound. He caught the sleeve of a servant and asked for some coffee to drink. Hopefully, it would help him sober up faster. He wandered over to the crowded Hazard table and watched the play for a moment.

The faces of the gamblers all blurred together into a conglomerate of excited young men and weary older ones. A few women were sprinkled in the mix, sweat dripping from their foreheads as much as the men in the heat and smoke. He knew most gaming hells wouldn't let women in the door, which was probably how Mary landed here.

Intermixed with the ambiance of excitement was a hint of desperation. Everyone at the Hazard table ogled the dice roll and held their breath. When the little ivory blocks landed, there was a roar of delight mingled with the groans of dashed hopes. Would anyone here be desperate enough to kill in order to pay off their debts?

The servant returned with his coffee. Henry sipped it while walking to an empty piquet table. He relaxed into the empty chair and gazed at the entrance, watching the players come and go. The man who greeted him extended welcomes and falsehoods about the house losing or fond farewells as needed.

"Fancy a game?" A young dandy slid into the seat across from him and picked up the deck of cards sitting there.

Henry frowned; this young man seemed familiar. Where had he seen him? He focused and began to laugh when his foggy brain caught up. "You're the man Mary caught cheating."

The young man's eyes widened and he cursed, losing his proper speech and accent. "The mort got me basted for it." He slapped down the deck and went to rise from the seat. Henry grabbed his cuff and told him to stay.

"I thought you wanted to play." Henry took the deck and scanned the cards to make sure they were all proper.

"I don't want another drubbing." The young man huffed and crossed his arms.

Henry pulled out his money. "I feel certain you'll win every hand tonight." The young man relaxed a little when Henry slid a bill across the table. "Do you work here?"

The bill was snatched up and disappeared into the young man's coat. "Every night. The owner likes my young and fresh face. Makes people feel safe and superior."

Henry fumbled the cards, abandoned his drunken attempt at shuffling, and dealt. "Do you know many of the customers?"

The young man shrugged. "There are quite a few regulars. Someone's always trying to win back what they lost, or come because they think they'll win big again. That's when we strip them of everything so they have to return."

Henry began the play with his worst card. The young man snorted. "You really are going to lose, eh?"

"As long as you keep talking," Henry said. "Do you know Lord Fletcher?"

"Who doesn't? He's so under the hatches we make him show his blunt before he enters the room." If Fletcher came here often it was probably how he heard about Mary's winnings that night, and why he was waiting outside her door to belittle her for funds.

Henry placed another poor card. "Did you let him in on credit?"

"For a bit, then his luck changed for the worse. He started begging for bigger IOUs, saying he's going to come into a fortune."

"How did he plan to do it?" Henry asked.

"Some fool scheme with his sister who married a duke. He

promised as soon as the old man died, he'd take over her welfare which came with a healthy portion. Didn't come about."

Now he was getting somewhere. "Seems like a long-term gamble. Was he trying to hurry it along?"

The young man stopped his play, his eyes snapping to Henry. "What are you getting at?"

"Did Lord Fletcher want his fortune faster? Enough to rush the old man's death?"

The young man's eyebrows furrowed. He set his cards down and rose to his feet. "I'm not singing for free."

Henry set his cards down and peeled off another bill. It was plucked up quickly and tucked away into the young man's pocket when he resumed his seat.

"There were rumors whispered about that he wanted a team to hasten the old man to his maker. But it never happened." The young man picked up his cards and fanned them to cool his face.

"Why not?"

"The old duke died before the baron put his plan in motion."

MARY WAVED out the window at the man from Bow Street who was hired to guard the house and guarantee she stayed in it. He glared at her as he did every day, but tipped his hat in acknowledgement.

"It's a cold day, perhaps we should invite him inside to patrol over me," she said to Miriam.

"I could sit him inside the front door. Much better than outside in the drizzle." Miriam put down her embroidery and rubbed her eyes in the dimming light. "I'll send him an invitation to join us for tea."

Mary laughed and then settled in close to the fire. She opened the package Constable Frost sent her filled with his notes from the investigation of Luke's murder. A cold little breeze tickled her ear and she wondered if Sarah was reading over her shoulder.

"I hope this will help us know what to do next," Mary whispered, squinting at the papers in her hand. Constable Frost's handwriting was neat but tiny. He recalled the facts of the night of Luke's death in a bloodless manner.

...His Grace was found face down with a paper knife lodged in his chest between the... Mary blinked away the sudden tears obstructing her vision. Every time she was certain of her emotions they would rise up and strangle her with a reminder of the past. She dug out a handkerchief and snorted at Henry's initials embroidered on the edge. One of the many he'd given her. She wiped her eyes, pressed the fabric to her nose and inhaled, pretending it smelled of his signature scent. It was enough to calm her and she returned to the notes.

Nothing stolen.

All of the household's whereabouts were confirmed, as well as those of Lord David Polk (now Duke of Fenwick) and Lord Jonathan Fletcher, Baron Fairley.

Her heart sank. Jonathan had been cleared by the law. Lord Carroll was mistaken, or he had simply lied to her.

She continued reading the report.

No blood on anyone's clothing or skin but the duke's.

No forced entry on the doors or windows.

Only signs of violence were the overturned desk, scattered papers, and a broken coffee cup.

A broken coffee cup.

Mary read the statement over and over. She'd only seen Luke drink coffee once when he was staying up late, working on estate business with Henry. Why was he drinking coffee at night? Was he staying up to speak with her when she returned from the opera? Was he meeting someone else who liked coffee?

A creeping finger of ice ran along her hands, prodding her to shuffle through the papers. She flipped through them and stopped when her hands were seized in an icy grip. She lifted the paper close to her face to decipher the writing.

Mr. William Merrill stated he had an appointment with His Grace earlier in the evening to speak about personal business. When asked if there had been any recent changes to His Grace's will or any other pending legal actions, Mr. Merrill refused to answer. With the generous provisions provided to all parties in the will, I did not see reason to pursue a writ of assistance to search Mr. Merrill's office.

Mary read the paragraph again and rubbed her skin when the ghostly hand released her. Luke spoke to Mr. Merrill privately in his study that night, but it wasn't anything out of the ordinary. Mr. Merrill was frequently at the house with papers to sign. Was he returning later to finish up? Was the coffee waiting for Mr. Merrill?

A loud pounding on the outside door made her jump. Miriam shrieked a little and dropped her work. Someone was shouting and kicking the door.

Mary and Miriam both rose and scurried to the foyer where the butler was opening the door. George was standing behind him, holding a club. A man burst into the house carrying a body and shouting for help. It took a moment for Mary to recognize the Bow Street guard keeping her on house arrest.

"In here, in here!" Miriam ushered him into the parlor, the butler and George following close behind.

The Bow Street man set the body on the couch and pulled off his damp hat and ran his fingers through his hair. "A carriage rumbled up to your porch, pushed the woman out, and took off. I think she's still alive."

Moaning came from the body wrapped in a dark cloak. A thin, bony hand pulled the fabric away from her face. A gaunt woman gasped for air while the scent of rot and human filth filled the room. Mary covered her nose and searched the woman's face for any recognition. Who dropped her here, and why?

"Send for the doctor," Miriam ordered the butler.

"Do you know her?" Mary asked. The woman was horribly thin, missing teeth and hair. There were no bruises or signs of abuse on her face or hands. She was simply wasting away.

George put his weapon down and moved closer to the stranger. He pulled the cloak gently from her and a letter fluttered to the ground from its folds.

Mary saw her name on the outside of the message. Her mouth went dry when she retrieved it.

"What is it?" Miriam asked while Mary broke the familiar seal she'd seen almost daily growing up.

Since you have plenty of time on your hands to have Mr. Church meddle in my affairs, I thought I'd bring you a gift to keep you busy.
-Lord Fletcher

A sob burst from Mary's lips. She covered her mouth while hot tears sprang forth to trickle down her face and she hugged her churning belly. She tried to steel herself but her heart broke a little more when she realized who the woman was. "I don't want to care. Luke said I can't do anything for her. He said..." More of Luke's words spun in her head. Oh, how she wished he was here!

"What's wrong? What does it say? Who is this?" Miriam reached for the note.

Mary's sobs made speaking almost impossible. "It's my mother."

Chapter Eighteen

❧

Vitiously - Not virtuously; corruptly.

HANDS behind his back and eyes on the floor, Henry paced outside the sick room. It had been three days since Mary's mother was dropped on the doorstep, and Mary had barely left her side since then. Three days of Henry feeling utterly helpless.

A doctor was called and wrinkled his nose at the sight of the dying woman. "Not much you can do at this point but keep her comfortable and wait for the end." He'd set out a bottle of laudanum. "Use this to keep her quiet. Not giving it to her at this point would be unkind."

David hired a nurse to help Mary wash and care for the doomed Baroness Fairley. At Henry's urging, the duke and his family left for Fenwick and the holiday season before the weather closed the roads. Henry would manage this new debacle without his uncle's aid.

The house was quiet without the family. Most of the servants had left with them. Agnes and George remained with their mistress. Mary's faithful maid was the only reason Mary had gotten any rest or food in the last three days, taking over vigil so Mary could eat or nap.

Henry heard George chatting in the foyer, playing cards with the Bow Street man. The offer to guard Mary inside a warm house with tea and food was a much better prospect than the cold outdoors. Henry should join their game, rather than wear a hole in the carpet.

He halted when the bedroom door opened and Mary appeared. Her hair was tied up in a tight turban and her gray dress was covered by an apron. She was carrying a basin of dirty water. Dark circles lined up underneath her eyes. Her pale skin was taking on an ashen color.

He reached out and took the basin from her. It slid from her grasp and her hands fell limply at her sides. "You should get some rest. Have Agnes and the nurse watch over her."

Mary nibbled on her lip. He saw the temptation in her face before she shook her head. "I need to do it." Her bright eyes lifted to meet his and her voice quivered. "It helps me not hate her so much if I'm helping her."

His heart hammered a painful thud. He wanted to throw the basin aside and embrace her. Then he'd lift her up and carry her from this place to somewhere she would rest, wear colorful clothing, and be surrounded by happiness. Someplace without dying parents and abusive brothers or Bow Street men and vindictive lords.

"You're too good for this world, Mary Fletcher Polk." Speaking her married name grounded him to reality.

"So are you, Henry Albert Church." There was silence while their hearts spoke to each other, saying everything they couldn't.

"I need to get some socks for her hands. She keeps scratching herself." Mary brushed past him. He placed the basin under one arm, reached out with his free hand, and cupped her elbow. Her arm slid through his grasp as she kept walking, her hand squeezing his quickly before she left.

He trudged to the kitchen with the dirty water, emptying it before making the return trip to the sick room.

Mary still hadn't returned when he opened the door. The nurse and Agnes were sitting nearby, working on knitting projects and conversing with each other. They glanced at him when he entered and he motioned for them to ignore him. He set the empty basin down and loomed over the sickbed.

Naomi Fletcher was writhing under the stack of blankets. Her eyes remained closed and her skeletal hands reached up and scratched at her cheeks. Red marks lined her wrists and neck. She gasped breathy moans, curling into a ball.

Henry crouched beside her and picked up the laudanum resting on the table next to her head. He examined the instructions written next to it. Naomi's eyes opened and rested on him. Her pupils were tiny pinpricks. Her lips moved, but no sound came forth.

The dark part of him he kept at bay by boxing in the ring rose up, and for once he embraced it. For Mary's sake, he would do anything.

"I ought to dump this whole bottle down your throat," he whispered. Naomi's eyes focused on the bottle, watching while he pulled out the cork. She began to drool.

"You don't even have the decency to die quickly for your daughter, do you? Somewhere in that rotten brain, you are

enjoying watching her serve you down to your last breath."
Henry leaned over and let one drop fall onto Naomi's lips. A
pale tongue lapped it up.

"Don't linger long in this world." Another drop. "Or I'll
take her away and have you dumped in a gutter where you
belong."

Naomi's eyes widened a little and she gasped.

"Do we understand one another?" Henry asked.

She managed a wisp of a nod and he administered the
remainder of her prescribed drops.

"Is something wrong?" Mary's sweet voice asked from
behind.

He straightened and handed her the bottle of laudanum.
"I gave her some drops to make her more comfortable."

Mary took the bottle. "Thank you." She set the bottle
down and pulled her mother's hands free from the mound of
blankets to cover them with socks. Red scabs covered the
dying woman's arms from where she'd attacked her skin
previously.

"Mary." He reached out and gently squeezed her shoulder.
He wouldn't allow her to run herself ragged for this creature.
"She'll rest now. You need to go get some sleep and let the
nurse watch over her with Agnes. Please."

She swallowed hard and touched the corner of her eye to
hide a tear. "Very well. I could use a nap."

Henry led her from the sick room, followed her to her
bedroom, and assured she went inside. He grabbed a chair
from the hallway and set it in front of her door, determined
no one would disturb her. A few glares from him had the
maids scurrying past the hallway when they came to do the
daily cleaning.

The butler shortly interrupted his vigil with a letter for

him. The seal imprinted on the red wax boiled his blood even further.

Lord Carroll.

He crumpled it in his hand for a moment, quelling down the hot belly of rage that was threatening to bubble over. Hadn't he made it clear he never wanted to see the man again in this lifetime?

Breaking the wax, he scanned the contents. It was brief and to the point.

Come and see me at White's to discuss dropping the criminal assault charges against the Dowager Duchess of Fenwick. - Lord C.

Damn, damn, damn! Henry stuffed the letter into his pocket and toppled the chair when he rose too quickly. He cringed, and listened for any sound from Mary's room. Silence.

He was careful not to stomp down the hallway while he retreated from Mary's door. He was less successful on the staircase. He'd just put on his hat and coat when Agnes appeared before him.

"Mr. Church, I know you persuaded Mary to sleep, but something's happened. There is a problem with Lady Fletcher."

Of course there was. When he had children, he vowed he would not follow the examples set by his corrupt sire and Mary's worthless mother. "What's happened?"

Agnes wrung her hands. "None of us thought the Baroness was strong enough to move, but she opened the bottle of laudanum and drank the whole thing before we could stop her."

Henry's sigh ended in a growl. If the dying baroness wanted one last show of control to make Mary come running to her side, he'd gladly stand in the way. "Don't wake Mary."

"It's lethal. She won't live much longer." Agnes shifted on her feet. "I don't want to bother my girl if she's finally resting. She's going to make herself ill. But she should know..."

"I'll take that burden from you. Mary's done enough. I won't have her fretting and crying over that selfish woman, waiting for her to die when there is nothing more to be done. Let her sleep. She needs it more."

He was certain he didn't imagine the relief on Agnes's face. "I'll see she's not disturbed."

Swooping up his walking stick, Henry set out into the cold toward White's, hoping to be in a more rational mood when he arrived.

He was not.

He stormed into the building, ignoring the servant who offered to take his coat. He scanned the rooms for his quarry and glared at the back of Lord Carroll's head. Henry marched to the table where the lord sat alone and refrained from breaking his walking stick over the man's skull.

Instead, he slapped his gloves and hat on the table and dropped into the chair opposite Lord Carroll. Henry took in the man's bruised eye and healing scratches on his face. Lord Carroll's nose was now crooked. What had Mary done? And how? "You'd better not be wasting my time."

Lord Carroll raised his brows. "This is our first ever private conversation, and that's what you're worried about?"

"This is our last *ever* conversation." Henry tapped his walking stick against the floor to relieve some agitation.

Lord Carroll inspected him for a moment. He pursed his lips before he spoke. "Are your siblings well?"

Jerking the letter out of his pocket, Henry tossed it on the table. "I'm not here to talk about them. I'm here to talk about this."

Lord Carroll frowned and picked up a glass of brandy next to his elbow. "Please, son, can't we have a civil conversation?"

Henry's walking stick clattered to the floor as he leaped across the table. He fisted Lord Carroll's cravat in his hands until the man began to choke. "Call me 'son' again and I'll kill you. Consequences be damned."

"Is there a problem here?" A voice spoke over Henry's shoulder.

Henry released Lord Carroll and returned to his seat. He glared at an anxious waiter. "No problems. I would like a glass of port." The waiter hesitated a moment before leaving him alone again with his sire. "What will it take to drop the charges against Mary?"

Lord Carroll's eyebrows lifted. "Mary, is it? I knew you were friends but do you have a greater affection toward her?"

Picking up his walking stick, Henry resumed tapping out his turmoil. If Lord Carroll expected an answer about Mary, he'd be waiting until the angels sounded their trumpets.

Lord Carroll exhaled and pushed forward a leather folder to Henry. "Open it."

Flipping it open, Henry glanced at the papers inside. "It's your will." He pushed it back to Lord Carroll.

Lord Carroll slapped his hand on it. "You're not in it."

"Good." Henry accepted the glass of port from the waiter and sent him scurrying with another glare.

"But you are my firstborn...offspring. And the grandson of a duke. The question of who gets my title could be brought into question after my death." Lord Carroll pushed the documents to Henry once more. "I want Benton to have the title."

"I agree, he should. What does this have to do with

Mary?"

Lord Carroll peeled a page away from the packet. "Sign this, stating the title goes to Benton and you won't contest it. I'll drop the charges against your lady."

Henry snorted. "That's all you want?" He snatched the paper from Lord Carroll's fingers and read it carefully.

It was a simple form, stating exactly what Lord Carroll wanted for Benton's future. Henry leaned over and plucked a quill from a nearby inkwell and signed his name with a flourish. "I want the Bow Street man out of the house by nightfall."

"He'll be gone," Lord Carroll promised.

Grabbing his hat, Henry turned to leave. Hopefully he'd never see this man's face again.

"Henry." Lord Carroll's voice was soft and trembled a bit. "Please tell me. Are the children well?"

While spinning around to give his sire a vocal drubbing, Mary popped into Henry's mind. Mary with her kindness and service to a dying woman who openly hated her. It softened his edges a bit, and he took a few deep breaths. If Mary was able to be decent to her monster, he could be decent to his own.

"They are healthy and well." Henry's words were curt and sharp. He took two steps toward the door but stopped when Lord Carroll asked, "And their mother, what of Penelope?"

Henry didn't turn around to face him again but tossed the response over his shoulder. "She's happy."

———

MARY APPROACHED the sick room with slow steps. Agnes stood outside the door waiting for her. One glance at Agnes's

face, and Mary knew her mother was dead. She heaved a great
sigh of relief and almost felt giddy with the freedom. She
didn't even want to enter the sick room again to verify it. At
least she owned plenty of black clothing to mark the
occasion.

"I need to arrange for an undertaker," she said. All the
overwhelming things that went with death flooded her brain
and she was instantly fatigued once more.

"I already did. He'll be here by morning." Henry's voice
came from behind. "I've announced it with the papers,
arranged for the services, and found her a grave to reside in."
His presence filled her with warmth and peace. She spun
around to greet him, taking his hands in hers. She peered into
his face, admired his crooked nose, and wanted to kiss him all
over.

She settled for a "thank you" and released his hands.

"We need to tell the cook there will be one less for dinner.
The charges against you have been dropped and our Bow
Street man is leaving." His mouth broadened into the most
wonderful smile.

"What?" Agnes gasped and wrapped an arm around Mary's
waist.

"They have? How?" Mary pulled Agnes a little closer.

Henry flicked his hand. "A title. Lord Carroll wanted to
make sure I wouldn't press for the title when he died and that
Benton would inherit. I assured him I never want to be asso-
ciated with his name in any way."

"This is wonderful." Agnes buried her face in Mary's neck.
Mary echoed the relief and wished again to cover Henry in
kisses. She hugged Agnes tightly and breathed easier for the
first time in weeks.

"I cannot ever repay you, Mr. Church," Mary said.

He wrinkled his nose. "You can repay me by never calling me that again. Even if we are not in private, I'm Henry to you."

She laughed a little and was ushered to dinner in her room by both Henry and Agnes, followed by the best night sleep in months.

Her heart beat a little easier when she stretched in bed the next morning. The Bow Street man was gone. The charges against her were dropped. And the undertaker had taken her mother's body away.

Lying in bed for a moment, she waited for any remaining tears or sobs on her mother's behalf to rise, and was elated when none came. She swung her feet out of bed and put on her slippers. Maybe now she could start thinking toward the holidays? There was plenty to do. She needed to return to the Sycamore estate and...

Her black lace shawl was in tatters on the floor. The torn pieces spelled out a name this time instead of an accusation. *Merrill.*

Mary's shoulders slumped and all the excitement drizzled away. Sarah had been oddly quiet for the last four days, enough to give Mary a respite from her haunting while her mother died. She supposed she should be grateful to the spirit for being so benevolent.

Picking up the shredded shawl, she retired it to the rag bin with her new found freedom. It wouldn't matter if she were in London, Fenwick, Hawthorne, or the Sycamore estate, Sarah would follow wherever she went. Until the ghost was at rest, Mary would never be free. "We'll go and pay a visit to Mr. Merrill today," she said softly. A subtle lilac scented breeze touched her nose and disappeared.

Chapter Nineteen

Covetousness - Avarice; inordinate desire of money; eagerness of gain.

DRESSED in her blackest black and a woeful expression, Mary entered the foyer of Mr. Merrill's office. Agnes followed her in while George waited outside.

A clerk greeted them and asked if they had an appointment.

"No, and I do apologize. I was hoping Mr. Merrill will see me on short notice. It shouldn't take long." She offered her card to the clerk. He read her name, and his brows shot to his hairline. "Of course, Your Grace. Let me go ask."

He left at a quick pace while Mary took a turn around the room. The walls were covered with wood instead of paper, and bookshelves were crammed into every nook they would fit. It smelled like paper and ink, of earthy wood with the faint hint of ... lilac.

Mary's shoulders slumped. Sarah was here. Mary muttered a quick whisper to the unpredictable spirit to stay silent. An icy finger ran along her cheek in response and she shuddered.

"Cold?" Agnes asked, peeling off her own shawl to hand to Mary.

"No, thank you. I'm nervous."

Agnes wrapped her shawl around her shoulders. "I'm still not sure what we're doing here."

"I need to ask Mr. Merrill about his business with Luke the day he died," Mary said.

Agnes's face paled. "The ghost is still pushing you?"

Mary bit her lip and nodded. The ghost was breathing down her neck.

Mr. Merrill interrupted their exchange. "Your Grace, this is a welcome surprise. Can I get you anything? Tea?"

"No, no thank you. I need a moment of your time if you have nothing pressing."

"Nothing at the moment, please come into my office." He ushered her back toward a warm and cheery room filled with files and books. Agnes followed and took a seat next to the door.

Mary sat in a comfortable chair in front of Mr. Merrill's large desk. He sat across from her, clasped his hands, and leaned forward. He focused on her face with sincerity. "Let me first offer my condolences on the passing of your mother."

She properly bowed her head. "Thank you, Mr. Merrill."

"Are you coming to inquire over any inheritance she might have left you? I will investigate the matter if you would like."

"I doubt very much she had any worldly goods left to leave me. I've actually come to ask about a meeting you held with my husband the day he died. Do you remember?"

Mr. Merrill slumped in his chair and scowled. "I do. It was a private matter not worth bringing up."

"He's dead, I don't think privacy matters much to him anymore."

"No, but it might matter to you."

"Pardon?"

Mr. Merrill grumbled and tapped his fingers on the desk. Mary waited in silence while Mr. Merrill's expressions wavered between indecision and contemplation.

He exhaled heavily before speaking. "It's a matter best left alone now, Your Grace. There's nothing you need to worry about."

"I need to know. I need to find who killed him and all my investigations have led me here."

"Good heavens! Do you think I did it?" Mr. Merrill began to pale, resting his hand on his chest.

Mary leaned across the desk. "No. Not at all. I know you and he were friends of a sort, and he trusted you. But all my questions have been answered except for why he met with you. I'm hoping it will open up further avenues of inquiry."

Mr. Merrill held her gaze, his eyes searching hers. For a moment it appeared he would tell her what she wanted. Then he shook his head and slid his hand out of her grasp. "My dear lady, I implore you to let this matter rest."

He rose from his seat to usher her out when the quill and ink on the huge desk toppled over. The black ink trickled and spread across the surface. Mr. Merrill jumped to mop up the mess when the cheery fire warming the room went out with a poof.

Everyone froze. The air cooled and the overwhelming scent of acrid lilacs crept into the room. Mr. Merrill sniffed twice and glanced at Mary with puzzlement. "What's happening?'

Agnes gasped from behind them. Mary bit back a sob and tried to keep her voice steady. "Please, Mr. Merrill. Please tell me. I beg you." She did not want a repeat performance of Sarah's violent tantrums.

Mr. Merrill came to stand by her chair and placed a hand on her shoulder. His eyes scanned the room. "What evil is this?"

"It'll go away if you tell me what I need," Mary said.

His skeptical face brought a shelf full of books crashing to the floor.

Agnes screamed and Mary ran to the door. It was locked tight. She leaned against it and pulled Agnes to her, tucking the maid's head out of the way when a decanter of spirits sailed across the room. A clerk outside began rattling the handle and pounding at the door.

"Mr. Merrill, tell me at once!" Mary screamed at him. The books on the floor began shredding their own pages.

The astounded solicitor was frozen until a large law book flew toward his face. He ducked before it hit him and he landed on the desk to keep from falling.

"He was seeking an annulment from you!" Mr. Merrill shouted.

Every object in motion halted and gently sank to the ground. The fire in the hearth burst back to life.

Mary's heart was beating in time to the buzzing in her ears. Her mouth went dry. "An annulment?" Luke wanted to dissolve their marriage? After all the trouble he'd gone to protect her?

She licked her lips and swallowed. "What- what had I

done to displease him?" Hot tears rose to the surface. Agnes's arms tightened around her.

"Oh my dear girl, you did nothing to displease him." Mr. Merrill picked his way through the debris on the floor to reach her side. "He thought you were delightful."

"Then why?" She harshly erased the tears from her face with her sleeve, digging into her skin hard to stop her emotions from leaking.

"He didn't say why. He said things were progressing faster than he'd thought they would and to start annulment proceedings."

"What things?" Her mind flipped through the past year, trying to remember anything troubling Luke.

"He didn't say and I didn't ask. Forgive me for sounding callous, but it was not my place to pry." He handed her a handkerchief and glanced around his damaged office. "But I demand to know; what is this madness I have witnessed?"

Mary took a moment to control her emotions and think of the right words to say. *I'm being haunted? The spirit of Luke's dead daughter wants justice for her father? I'm a witch and you should hang me?* "Someone wants justice for the murder of my husband. And they will go to any lengths to get it."

Mr. Merrill focused on her, then on Agnes, and the mayhem in the room. "Someone not of this world?"

"Someone with a great amount of anger," Mary added.

The clerk outside pounded on the door, calling out for Mr. Merrill to respond.

Mary clutched at his arm. "Mr. Merrill, I need your discretion on this. Please. If word got back to my brother or the constabulary..."

"I am the definition of discretion, Your Grace. I'll tell my clerk you are a passionate lady with a temper. But I want you to tell Mr. Church about all this. You need his help."

Mary threw the advice away. She couldn't imagine starting a conversation with Henry about his deceased mother haunting her, not to mention how Sarah mercilessly treated anyone who got in her way. "Please bill me for the damages."

The door suddenly unlocked and the clerk stumbled into the room. He took immediate stock of the damage and gaped at Mary, then at his employer. "There were horrible noises. And..." he ran his fingers through his hair, "What a mess. Why would you..." He pointed a finger at Mary, remembered her station and stormed out of the room.

Mary readied to leave and tucked Agnes's arm in her elbow. "Good day, Mr. Merrill."

"God bless, Your Grace." The earnestness in his voice almost undid her.

They quickly exited the office and met George outside at the carriage. He scowled at Agnes's pale face and Mary's tear-streaked cheeks. "Everything all right, Your Grace?" He hardened two fists and looked ready to pummel anyone who upset her. How did she ever think of him as a heartless murderer?

Mary improperly brushed his sleeve with her hand to show her appreciation. "Thank you, no. Everything is fine."

It wasn't. It was horrible. It was gut-wrenching, brain-melting, heartbreaking, and horrendous. But she steeled her spine once again, hoping it wouldn't shatter under the weight on her shoulders, and let George help her into the carriage.

Agnes followed and sat across from her. Once George climbed up top and they began to roll, the maid spoke. "I had no idea how wicked the spirit is. I hope that's the worst of it?"

"I wish it was." Mary's lip trembled while the words tumbled from her lips about black-eyed children and torn books, demolished clothing and icy grips on her body, candles lit on their own accord and a lady in white who sang to the children and possessed Henry to give him added strength and agility. "I am heartily sick of it." Mary leaned into the squabs and closed her eyes.

Agnes's gloved hand caressed Mary's cheek and rubbed her neck, so warm and familiar. From the time she was a babe, she never doubted Agnes's love. She leaned into her maid's embrace and let her take the weight of the world for as long as the ride to the house lasted.

———

HENRY THOUGHT he would be the only one attending the hasty funeral of Baroness Naomi Fletcher when an unwelcome mourner showed up at the burial. Lord Jonathan Fletcher, Baron Fairley, stepped up to the grave on the opposite side from Henry while the coffin was being placed in the ground by the hired pallbearers.

The words of the clergyman were ignored as the two men glared at each other across the open tomb. Henry was sorely tempted to throw the baron in with his mother. He received a withering stare from Lord Fletcher and was certain the man was having similar thoughts.

Henry smirked. The man wasn't worth the effort.

He threw his sprig of rosemary onto the coffin while the churchman and the pallbearers left. Another tiny bundle of the fragrant plant joined it. The tension between them rose until the gravedigger approached and threw the first shovel of dirt into the grave.

"Didn't think you'd show up," Henry spoke first.

"Believe it or not, I liked my mother." Lord Fletcher sneered.

Henry scoffed. "Liked her so much you dropped her dying bones on the doorstep and ran?"

"She was dying and I had no funds or means to care for her properly. I could barely afford the drops to keep her comfortable. Once she became incapacitated, I knew Mary would open her arms and do what's right for her family. It was also a way to warn you away from my affairs."

"You're a scab. And your mother was a wretched woman. I'll leave you to your mourning." Henry spat on the ground and turned to leave.

"Go back to prigging my sister, the doxy," Fletcher called after him.

Henry's steps slowed until he came to a stop. His fists bunched and the world tinged around the edges with red. Lord Fletcher might be joining his mother in the grave after all.

He swung around to face the lout. "I'd snap your neck now, but there are witnesses." He motioned to the gravedigger who ceased his work and was leaning on his shovel, listening intently.

"Coward." Fletcher taunted. Maybe the dolt did want to die today?

Instead, Henry tipped his hat. "I'll be off then, to the constabulary. I'll bet he'd be interested in knowing you were planning to expend the duke's life. I'll bet he can find the others who agreed to join you for a cut. I wonder what the penalty is for merely planning to assassinate a duke, even if you never carried it out."

Lord Fletcher's face became ashen but he puffed out his chest like a rooster. "Try it. I'm not afraid of you. Without your uncle here, you're a nobody. And none of this would have happened if Mary would have given me what I needed."

"Don't blame Mary for your incompetence." Henry snarled. He tossed a coin to the gravedigger. The dirty man caught it with a questioning expression.

"For your silence on this conversation, and for having to endure this beetle head's company." Henry marched away.

"Mary will do right by her family. She'll do right by me. I'll see to it she does!" Fletcher shouted.

Without breaking stride, Henry spun, bit his thumb at the Lord Fletcher, and continued walking to his carriage.

"Where's Her Grace?" Henry asked as soon as he entered the house. The butler helped him remove his outerwear and directed him to the library.

Henry found Mary sitting in the dark among the rows and columns of books. The only light came from the fireplace, illuminating her form. She sat in a large chair with a side table next to it holding a bottle of port and a full glass. She glanced at him, the firelight making the shadows of despair on her face starkly stand out.

Wordlessly, he moved another chair next to hers and plunked down into it. He stared at the fire and let out a deep breath. "I'm in a bad skin, how about you?"

Silently, she handed him her glass of port.

He snorted and took a long swig before passing it back. She took a little sip and set it down on the table. She placed both hands on the armrest of her chair and sank into the cushions. "I'm not nearly drunk enough to have a polite conversation yet, so I hope you like silence."

Henry leaned over and covered her hand with his. She turned her palm over. One by one, she linked her fingers through his. He closed his eyes and basked in the sheer pleasure of touching her. "This is nice." He settled into his seat and imagined more nights like this, sitting beside her, holding her hand.

"It is."

"Would you like to unburden yourself?" he asked.

She let out a sigh that ended in a disgruntled moan. "You go first."

He opened his eyes and stared at the fire dancing in the grate. "I am happy to report I have taken care of your mother's earthly remains. I had them dig a deeper grave to try to keep out the resurrectionists. She had a few nice words from a clergyman, and two sprigs of rosemary on her coffin."

"Two? Who gave the other?"

"Lord Fletcher."

Her fingers contracted around his. "Come out from under his rock, did he?"

"And as charming as ever."

She scoffed and took another drink of port before handing the glass to him again. There was something intimate about sharing the same vessel. As if he was kissing her vicariously through touching his lips to the same place she'd laid hers.

He finished a swallow and continued. "I may have insulted him."

"I hope so."

"Bit my thumb at him."

She gasped then giggled. "Did you really?"

He closed his eyes again, heart lighter at the sound of her merriment. "I imagine he'll want to duel, but I doubt he could find a second because he's such a hog grubber."

"A blackguard," Mary chimed in.

"A scaly cove," he said.

"A scrub," Mary added and giggled louder.

"A slubber de gullion," Henry spoke in a deep accent. She laughed again and he squeezed her fingers. "Feeling better?"

She sobered a little. "Somewhat."

"What's got you in the blue devils?"

She was silent, gazing at the flames. He waited. He'd wait forever.

Her voice wavered a little when she spoke. "Luke was going to have our marriage annulled."

A lightning bolt striking him would have been less shocking. "What?!"

She bit her lip. "You're squeezing too tightly."

Releasing her hand, he stood, pacing before the fireplace while his mind tried to catch up. Annulment? What was the old man thinking? How dare he try to leave Mary again with no protection.

"Who told you this?" he asked.

"Mr. Merrill. I went to his office to question him about the meeting with Luke the day he died. He was summoned to start annulment proceedings. I assume since Luke died the next day, he dropped the whole matter."

Henry ran his fingers through his hair, wishing he could throttle his dead grandfather. "You should not have gone there."

"I had to. Once the trail went cold after verifying Jonathan's activities, it was the next place to seek a new line of inquiry."

"No, I mean I should have gone. I should have been there to protect you from such horrible news. You should have come to me first."

"You were taking care of my mother's remains. I didn't want to put another burden onto you," she protested.

He knelt by her chair and took her hands. He memorized

her features in the firelight. Her bright copper curls, her shining eyes, her pink plump lips open a little. "I want you to place as many burdens as you have on me. All of them. I want them all." He leaned down and kissed each of her fingers gently. He wouldn't muck it up this time. "Please, my darling Mary. I still want to take you away from all this. Say the word, and we'll be off. Just the two of us, to wherever happiness is found."

Her breathing was rapid and her lips shifted up. "Truly?" she asked.

"This very moment if you wish it." His heart began to pound and he willed her to accept.

She opened her mouth to speak when the empty glass they shared tipped and fell off the side table. It fell onto the carpet with a light thud and rolled toward the fire.

Mary's face went pale. She pulled her hands from his sharply and stood. "I - I cannot."

He rose to face her. "You cannot?"

Her shoulders slumped. "Not yet."

Henry closed his eyes and pinched his nose at the headache forming there. "Not until you find Luke's murderer?"

"Not until then." She swept up her skirts and moved past him. "I'm feeling tired. Goodnight, Henry."

He didn't watch while she exited the room and waited for the door to shut before he answered softly. "Goodnight, my love."

Needing to do something before he exploded with frustration, he built up the fire to a roaring blaze and dropped down into the chair with the bottle of port.

He took a swig and stared at the fallen glass. Mary was receptive to running with him until it fell over, then she couldn't get away from him fast enough. He toed the glass and rolled it back and forth under his boot. He briefly thought about crushing it. Perhaps it would break whatever spell had come over her.

Henry rolled it away and nestled down into his chair with the bottle of port for company. His eyes became heavy and he let the warmth of the drink lull him to sleep.

———

HENRY WAS deep inside a lovely dream. Mary sat beside him in a gig, racing along the roads near Fenwick. She held onto her hat with one hand and his arm with another. Her sunny pale-yellow dress fluttered in the wind. She laughed and squealed when they turned a corner and saw Lou-Lou standing at the side of the road, bouncing up and down and begging for a turn. Henry stood up to lift his sister into the gig when he fell out of the vehicle.

With a start and a snort he awoke on the floor. Pushing himself up, Henry chuckled. Not since childhood had he fallen out of bed and onto the floor. Too much port.

He stretched and glanced at the waning fire. There was enough flame to catch the candle someone left him to find his way to bed. He leaned over the fireplace to light it when he heard the floorboards creak.

Before he could turn his head, an overwhelming blow to the back of the head had him seeing black, then stars, then black, and stars mixed together. He crashed to the ground and struggled to keep his senses, waiting for his opponent to strike again.

"That's for the time you cheated me in the ring," Lord Fletcher's familiar voice mocked him.

Henry staggered to his feet and searched for his foe. The world was still spinning when the second strike came. Not a blow this time, but a slice with something sharp across the ribs. Henry cried out and shifted into a defensive stance while grabbing his wound. His vision was still too blurry to make out where the attack was coming from.

"That's for meddling in my affairs." Lord Fletcher grabbed him by the hair and slammed his head into the mantel.

Henry grunted and blinked. His wound stung and hot blood covered his hands.

With his vision still blurred, he reached out toward his attacker and managed to grab a handful of clothing. With all his might he slammed a bloody fist into Lord Fletcher's throat.

Lord Fletcher gagged while Henry stumbled away and searched to find something to hold onto while his sight came back into focus.

"Cur!" A kick to Henry's knees and he hit the floor with a grunt. Another kick to his ribs forced out a groan and he instinctively covered his head.

"I'm going to take you apart one piece at a time. Then I'm going to take my sister." Lord Fletcher's voice was near his ear. The sharp tip of a knife began to slice off Henry's earlobe.

The acute pain of the knife worked like a splash of cold water on his senses. His vision returned as he struggled against Lord Fletcher, pushing and wheezing when he saw something emerging from the darkness.

Two women silently moved side by side behind Lord Fletcher. One dressed in black with neat copper hair, bright eyes, and creamy skin. Mary. The other was dressed in white, her hair long and dark, her skin gray. Her black eyes bore into him. He froze in fear as what was left of his earlobe dropped to the floor.

The black-eyed woman moved nearer to Mary, closer and closer until she disappeared inside Mary's skin. Was he hallucinating? Mary's bright eyes turned hard and her steps quickened. She held in her hand a long brass candlestick.

Henry's angel of death slammed the candlestick into Lord Fletcher's head. He cried out and fell next to Henry. Mary stood over her brother with the candlestick raised like the Celtic warrior queen taking her vengeance on the Romans. He glared up at her and snarled. "Worthless bitch."

The candlestick came down again, slamming against the side of his skull with a crunch. Her blow knocked Lord Fletcher sideways. He had no time to recover before she smashed it into him again, and again. The sound of thumps and rapid breathing with the occasional crack of breaking bones rang through the still air of the library. Only when Lord Fletcher stilled completely did she stop her work of destruction.

His angel stared at her handiwork. The candlestick clattered to the floor. Mary examined the blood splattered up her hands and arms.

Henry wobbled to his feet with a groan, pressing hard at the wound in his side.

Mary's gaze didn't leave her brother's fallen form. The angel of death had a voice sweeter than that of a dove. "Henry," she swallowed, "I believe I have committed fratricide."

"He was an unnatural human and the world is better without him," Henry grunted, pulled his cravat off with one hand, and stuffed it against his ribs.

"I'm covered in blood," she announced, staring down at her skirts. "I don't think it shows on my gown."

"Bombazine covers many sins." Henry limped toward her.

"I'll have another year of it, mourning him. I am so tired of wearing black. I guess it won't matter when they hang me for this. Oh, what a mess!"

"No, you won't. Not for him." Henry promised.

Now his angel began to cry, wiping her eyes furiously and leaving smears of blood on her cheeks and hands. "We need to call the constable. You need a doctor. Oh, what did he do to you?" Mary's blood-stained hands began to run over his frame and face, cupping his torn ear.

He reached up and caressed her face. She stopped her rambling and gazed up at him, tears swimming in her eyes.

He wanted to kiss her face, blood and all. He wanted to hold her little body close and praise her heroism. He wanted to love her with everything he had, starting by protecting her from this new upset in her life.

"No constables, no doctors. Wash up and go to bed. I'll take care of this," he promised.

"This is too much," she ended with a sob.

He stroked her face again. "Go to your room, clean up, and go to bed," he said more forcefully.

She closed her eyes and leaned into his touch briefly, before backing away. Hands on her hips and her voice firm, she said, "I'm not going anywhere. I made this mess and I'll clean it up."

Chapter Twenty

꧁꧂

Nightrule - A tumult in the night

ALL MARY SMELLED WAS LILACS. A feeling of invincibility
sank into her bones. Her sight was brighter, clearer. Her skin
felt stretched tight and her muscles were superhuman. Faster.
Invincible.

If only she remembered everything she'd done.

Memories came to her in flashes. She'd fallen asleep with
her clothes on when icy cold hands jolted her awake. The
sound of a thud and the sight of Henry being attacked. A
candlestick in her hand. Jonathan. She hit him once, then
nothing. Nothing, until she was staring down at his mutilated
head and a wave of shock washed over her. She was ready to
fall to pieces when Sarah took over again, shoving her
emotions aside and replacing them with a cold, hard logic she
couldn't break free of.

Sarah was still inside her. A presence lurked in the back of her mind, ready to take over if she faltered. At the same time, Sarah filled her body with more strength and vitality than she'd ever known. Was this how Sarah helped Henry fight in the ring?

Well then, if Mary was possessed, she'd make use of it.

"Let me see your wounds." She pulled Henry over to the dim firelight. She peeled off his jacket and waistcoat to examine his ribs.

He flinched when she touched the wound. There was no bone gaping at her, but it was bleeding. His clothing had taken the brunt of it. "Give me your cravat."

He handed her the bloodied wad and she wrapped it around his torso. She pulled out her handkerchief and held it to his ear to staunch the flow there.

"Look at me," Henry said. She tipped her face up and he swiped his handkerchief over her face. It came away smeared with spots of blood.

"I don't know how we're going to get it all cleaned up." Mary glanced down at her brother's body. She'd smashed Jonathan's head open on the hearth instead of the carpet. It should be easier to clean. What a logically morbid thought to have!

Henry pulled her hand from his ear and kissed her dirty palm. "Go to the kitchen and get some water. Grab a pair of Josiah's clothing from the laundry while you're there."

She followed his directions and returned with a bucket of water and rags. Henry enclosed Jonathan's head in his jacket when she returned. It made the sight easier to bear. Covered up, he appeared to be sleeping.

Together they got on their hands and knees and tackled the bloody task.

"How are you?" Henry asked while she wiped the candlestick.

Possessed? Probably not the answer he was searching for. Sarah's power surged through her, locking her emotions firmly away from the turmoil.

"I'm sure I'll have a proper display of hysterics later," Mary promised.

"I'll be there for you when you do." Sweat beaded his brow and he stopped scrubbing. "That's good enough. We need to get going. Go dump out the water and meet me in the mews."

She hurried to complete her task and found him dragging the body outside. "Here." she lifted the body's feet and they carried it into the stables.

The horses whickered when they entered. A few stomped at having their rest disturbed. They dropped the corpse next to a small cart, Henry panting with the exertion.

"This is all too much. You're hurt. We should get help," she rested a hand on his back and he straightened.

"You're not going to Newgate and hanging for this scab. I'll be all right in a moment. Do you have Josiah's clothes?" he asked. She lifted the bundle. "Good, go change and I'll get the cart hitched up."

She hid behind an empty stall door and slid into Josiah's clothes while Henry led a pony into position in front of the cart. He took her soiled dress and tossed it inside the cart.

"I hate to have you do this, but we need to strip him down. There can't be anything on him to hint at who he might be." Henry blocked her view from the head and began taking off the corpse's waistcoat. She started with the boots. Once the body was stripped, they wrapped it in oilcloth. Henry dragged the carcass to the end of the cart and together they lifted it in.

Henry drove the small cart out of the mews. It wobbled over the stones and she touched him at every jounce, getting little waves of heat from his body. She glanced at him often, worried about the bump on his head and the deep slice on his ribs. He was still sweating in the cold night air from his exertions.

He caught her staring. "You keep watching me like I'm about to fall over."

"It's a concern I have at the moment. How's your head?"

"I took a nobbler like that once in the ring and came out all right. I'm not worried."

"And your ribs?" Mary resisted the urge to reach out and make sure her bandage work was holding up well.

He flinched and pressed a couple of fingers against his wound. "Tender, but I think I'll mend. It's not bleeding through." He scanned the road ahead and their destination. "We're here."

It took most of the night to drive to St Bartholomew's Hospital. Granted, they weren't traveling very fast in a cart with an old mule plodding along and they'd made a few extra stops dispersing her and Jonathan's clothing to any sleeping beggar they came across who needed it. The poor didn't care about bloodstains.

The pale brick of the giant edifice shone in the moonlight when they approached the courtyard. Henry drove the cart around to the rear of the hospital. Mary expected it to be dark and dismal, but it was well lit. They weren't the only ones dropping off bodies. A small row of carts and men were lined up at the door. A young man with a bloody apron appeared, asked a few questions, and then led them into the hospital with their corpse.

Henry rubbed his neck. "I'm sorry. This is disgusting and

MEL STONE

not a place for you. But I didn't know of a better way to dispose of your brother's body without anyone asking questions." He winced as he climbed off the cart.

Mary pulled her steenkirk above her nose to hide her face and leaped down. She moved much easier in Josiah's borrowed clothing. She raced to the end of the cart and climbed in before Henry strained himself further.

"I'll do it." She spoke quietly so her voice wouldn't carry to the others in line.

"You won't be able to carry him by yourself," Henry said.

"I'll push him off." Mary surprised them both by lifting Jonathan's torso and easily dragging him to the edge. Sarah's strength filled her limbs. Would the ghost ever let her go? For now, she seemed content to lurk in the background of Mary's consciousness.

Mary buried her thoughts and hopped down from the cart. She took hold of the body and pulled the torso her way. "Get his feet." She directed Henry.

He was watching her with a little suspicion. "I should take the head."

"It's heavier and I won't have you hurting yourself further. Now do what I say."

He hesitated before obeying, and together they wrestled the body to a place in the gruesome queue.

"Do you smell lilacs?" he asked her quietly.

She was glad for the cover of darkness, her cap, and the steenkirk around her face. She was sure her eyes were bulging and her mouth was gaping like a fish with surprise. "How did you know?"

"I smell it when I fight. It comes out of nowhere but I always know I've got a sure win when I smell lilacs. It makes me faster, stronger. Capable of anything. Like a lady being suddenly able to annihilate a Lord's house when asking for information."

Mary gulped and chewed on her lip. "We need to have a long talk."

"We certainly do."

When it was their turn at the door, the tired young man with the apron glanced at the wrapped body and asked Henry. "Man or woman?"

"Man. Poor clump was run over by a cart. His head's not in good shape but the rest of him is prime." Mary was impressed with Henry's sudden change of accent. She remained silent.

The young man ushered them in and directed them to set Jonathan's body on a table. He wordlessly unwrapped it and wrinkled his nose at the misshapen form. "Five pounds due to the damage."

Henry bobbed his head and received payment. Mary followed him out of the hospital, stiff with shock at how easy it was to dispose of Jonathan's body.

They climbed up on the cart and Henry handed her the money. "Here. You should have it."

Mary stared at the bills while the cart rolled into motion. Five pounds. The total worth of her good-for-nothing brother was five pounds.

The sky was lightening into a pre-dawn grey when they exited the courtyard of St. Bartholomew. Once the cart turned onto the street, a lightness swept over her, a release of something heavy from her soul, followed by a crushing sense of exhaustion and sorrow. She pulled the steenkirk off her face and inhaled the less than pure London air. No more lilacs.

"She's gone."

"Who's gone?"

"Sarah."

Henry side-eyed her. "What are you talking about?"

Mary swallowed. Now was the time for that long talk. "We've been haunted."

"We?"

Mary shrugged and shivered. "You've been frequented by her longer than I have. Your mother, Sarah. She never left you."

Henry's lips tightened. She wished he would face her, give her some sign on what he was thinking, but his eyes were fixed firmly ahead. She slowly leaned toward him and rested her head on his shoulder, absorbing his warmth and inhaling his scent. As long as she stayed in this exact position, she'd let him take as much time as he needed to figure it out.

"Lilacs," he said finally. "And a white lady who hums lullabies."

"Yes."

"She helped me fight, all those years."

"She was protecting you. Although, I'm not sure why she chose me to come to your defense instead of helping you as usual."

Henry gingerly touched his head. "That first hit rendered me senseless. I doubt she could have helped much." He then snorted. "George and Peter will be smarting when they learn I'm not a boxing prodigy."

Mary managed a brief smile. "She began haunting me when Luke died. I think after all that happened to her, she doesn't want her father's death to go unsolved, unpunished."

"I assume she did more than sing lullabies to you."

Mary buried her face into his shoulder. "I don't want to talk about it. She frightens me."

Henry's arm wrapped around her and pulled her in close.

His lips kissed her brow. "My dear girl, why didn't you tell me?"

"Jonathan was trying to declare me mad. I couldn't go about telling everyone I was seeing a ghost."

"Not everyone, just me. You told me once you'd do anything to keep me from pain. Don't you think I'd do the same for you?"

Mary sniffed and wiped her nose on her sleeve. Her emotions rose to the surface to mix with her exhaustion. "I don't know anything when it comes to you. I want so much from you, but I'm afraid to ask."

Henry stopped the cart and faced her, taking both of her hands in his. "Afraid of what?"

"Afraid you'll always see me as a little girl when I want you to look at me as a woman. A woman who is in love with you."

A heartbeat of silence, then he dove for her lips, her face in his hands and his mouth devouring hers. She sighed deeply and kissed him, her arms wrapping tightly around his neck. They pressed into each other with equal fervor, both trying to get as close as possible.

When he released her, he rested his forehead against hers, rubbing his hands up and down her arms. "I have loved you for... forever."

She gazed at him, her heart galloping. "You have?"

He kissed her again. "Back when you were Mary Fletcher of Fairley Park."

———

HENRY WAS ITCHY, sore, had a devil of a headache, but he couldn't remember being happier. Mary was in his arms.

At the moment, she was tucked up under his chin,

sleeping on his chest while he sat on a lumpy seat of straw in the mews. Neither one of them wanted to return to the house with reality waiting for them there.

He removed her stolen cap to let her copper curls free and kissed her bare head. She snuggled closer to him with a little snore. Adorable.

As much as he wanted to remain in their little magic spell, the pressures of the real world were closing in. He frowned, shifted his weight to a more comfortable spot and held Mary tighter. He could prevail against a country that wouldn't allow them to marry. It was easy enough to move away. He could overcome her fears about his love for her and was anxious to prove it. He could help her fight her past and sorrows and fears, and keep the secret of her brother's death safe. But he couldn't fight a ghost set on revenge.

Especially the ghost of his mother.

With a weary sigh, he closed his eyes and let his thoughts bombard him while searching for an answer.

The door to the mews opened with a crash and the stableboy sprinted in, wide-eyed and whimpering. He ran to the ladder leading to the loft and speedily climbed up.

Henry sat up while Mary stirred in his embrace. "What's wrong, boy?" he called out.

A fearful face peered over the edge of the loft. The boy gulped at the sight of Henry below. "What you doin' in here? The whole house is searching for you two." The boy glanced at the door to the house and paled. "I ain't going in there to tell them I found you." His head disappeared into the loft.

Mary pulled away from Henry and rubbed her bleary eyes. "What's going on?"

"Not sure." Henry stiffly rose to his feet with a grunt and lowered a hand to help her up. "Let's go find out."

A group of pale and grim servants were all in the upper hallway when they returned, clustered together and whispering. Henry scanned the room and rested on George's thin-lipped face. "What's happened?"

George shook his head. "Old Scratch himself is in the house. 'Tis the devil's work, and I'm about to search out some holy water and a Levite, papal laws be damned."

A loud crash came from behind the doors of the gallery. A few of the maids jumped and whimpered, hugging each other. The rest of the household stared at the door with wide eyed horror, their bodies tightly strung for fight or flight.

Mary slipped a hand into his elbow. "Where's Agnes?" she asked softly.

Henry scanned the faces again. Mary's beloved friend was missing. "Agnes?"

"She's with the beast." George motioned at the closed room. "Agnes started screaming like a banshee early this morning an' locked herself up in the gallery. That's when the ruckus started. I tried going in and got hit in the eye with a vase for my trouble." George gently touched a swelling bruise at his eyebrow.

Henry faced Mary when she gasped. Her cheeks were as pale as the servants'.

"Sarah," she whispered. She swayed a bit on her feet. Henry supported her weight while she clutched at his arm. "What is she doing to Agnes?"

"Let's find out." Henry hid any bit of fear niggling at the back of his skull. He held Mary's hand and they faced the gallery door together. Hand trembling, he turned the knob and entered first.

Paintings were strewn about the room. Some were upright, some face down, others slanted at various angles.

Every portrait seemed to be glaring at him for the injustice they'd received. A few broken frames lay on the floor with shards of glass and pottery. A couple of busts laid on their sides with broken noses and ears.

Agnes' limp body lay sprawled at the end of the galley. The neat and tidy maid's clothing was torn, her hair in disarray. Her eyes were closed and little drops of blood covered her face and hands.

Mary cried out and dropped Henry's hand to rush to her friend.

"Agnes, dearest, please wake up." Mary pulled Agnes into her lap.

Henry knelt beside them and took Agnes's hand. It was cold. Had the ghost killed her? Why?

Mary shook Agnes. "Agnes, please. Please talk to me!"

Placing a hand gently over the maid's face, a tiny breath brushed against Henry's skin. He pressed a touch over her pulse at the throat. It beat hard and fast under his fingers. "She's alive."

Mary sobbed and cradled Agnes to her. "Sarah! Sarah, why?" she cried out.

The gallery door slammed shut. Henry jumped when the lock clicked tightly in place and the servants outside shrieked. The paintings began rattling in their places, vibrating with such force that more frames cracked. Another bust toppled to the ground, shattering into pieces. The shards lifted from the ground and flew across the room, pelting Agnes and Mary.

Henry threw his arms around both of them, tucking them in tight for protection. The cacophony of sounds was deafening as more glass broke, more frames split, and even the rugs began to shred themselves. Mary's weeping rose above it all, piercing his heart. He released her and stood, facing the empty room. He wished for something to fight head-on when he saw the only remaining portrait on the wall.

Sarah Polk Carroll's face warped into something other-worldly and angry. The blue dress was now white, her creamy skin sallow and grey with dark veins running through her flesh. Once bright and beautiful eyes were black and hollow, the lips pulled back in a scream.

"Mother," he said softly but firmly.

The ruckus stopped. Everything in motion clattered to the floor. The silence was like a great storm holding its breath before unleashing its fury. It was more prominent when mingled with Mary's soft crying.

He approached the painting and reached a hand to it; the canvas was ice under his fingers. "Mother, you have to stop this."

The figure in the portrait began to grow, filling the frame. Henry stepped away when the entity spilled forth out of the picture and took form in front of him. A pale hand reached out toward his face. He flinched but didn't move as icy fingers touched his cheek.

"Hello, Mother," he whispered.

Another hand joined the first, cradling his face in a frigid caress. It appeared as if the creature's face softened a little. He paused, then reached up to touch her hands, his fingers passing through her ghostly shape. The hollow blackness swallowing her eyes receded a little. The veins on her face faded.

"Let us help you," he said.

Sarah lowered her hands and scowled. Henry braced himself for another attack, but all she did was point at Agnes.

"Agnes? What did Agnes do?"

Sarah opened her mouth to speak and nothing came out.

The veins began to spread again and her anger rose again and the broken objects in the room clattered.

"Shhh, shhh, shhh. We'll figure it out." He made more soothing noises until the room fell into silence once more. Sarah's glower and accusing finger never shifted from Agnes.

The maid gasped loud and long before she opened her eyes. "I killed the duke," she announced.

Henry's heart sank into his shoes. "You did what?" he whispered.

Agnes gazed at Mary, weakly bringing her hand up to Mary's cheek. Mary was still and wide-eyed.

"I killed the duke." Agnes stroked Mary's cheek. "He was going to have my dear girl's marriage annulled. Leave you with no protection."

Tears fell onto Agnes's face from Mary's eyes. She choked when she spoke, "No. No, he would have taken care of me."

"I knew he provided for you in his will. So I poisoned him before he started any annulment." Agnes's voice shook.

Poison? Henry remembered the paper knife in Luke's chest, the blood, the overturned furniture.

"The duke figured it out." Agnes's hand fell from Mary's cheek. "I was watching, waiting to dispose of the cup when he realized he was dying. He ranted and stabbed himself to make sure everyone knew he was murdered."

Every creative curse Henry knew flew out of his mouth. Of course the old man stabbed himself! Stubborn old fox.

Agnes continued, tears streaming from her face, down her cheeks, and into her hair. "I thought it would all be well. But then the hauntings started. The ghost is getting worse and worse. After what I saw at Mr. Merrill's office, I knew she wouldn't let you alone without answers. So I confessed to her."

The ghost's hand dropped. The dark veins on Sarah's face receded and the room descended into peace once Agnes confessed.

"I called out to the ghost this morning. I told her I knew who killed her father and told her everything. She was very angry." Agnes gasped and closed her eyes.

"What did she do to you?" Mary demanded, shaking Agnes. "Are you dying? Where did she hurt you?"

Agnes' eyes fluttered open. "Hurt me? My dear little duck, she didn't hurt me. I took the poison I gave the duke."

"What? Why!"

"So she'll stop haunting you. So you can be happy." Agnes's voice grew faint. "You're the daughter of my heart. I love you." Her hand fell from Mary's cheeks, and she closed her eyes. A little gasp escaped her lips and her body stilled completely.

"Agnes?" Mary shook her dear friend's body, hands roaming over the still form frantically. "Please, please don't leave me."

Henry pulled Mary from Agnes's body, Her arms locked around his neck and she began to wail.

He crushed Mary's body to his, muttering useless words to console her.

Movement out of the corner of his eye caught his attention. Sarah stood before him. The black holes that filled her sockets were replaced with bright eyes. Her pale gray skin lightened into creamy white. She bent over them both, brushing cool hands over Henry's head before disappearing.

Henry lifted Mary and stood. Enough of this madness. Enough of heartache and pain and secrets. He was finished with it all.

He winced at the pull of his wounded ribs. Mary buried

her face in his neck and continued her uncontrollable crying. He walked them both to the door of the gallery and threw it open.

The servants yelped when he strode through them. He didn't pause as they peppered him with questions. His goal was firmly set. He was leaving with his love and no one would stop him.

George was the most insistent. "What's going on? What are you doing?"

"I'm taking Mary and I'm leaving this country for good." Henry barked and left the house forever.

Epilogue

Oxymel – A mixture of vinegar and honey

MARY ROLLED over and slowly opened her eyes. Her vision filled with the sight of a broad back distinctly marked with thin red streaks from her fingernails. Apparently, she'd been too passionate last night.

"Oh, my." She sat up and reached out a hesitant hand toward her husband's skin. "Henry?" she spoke softly. "Henry, I think I damaged you."

He rolled over with a groan. "You did. In all the best ways." He smiled at her and the warmth in her chest spread out to all her limbs.

He reached out a hand and cupped her face, brushing a thumb over her cheek. "All right there, wife?" he asked.

The warm feeling within her swelled and she leaned down

to kiss him, then wedged herself into his embrace. "I'm perfect."

The warm Caribbean breeze came through the open windows and brought with it the scent of the sea.

Henry surrounded her with light. Light beaches and trees and flowers, light blue water, and colorful creatures. A bright yellow house with plenty of room for...

A thud against the bedroom door interrupted her thoughts.

"Papa! Are you awake? The crabs are here!"

Henry chuckled, kissing her before reaching for his robe. "It sounds like I'm off to catch crabs for the day."

Mary re-adjusted the sheets and readied herself for their morning ritual.

Henry opened the door and three little bodies tumbled in. The two little brown-skinned boys raced past Henry and leaped onto the bed. They bounced up to their mother where she welcomed them into her arms. Henry picked up their shorter little sister, kissed her smooth dark cheek, brushed the tight curls from her beautiful *normal* brown eyes, and set her on the bed to join her brothers.

Charles, Antony, and Isadora. Three little orphans who took refuge under their steps during the last huge storm. They also took Mary's heart. She squeezed them tighter to her and wrestled with the boys when they tried to break free from her embrace. "I need more kisses," she teased.

"Mama, let go! We need to catch the crabs. Get dressed, Papa." Charles managed to duck out of Mary's grip and pull Antony away from her relentless kissing.

The boys threw articles of clothing at Henry and "helped" him get dressed while Isadora snuggled up to her mother and rested her head on Mary's breast, tucking a thumb in her mouth.

Mary stroked the toddler's hair while the boys tugged Henry from the room with a great deal of commotion. They sighed as one when the noisy males left.

Mary kissed Isadora's head, "Did you sleep well, my girl?" Her daughter had been suffering from nightmares for the past week.

Isadora nodded and pulled her thumb out with a pop. "When I got scared, a beautiful lady in white came into my room. She sang to me..."

Author's Notes

If you've made it this far, I know what you're thinking. "Mel, it's 'chip off the old block' not 'chip of the old block'." And you'd be right! Why? Because you were born after 1870 (I hope).

The phrase was originally used in a sermon back in 1621, where it was written as - "a chip of the same block". Fast forward to 1811 and *Grose's Dictionary of the Vulgar Tongue* (which I referred to many times to write this book) and it is written as - CHIP. A child. A chip of the old block; a child who either in person or sentiments resembles its father or mother. So when this book took place, that's what would have been said. Fast forward again to 1870 and a newspaper in Ohio changed it to "the child is too often a chip off the old block" which is what we say now.

Words and phrases are always changing and evolving. And I LOVE it. Finding the history behind them is a thrilling little treasure hunt I get to go on every time I write. I hope you enjoyed the little snippets from Samuel Johnson's Dictionary with words we don't usually hear anymore and thank you for going on this journey with me.

Acknowledgments

Many thanks, hugs, and kisses to my Beta army: Jess, Ruth, Kirsten, Julie, Allie, Raneé, Randi, and Victoria. You are all amazing, helpful, and fabulous cheerleaders. My critique group Robin, Sarah, Carole, Amy, and Kierstin for all their help polishing a really rough draft. My son, Jefferson, for listening to the entire plot of my book while on a road trip. My Bubby for calling me out when there are gaping plot holes. My editor Julia at Better Than Spell Check for making my words look shiny and finding those little historical details I miss. Raneé, for her beautiful formatting work. Boo for keeping my feet warm while I work. And last, but not least, my hubbyman Dell who is my own December to May romance. (There is only 16 years between us, not 50.)

About the Author

Mel wrote, illustrated, and published her first book at the age of five. It was not a huge success and she only sold one copy to her mother. Undaunted, she plunged herself into reading every book she could get her hands on. She found a love for ghost stories and gothic tales, suspense-driven works of fiction, and of course a little romance never hurt. Now she combines all three of her favorite genres and writes up tales that feel familiar until you find out things are not what they seem. She lives in the Wasatch Mountains and enjoys time with her children, her husband, and her 100-pound lab/mastiff/dane, Boudica, who thinks she's a lap dog. She also has a serious addiction to yarn, fiber arts, and crochet hooks.

More Books by Mel Stone

The House that Death Built

Norfolk, 1816

Joy's idea of a happily ever after was simple: A comfortable home, a loving husband, children of her own, and plenty of spaniel puppies to trip over. When Arthur Marco promises her the life she dreams of she happily accepts his proposal.

When she joins him at his ancestral home she finds her passionate and loving husband has become irrational and tyrannical. She becomes a prisoner in his presence while he rips the house apart searching for something.

Joy begins her own quiet search for answers. She dives into the Marco family past of the young brides who have all died there. Every truth she reveals brings her one step closer to the evil in the house, and the death that will follow.

Now available on Amazon for ebook, paperback, and audio.

Connect with me on Facebook and Instagram, @AuthorMelStone. I'm also a member of the FB group: Gothic Romance Readers and Authors. Come join us and find more great reads and fun people who like spooky stories.

Visit authormelstone.com and sign up for my newsletter to get a free copy of my novella, *From the Ashes of June*.

Made in United States
North Haven, CT
07 May 2023

36329057R00150